CW01011233

BEDTIME STORIES FOR CHILDREN

Fantastic Fun Adventures with Fairies, Wizards, Dragons, Unicorns, Princesses and Enchanted Lands to Make Bedtime A Magical and Easy Experience for Kids and Parents

Rosa Knight

Table of Contents

Part 1

BEDTIME STORIES FOR CHILDREN

Fantastic Short Stories of Fairies, Wizards, Dragons, Unicorns, Princesses and Enchanted Lands to Make Bedtime a Fun and Magical Experience for Kids and Parents

Introduction

Courage is something children learn by failing and there must be many stories in the world talking about how a child can grow to be braver. The stories of legends and origins make the world more fantastical and inviting. By talking about how people in the past looked at the world, a child can learn about how times have changed from then to now.

This time, in a child's life, is full of wonder and mystery. When you are processing new information all the time, everything seems profound and magical. It is up to us to encourage that imagination.

Reading to your child can allow you to channel their creativity in a healthy and exciting way. You can be the guide that ushers your little one away to magical lands. Introduce them to characters that they will fall in love with. You can control the content that they are consuming while also adventuring right alongside them.

Each of these tales was written to teach the morals and values that you are already working to instill in your children. The easiest way to learn is through entertainment. As the parent, you can pass on these lessons without your child even realizing that they are being taught. There is so much imaginative literature for children on the market. Thank you again for choosing this book, and I hope that it offers a lot of joy to you and your little one.

Chapter 1: The Little Girl with the Missing Eye

A little girl woke up one morning and opened her eye. The little girl only had one eye to open when she woke up in the morning, for she had lost the other eye, when she was very small. The girl did not remember losing her eye and so it never really bothered her that she didn't look just like everyone else.

In fact, her mother always told her that she had lost her eye to see better. When the little girl asked her mother what she meant, she said, "You may be missing an eye to see the world around you, but you have so much inner focus and wonderful intelligence because you work hard to know more through your one good eye. You can see the world differently than other people do. You can see more deeply because of your loss."

As the girl grew older, she began to understand what her mother meant more and more. It was clear to her that she always had a good line of sight on what was going on underneath the surface of anyone that she met.

She could read people easily because her mind was better at listening than at seeing.

She and her mother and father and little sister and little brother decided to move closer to the village that spring so that she could have people around her closer to her age and so that her family could have a better life.

She was excited to make friends with other girls like her, and she was eager to find out what it was like to live in a new place.

When the Spring came, her family packed up their wagon with all of their belongings and began the long road into their new lives.

She was amazed by everything along the way.

Everything looked new and exciting to her eye.

Inside her mind, she was full of inspiration and happiness.

She was able to love her way of looking at life through her one eye, and she felt so happy to be with her family on this journey.

When they got to the village, her mother and father took them straight to their new cottage.

It was close to where her mother and father had found work that they could both do in the community.

"When we are at work, you will start to go to school.

We have been teaching you at home this whole time, and now you will learn new life lessons and have new people to play with.

Your little brother and little sister will go to another school for younger children.

This is the way of village life," the mother told the girl.

"I cannot wait to make new friends.

I have always dreamed of this moment."

She was so happy that she could barely rest the night before her first day of school.

The next morning her mother sent her off with food and a kiss.

"Farewell, my sweet child. Always remember that you are the one who can see beyond the surface of things."

She walked up the path to her new school.

Along the way, she saw many people in the street, walking to and for and going this way and that.

It was a whole new adventure and she was on her way, one eye focused on the road ahead.

Most people didn't pay much attention to her, but she noticed that when they did look at her face, they stared at her and looked uncomfortable in their faces.

She wondered why and thought maybe everyone was grouchy in the morning in this village.

When she got to the schoolhouse, she was met with the same looks, and even the teacher was making her suddenly feel very uncomfortable.

What was wrong with everyone?

Didn't anyone in this village have manners?

She quickly understood why.

It was because of her missing eye and that she looked different from everyone else.

She decided to be brave and full of courage, remembering what her mother told her as she stepped out the door this morning.

She could see beyond the surface of things, and these people were uncomfortable because of her eye.

She took a seat at the back of the class and felt disappointed that there wasn't more of an introduction from anyone in the room.

The teacher came over to her desk as the others took their seats in the schoolroom.

"You are a new student. Welcome to your first day.

Just copy your work out of this book and follow each lesson."

The teacher walked away and asked her nothing about herself, her name, and she suddenly felt very lost.

She had never been treated this way before.

If people weren't staring at her, then they were ignoring her.

What she hoped would be an exciting first day of making new friends turned out to be her first feelings of shame for her missing eye.

Her mother told her when she got home that night that people aren't used to seeing someone so special and that in time, they would all learn of just how much she knew.

The next day she walked into the classroom, and as the children took their seats and the teacher began to write on the chalkboard, she walked right to the front of the room and began to speak...

"I would like to say hello to you all and tell you what I know.

I know that you are afraid to talk to me because of my missing eye.

I know you are all really kind at heart.

I know that you are just uncomfortable around someone who is different from you, and I know that when you are ready to make my acquaintance, we are going to be great friends."

The little girl walked back to her desk at the back of the classroom to the sounds of giggling, murmurs, and chit chat.

The teacher asked for silence from the students.

"Thank you for sharing with us.

We are glad you are here and we accept you into our school with open arms."

The other children turned to look at the girl once more before turning back to the class lesson.

She worked very hard to answer all the questions well.

At the end of the day, the teacher reported back all of the graded lessons.

“Our new student is the only one who got every answer correct.

Congratulations, you are our new top student.”

The little girl blushed.

She felt proud of herself, no matter what anyone else may have thought about her.

She walked home after the bell rang, and as she was making her way up the cobblestone street, she felt a tug on her jacket.

“Excuse me,” said another little girl.

“My name is Sue, and I wondered if we could be friends.

Maybe we can study together. I really enjoy learning new things.”

The little girl felt elated.

Someone wanted to be her friend.

“That would be wonderful,” she said.

“I know it might sound rude, but is it okay if I ask what happened to your eye?

Were you born like that?”

The new friend was curious.

“I had an accident when I was a baby.

I don’t remember it at all.

I just learned how to see with only one eye, but I am just like everyone else.”

The two girls walked a little further up the road and got to know each other better.

Just then, they heard the voice of another child calling out to them as they walked...

“Hey! Wait up!”

A young boy ran over and up to the two girls who had stopped in the path to wait for him.

“My name’s John.

I really like what you said at the front of the class today.

You seem really nice and smart.”

The little girl smiled.

She knew what he wanted to ask next, and she beat him to the punch.

“Go ahead, you can ask about my eye. I know you want to.”

She smiled, and the three of them laughed.

She was so glad to be meeting children her age who she could talk to and learn new things with.

They walked on for a while longer until they came to her house.

“Well, this is my home. I guess I will see you tomorrow at school.”

She started to head inside when Sue said, “I will meet you here in the morning, and we can walk together.”

“Me too!” said John.

The little girl was so happy, she rushed inside and told her mother what had happened that day.

Her mother wrapped her arms around her and gave her a big hug.

“I knew you would see more than what others could.

You were so brave to share what you know and who you are."

The little girl hugged her mother and yawned, stretching out her arms.

It had been a long day, and she was tired.

She ate her supper and took a bath, and when her mother tucked her into bed that night, she told her the bedtime tale of a little girl with a missing eye who taught others to see more clearly.

She yawned and stretched again, closed her eyes, and began to drift off to a wonderful and restful sleep.

Tomorrow, when she woke up, there would be friends at her door, and she would continue to find new adventures, looking out ahead through her one, good eye, seeing all she can from the outside to the inside and back again.

Sweet Dreams!

Chapter 2: The Princess in the Flammenburg

Once upon a time there was a poor man who had had as many children as holes in a sieve and all the people in his village as godparents. When he was again born a son, he sat down on the road to ask the first best to be godfather. Then an old man in a gray cloak came to meet him, he asked, and he agreed and went to the baptism. As a baptismal gift, the old man gave the father a cow with a calf. That was born the same day as the boy and had a golden star on his forehead. The boy grew older and bigger and the calf also grew, became a big bull and the boy led him every day to the mountain meadow. But the bull was able to speak, and when they were on the top of the mountain, the bull spoke: "Stay here and sleep, I want to find my own willow!" As soon as the boy fell asleep, the bull ran like lightning on the big one Sky meadow and eats golden star flowers. When the sun went down, he hurried back, woke the boy, and then they went home. So, it happened every day until the boy was twenty years old. One day the bull spoke to him: "Now sit between my horns, I carry you to the king. Demand from him a seven-meter-long iron sword and tell him that you want to save his daughter. " Soon they arrived at the castle. The boy dismounted, went to the king and said why he had come. He gladly gave the shepherd boy the required sword. But he had no hope of ever seeing his daughter again. Already many brave youths had tried in vain to rescue them, because a twelve-headed dragon had kidnapped them, and it lived far away, where nobody could get to. First, there was a high, insurmountable mountain on the way there, secondly, a wide and stormy sea, and third, the dragon lived in a castle of flame. If anyone had succeeded in crossing the mountains and the sea, he would not have been able to penetrate through the mighty flames, and if he had succeeded, the dragon would have killed him. When the boy had the sword, he sat down between the horns of the bull, and in no time, they were before the great mountain. "Now we have to turn back," he said to the bull, for it seemed impossible for him to get across. But the bull said: "Wait a minute!", Put the boy on the ground, and as soon as that happened, he took a start and pushed with his huge horns the whole mountain on the side. Now the bull again put the boy between the horns. They moved on and came to the sea. "Now we have to turn back!" Said the boy, "because no one can go over there!" "Wait a minute," said the bull, "and hold on to my horns." He bent his head to the water and soffit and soothed the whole sea, so that they moved on dry feet as in a meadow. Now they were soon at the Flammenburg. From afar, they were met with such a glow that the boy could not stand it anymore. "Stop!" He shouted to the bull, "no farther, or we'll have to burn." The bull, however, ran very close and poured the sea he had drunk into the flames, so that they soon extinguished and a more powerful one Smoke arose that darkened the whole sky. Then the twelve-headed dragon rushed out of the black clouds angrily. "Now it's up to you!" Cried the bull to the boy, "make sure you knock all the heads off the monster!" He took all his strength, grasping the mighty sword in both hands, and giving the dragon one like that quick blow that blew all heads off. But now the monster struck and curled on the earth, causing her to tremble. The bull took the dragon's trunk on its horns and hurled it so high up to the clouds, until no trace of it was to be seen. Then he spoke to the boy: "My service is now over. Now go to the castle, there you will find the princess and lead her home to her father! "With that he ran away to the sky meadow, and the boy did not see him again. He found the princess, and she was very glad that she was redeemed from the terrible dragon. They drove to their father, held a wedding, and it was a great joy throughout the kingdom.

Chapter 3: The Unicorn and the Caterpillar

Brindle the magic unicorn was a beautiful white unicorn with a special golden horn that sparkled in the light more than anything else in the whole world, Brindle loved helping people, learning new things, and making new friends!

One day, when Brindle was walking along in the sunshine, she heard a little voice crying. Because she was a magic unicorn, she could also feel how sad and afraid the person was. Brindle looked around until she spotted a tiny fuzzy creature with a bunch of legs sitting on the leaf of a nearby plant.

It made Brindle feel unhappy whenever someone else was unhappy or sad, so she went over to see whether there was anything that she could do to help.

"What is the matter, little friend?" Brindle asked the fuzzy little creature. The little creature looked up at Brindle, stopping what he was doing.

"I am afraid," the little creature replied. "My mommy told me that everything is about to change, and I am afraid of change. I like things the way they are. New things scare me."

"Well, what kind of change is going to happen?" Brindle asked.

"I d-d-don't know!" The little creature sobbed. "I didn't understand what my mommy was trying to tell me. It all sounded so scary!"

"Ahhh, I see." Brindle nodded in understanding. "You are afraid of the unknown."

"The unknown... is that some kind of monster?" The little creature shivered.

“No,” Brindle giggled. “The unknown is just things we don’t know. When we don’t know things or understand things, it makes them feel very scary. But really, the unknown is just a big, new adventure!”

“Really?” The little creature asked, hopefully.

“Really.” Brindle nodded. “What is your name?”

“I am Cal,” the little creature answered. “And I am a caterpillar.”

“A caterpillar! How wonderful!” Brindle smiled. “My name is Brindle, and I’m a unicorn.”

“I have never seen a unicorn before,” Cal said with a smile. Then he gave a big yawn.

“Are you sleepy?” Brindle asked with concern.

“Yes,” Cal said. “When I started getting really sleepy, that’s when my mommy said that I had a change coming in my life. She showed me how to make this blanket I have been working on to keep me safe.”

“Well, I can help keep you safe, if you’d like,” Brindle offered. “I can stand and watch over you while you sleep.”

“That would be wonderful!” Cal said excitedly. He started working on his blanket even faster to get it done.

“How fun!” Brindle said, watching him work. “You are building the blanket around you and wrapping it all around yourself!”

“My mommy told me that it was called a cocoon,” Cal said, close to finishing his work.

“Okay,” Brindle said with a smile. “You finish that last little bit to get your head covered and go to sleep. I will protect you and be here when you wake up.”

"Thank you, Brindle," Cal said, his eyes getting very sleepy. "You are a very good friend. I am glad we met."

Cal finished his cocoon and wrapped the last bits of himself uptight. Brindle gave him a gentle little touch of her horn, and a magic glow surrounded Cal's cocoon to protect him.

Brindle waited and waited while several days passed, and Cal was still asleep. She never left her friend's side the whole time. Then one day, the little cocoon surrounding Cal started to move.

Brindle was excited to watch as Cal's cocoon split open and he started struggling to come out. When he was finished, Brindle jumped and danced and laughed.

"Cal, change really did happen to you!" Brindle said happily.

"It did?" Cal looked around. "I don't feel any different."

"Oh my, you should!" Brindle said, lowering her horn down to her friend. "See how shiny my horn is? Use it as a mirror to look at yourself."

Cal leaned in close toward Brindle's horn and then jumped back, startled. He looked again and was in awe. Cal's body had grown really skinny while he slept, and beautiful wings sprouted from his back.

"I look like my mommy now!" Cal said happily. "I thought you were a caterpillar," Brindle smiled. "I didn't know that caterpillars and butterflies were the same!"

"They are!" Cal said. "I just didn't know that change could be beautiful, and that's how I became a butterfly."

"See?" Brindle said. "Change doesn't have to be scary. It can be an adventure." "And it's a wonderful end to an adventure," Cal smiled, flapping his wings to dry them off.

"Silly, Cal," Brindle laughed. "You're about to fly. Your adventure is only just beginning!"

"It is!" Cal laughed as he launched himself into the air. "Thank you, Brindle, for staying by me and being my friend!"

"We will see each other again!" Brindle smiled as the little butterfly went off on his new adventure.

Chapter 4:
The spring's Magic

For a week and three days, the shreds had been flying in the house of the four seasons. Not because they were arguing—no, no. The room of Spring, the spring fairy, hissed, bubbled and popped. Sometimes black smoke smoked from the door and windows; sometimes it was whiter. And now and then there was even smoke with glittering stars and colorful bubbles. When that happened, Spring didn't scold immediately, but only after checking the glittering fog. Spring was desperate. The right mix of fairy dust, which she so urgently needed for the spring magic, simply did not want to succeed this year. The three other fairies were seriously worried about their fairy friend. "Spring is falling this year," Spring said at breakfast the next morning.

"Something is wrong. The fairy dust always explodes when I stir it." Sullen, she dropped her spoon into the cocoa. The chocolate milk splashed in all directions. Chair, the winter fairy, suddenly had brown spots all over her face. "Fine, your new freckles," said summer fairy Sunny, and laughed. "I couldn't have done it any better!" "Very funny," said Spring. "Lucky you. It's not your turn with your magic season, either. And you always got it right year after year, you got even better." She jealously glanced at the many certificates hanging on the wall. Chair had been awarded several times for their snow that was particularly suitable for snowmen. Marine, the autumn fairy, had received a prize for her dragon wind, and Sunny made the wonderfully refreshing summer storm after a hot day.

Only Spring had never received a certificate. After all, she had managed to trigger spring every year so far. But didn't even seem to succeed this year. "If this continues, I have to quit," she said sadly. Chair hugged Spring. "Oh, don't talk nonsense," she comforted the little spring fairy. "I'm sure your spring magic will be ready in a few days!" Spring sobbed. "I'm so sorry," she whispered in Chair’s ear. "I know you can't go to this year's snowflake party if spring doesn't come soon." "All right, Spring," said Chair. "You're not doing this on purpose. I still hold out a bit. This year the kids can go sledding until March!" Spring looked gratefully at Chair. Then she went back to her room with her head bowed. "I'll keep practicing," she murmured, closing the door behind her.

The other fairies looked at each other. "We have to help her," said Marine. "This cannot continue like that. Do you have any idea why your fairy dust won't work this year?" "Mm," Sunny thought. »I always think of a special surprise for the season. Last year I added a little more flower seeds, and that made summer particularly colorful!" "And it smelled good, too," Chair recalled. "I always change an ingredient," said Marine. "You too, Chair?" Chair nodded. "Yes, the recipe is never the same," she said. "Spring may be missing a new ingredient” But Spring has to find out which ingredient that is, "Marine said. The three fairies sipped their cocoa. "I have an idea!" Sunny called. »What do you think of it when we celebrate a spring festival? Spring is sure to change her mind."

"Yeah, that sounds good!" Said Marine and Chair at the same time, giggling. "Unfortunately, I don't understand much about spring," said Sunny. "Come on, think about what you think of spring?" The two fairies thought hard. "Being outside, the first flowers, sunbeams." Marine thought. "Looking for chocolate Easter bunnies and brightly painted eggs in the grass and the smell of wet earth," added Chair. Sunny laughed. "Great, that's a lot," she said. "And there are spring rolls with spring curd for dinner." and before we sip spring soup," said Marine enthusiastically. The three seasons fairies started preparing right away.

Chair peeked into her candy drawer and scolded, "Crap, there are no chocolate rabbits, only chocolate Santa Clauses. It was clear! Well, let's take them." And because there was still deep snow outside, she preferred to hide Easter Santa Clauses in the rooms. Sunny dragged all the flowerpots into the kitchen and watered the plants extensively. Soon the smell of damp earth spread everywhere. Marine fetched all the lamps she could find and made a festive sunbeam lighting for the potted jungle. Finally, Chair placed a pack of frozen spring rolls in the oven and stirred the curd cheese while the soup was simmering on the stove. All that was missing now was only Spring. Sunny knocked on her door. At that moment, there was a bang inside.

Sunny opened carefully. The black smoke was so thick that Sunny couldn't even see the little spring fairy. She put her hand over her mouth and coughed: " Spring? Let go of your experiments. We have a surprise for you!" Spring came closer, her face smeared with soot. »What is it? I don't feel like trying around anymore," she said. "Then come," said Sunny mysteriously. When Spring entered the kitchen, Marine aimed one of the lamps at her face. "May the spring sun be with you from now on!" She cried. Chair held a flowerpot under Spring's nose. "May the smell of soft, wet earth remind you of melting snow and the first flowers," she said solemnly. "And may the spring rolls fill your hungry belly," said Sunny.

Spring laughed. "You are the best. I have to admit, my bad mood has blown away!" The three fairies were pleased that their surprise had worked so well. Sunny clapped her hands. "Before we eat, we're looking for the Easter chocolate Santa Clauses. We need a dessert, after all!" She shouted and stormed off. Spring could not be said twice and chased after her. In no time she had found two Santa Clauses! She proudly held up her prey and cheered: "I have it! Delicious Easter Santa Clauses!" Exuberantly, she danced with them into her room and around the cauldron of fairy dust. And again. And again. She circled the cauldron three times. Suddenly, colorful bubbles emerged from it. Then there were a hiss and silver stars danced all over the room that her surprise had worked so well.

"Hu, what's going on now?" Spring said, startled. "Quick, come here!" Sunny, Marine and Chair rushed into Spring's room and looked curiously into the cauldron. "Well, looks like the fairy dust does," Sunny chirped. Spring looked at her friends helplessly. "But how is that possible?" She asked baffled. "You put the missing ingredient in it," answered Marine. Spring shook her head. "It cannot be. I didn't do anything," she murmured, staring incredulously at the pink, sparkling dust in the cauldron. Chair laughed. "Yes, you added something. Even if you didn't notice fun! And good mood!" Spring's eyes lit up. "You're right! Spring magic mixed with dark thoughts. That couldn't work in the morning.

Chapter 5:
The Elven Queen Has Her Birthday

The two elven girls Luna and Violina sit on a branch over the river and wash their Sunday clothes. "Tomorrow is the time," says Luna. "I'm so excited!" Violina nods. "Me too. We have never played in front of so many people. And then also for the Elven Queen's birthday! Hopefully, everything will go well." Luna smiles. Everything will go well for sure. At least that's what she hopes. After all, they practiced so much! She pulls her dress out of the water. It is embroidered all over with shiny silver notes, as it should be for a singing elf. The skirt shimmers in the sun. "Done," calls Luna. "I'll hang it up to dry!" Then Violina lifts her dress out of the water. Because she is a violin elf, little golden violins embroider on her dress. Luna and Violina quickly hang their clothes over a rose bush.

When they dry there, they smell lovely of roses tomorrow! "Are we going to the island again and do some practice?" Asks Violina. Luna agrees. They climb into their flower boat and flap their wings. They arrived at the small island in no time. "How good that none of the other elves can hear us here," says Luna. "

You are the most beautiful elf here,

thank you for your kindness.

You rule us royally,

all elves love you.

We wish you

sunshine and luck and blessings on your ways!

The little elves practice their song over and over again. Soon, many small beetles, caterpillars, bees and butterflies gather around them, listening to them spellbound. They clap enthusiastically again and again. And Violina and Luna keep singing. They don't even notice that the sun is setting, and their listeners are disappearing one by one. They sing and play until they finally fall asleep, and the next morning they are awakened by the hum of a fat bumblebee. Violina tiredly presses her furry bumblebee. "Shut up, your old alarm clock!" She growls sleepily. "Well, I have to ask very much," complains the bumblebee indignantly. Violina opens her eyes in surprise. How long has your alarm clock been able to speak? Then she discovers that she is not lying in her bed at all.

"Oh dear," she calls loudly and shakes Luna on the shoulder. "Luna, we fell asleep! We have to hurry! The festival is about to start, and we wanted to help with the preparations." Luna nods sleepily. Violina presses the violin into her hand and pushes it into the boat. Then she quickly directs it across the river to her clothes. “Here, it's still a bit damp from the morning dew, but you can put it on," says Violina and hands her dress to Luna. Luna’s eyes are still half-closed. "Well, you might be a sleeping cap for me," Violina murmurs and helps Luna put on the dress. Then she continues to steer the boat to the fairground. You are lucky. The festival has not started yet, and the preparations are in full swing. All elves have something to do and run around excitedly.

Long tables with white ceilings stand around the large stage. Some elves bring shiny crystal glasses to the tables; others distribute silver cutlery. Elves with high white chef hats place huge pies with strawberries and cherries on the charts. And the smallest elves scurry around in between and scatter colorful flowers. Next to the stage is the elven Queen's throne, which already adorned with flowers. "Oh, that's nice!" Violina whispers. "Come on, Luna, let's practice again quickly," she says, reaching for her violin. "One, two, three, go! “But what is it? You only hear a croak. Luna has opened her mouth wide, but not a single sound comes out. She tries so hard that her head turns completely red. Violina also tries to elicit some beautiful sounds from her violin.

But there is only a loud squeak. "What will it be? Is that your surprise?" Giggles, a dark voice Elf Teacher Jackal stands behind them and laughs. "Oh, Mr. Jackal, you have to help us," Violina says desperately. "We slept outside tonight, and my violin got soaked from the rope! And I think Luna got a cold; she can't sing a sound!" Thick elven tears are already rolling down Violin’s cheeks.

Mr. Jackal comfortably puts his arm around her shoulders. "Oh, we'll have it right away," he says reassuringly. "You can borrow my violin; I'll get it from home. And Luna first drinks hot tea. Violina nods and fetches tea for Luna. The elves sit sadly on a sheet, waiting for teacher jackal and drinking tea." Can you already say something? ", Violina asks after every sip Luna takes. But Luna shakes her head again and again. Finally, Mr. Jackal comes back. He hands Violina his violin." Here, practice a little more so that you can take care of yourself she's used to, "he says with a smile. Violina carefully strokes the bow over the strings. Soon it sounds perfect." It's a shame that you can't lend your voice to Luna, "says Violina sadly." Yes, that would be good" says Luna. Mr. Jackal grins. "Why are you laughing?" Asks Luna. "It's not funny!"

Mr. Jackal grins even more. "The voice is already back!" "Right," says Luna, "I said something!" Now she has to laugh too. "Well, now quickly to your seats," murmurs Mr. Jackal. "The elf queen has just come; the festival is starting!" they have not even noticed that all the other elves are already sitting at the tables. The elf queen is now majestically walking to her throne.

Luna and Violina dash to the stage. They excitedly wait behind the curtain until it's their turn. The ceremonial elf is saying: "Dear Queen, we are delighted that you are celebrating your one hundred and twenty-seventh birthday with us. All fairies congratulate you from the bottom of their heart and wish you a wonderful celebration. And at the beginning of our anniversary, two little elves want to recite the poem for you. Raise the curtain for Luna and Violina!"

The two elves step forward solemnly. Then they play and sing their little melody. It sounds beautiful and magical. The whole Elf people cheer, and even the Queen says this is the most beautiful song she has ever heard. The little elves shine. They hug and thankfully wave to Mr. Jackal. They have never been so happy in their lives!

Chapter 6: Where's Mom Duck

At a large pond in the middle of the green, Mama Duck is standing in her nest and is very proud when the offspring hatch from the eggs. The little ducks break the shells and stick out their little heads. Then they wiggle their butts and shake the rest of the bowl off their bottom. Mama Duck nudges each of them lovingly with her beak. The little ones immediately know that this is the mom. Then the mom jumps into the water and one after the other jumps after. They swim in a line across the pond—the proud mom away from the front. But, oh dear, what is that? A chick has not yet hatched. It rumbles back and forth and rolls back and forth in the nest. With a lot of momentum, it tumbles onto the meadow, and the egg breaks on a stone.

The eggshell flies around, and the little duck shakes a lot. It looks around carefully. Well, there is nobody there. Hmm, weird. So, the duckling waddles off to find his mom. After a short time, the duckling meets a frog. The frog sits on a branch by the water and croaks. "Hooray!" Thinks the duckling. "It has to be a mom." It runs to the frog and happily croaks with it. The frog looks at the duck: "What are you doing here?" Asks the frog. The duckling replies: "I croak with you, mom!" The frog shakes his head: "I'm not your mom!" He says and hops away. The duckling is sad, he thought it found Its mom. It continues to waddle with its head hanging. After a few steps, it encounters a bird. The bird is chirping happily. The duckling looks at the bird and thinks: "This is not croaking, but it has feathers.

Maybe that's my mom." And then it sits down next to the bird and croaks loudly. The bird is outraged: "Why are you covering my beautiful singing with your quack?" He asks. Then he pecks the duckling on the head and flies away. Now the duckling is sad, and tears roll down his cheeks. "I will never find my mom again!" She sobs softly to herself. A fox comes to the duckling. "Well, duckling, why are you so sad?" Asks the fox. "I'm looking for my mom. I'm all alone!" Says the duckling. The fox grins sneakily and says: "Come with me. Together we will find your mom. "The duckling is happy: "Hooray!" and runs after the fox. After a while, the duckling asks the fox: "How long are we going to run? We're almost in the forest. "The fox answers:" Don't worry. Your mom is there and waiting for you. "

The fox has no intention of finding the mom. He wants to lure the duckling into the forest to eat it under the protection of the trees. The fox grins and thinks: "It's too easy. I don't even have to wear the duckling; it runs into the forest on its own. "Once at the edge of the forest, the duckling stops: "But it is dark there in the forest!" It says fearfully. "You don't have to be afraid!" Says the fox. "I hid your mom there, so she's safe. "Sure, what from?" Asks the duckling. The fox answers in a worried voice: "You know, there are many angry animals that would love to eat you. But don't be afraid, I'm not one of them! "Just as they wanted to continue, a bear stands in the way: "Well, fox? Where do you want to go with the duckling?"

He asks. The fox ducks in terror: "Hello, big bear, where are you from so suddenly? I only help the duckling to find his mom!" The bear looks at the duckling. Then he asks in a growl, "Is the little duckling, right?" The duckling jumps up and down: "Yes! The fox hid them in the forest because there are so many angry animals. "The bear immediately suspects what the fox is up to." “So, there are a lot of bad animals here," he grumbles. Then he looks at the fox suspiciously: "Well, luckily you are not one of them, fox. Right? "The fox shakes his head quickly:" No, no, but of course not. I just wanted to help poor duckling. "The bear takes the duckling protectively in his paws and says:" Well, that's great that the fox helped you here. Now, I'm going to make it better.

Your mom is no longer in the forest. I think she went to the pond to look for you. She misses you very much, you know? "Then he looks at the fox again and asks with a threatening look:" Is it true, fox? "The fox nods his head very quickly:" Yes, now that you say it falls it me again. She ran to the pond earlier. "Then the fox looks at the duckling:" Your mom is back at the lake. I had completely forgotten that, yes, yes. "So, the bear takes the duckling with it. The two meet the bird on the way to the pond. The duckling trembles. "What have you got?" Asks the bear. The duckling ducks and whispers: "The bird pecked me because I thought it was my mom." The bear looks at the bird angrily and grumbles: "I look into your face here; the duckling probably speaks the truth.

You also must help, but you didn't help poor duckling!" Then he takes a deep breath: "We'll talk about that when I come back," he says, and carries the duckling on. The bird flutters away quickly. Next, the two meet the frog. The bear looks at the duckling: "Did the frog hurt you too?" The duckling replies: "No, he just jumped away." The bear looks at the frog angrily and grumbles: "I look at your face here; the duckling probably speaks the truth. You also must help, but you didn't help poor duckling!" Then he takes a deep breath: "We'll talk about that when I come back," he says, and carries the duckling on. The frog hops away quickly. When the two arrive at the pond, the duckling is very happy when it sees the mom.

It cheers and jumps headlong into the lake: "Thank you, dear bear! Calls it to the bear. "And please also thank the fox of mine." The bear grumbles back loudly: "Little ducks are welcome. And don't worry, I will indeed thank the fox powerfully from you. "When the fox hears this, he picks up his ears, startled. "Oh dear, now I'm still on the collar." He thinks and runs as fast as he can over all mountains. The fox has never been seen since. The bear still keeps a watchful eye on the little duckling, so that a clever fox never gets stupid thoughts again.

Chapter 7: A Snowman Saves Christmas

Once upon a time, there was a snowman who lived in the Christmas wonderland. But it wasn't a treehouse. It was a real house in a tree. It was normal in the Christmas wonderland, and there were also gingerbread houses, huge Christmas trees and a lot more fantastic. But let's get back to our snowman, whose greatest wish was to be a Christmas elf. However, only elves could become Christmas elves. So, it was written in the big Christmas book. Still, the snowman tried year after year. The boy even disguised himself once as an elf to get to the great Christmas factory. But he noticed the Nachleben at the gate. Maybe his carrot had betrayed him on the face? Or perhaps he was just more spherical than everyone else. It would work this year because the snowman had a great idea.

The boy wanted to pack gifts himself and distribute them to the children. Could Santa not be angry with him for that? And he could finally put the smile so longed for on the children's faces. The first thing was to get the presents. But where to get from and not steal? He had to make money somehow. But what should he do? He was incredibly good at sledding. But you couldn't make money from it. Then he thought of something. He slipped happily and began to form little snowballs. Then he took a sign and sat in the snow. The sign read: "Every ball three thalers." That should work. Everyone likes snowball fights, but the snowman sat in a vain hour after hour. Nobody even bought a snowball. So, he asked the blacksmith if he could help. But he only laughed out loud.

"What do you want to help me?" Asked the smith. "If you stand by the fire with me, you will melt. Do you want to serve me as drinking water?" "That's right." Thought the snowman, it had to be something where it was cold. So, he went to the ice cream factory. Large ice blocks made there to build igloos. But here too, the snowman was laughed at. "How do you want to help me?" Asked the factory manager. "The blocks are so heavy if you want to push them, your thin stick arms break." "That's right." Thought the snowman again, it has to be something where it is cold, and the work is not too difficult. So, the snowman went to the ice-cream seller. He was taken with the idea and said: "You are a good ice cream seller! You are never too cold, and if ice is missing for cooling, we simply take something from you. "

When the snowman heard this, he was startled. "Ice cream from me?" He asked. "I think I was wrong in the door," he said, running away quickly. The snowman was sad now. Nothing boy tried worked. The boy sank to the ground in the middle of the city; His hat slipped over his sad button eyes. He took his violin and played a Christmas carol. It had always helped him when he was sorry. When he was playing, he was so thoughtful that he didn't even notice the people passing him throwing some change. It was when a stranger given by said: "A wonderful Christmas carol. It is one of my favorites. Keep playing snowman," he listened. He pushed his hat up and saw the change in front of him. "That's money!" He said softly and kept playing. "That's money!"

He cried out and continued playing. He grinned all over his face and sang with all his heart's content: "Tomorrow there will be something for children. Tomorrow we will be happy. "With the newly earned money, he bought gifts and wrapping paper on a doll there and a car here. It was packed and laced diligently and passed the cord through the hole. "One on the right, one on the left—yes, the snowman comes and brings it!" But wait. How are the gifts supposed to get to the children from here? The snowman considered. "I can't wear it. But I don't have a Christmas sleigh either. And Santa Claus will hardly lend me his. The reindeer would also want to eat my carrot." The snowman was incredibly good at sledding on a sled, but it wasn't always just downhill. So, what to do? The snowman also had a great idea here. He tied the presents onto a snail. Snails can carry a lot. That would work. Just when he does, a Christmas elf came by.

"What will it be when it's done?" Asked the Christmas elf. The snowman proudly stood next to his snail. "This is my Christmas snail! And I'm handing out gifts to the kids this year." The Christmas elf looked at the snowman and the snail in amazement. "I'd laugh now if it weren't so sad," he said then. "You already know that a snail is too slow to deliver gifts to all the children in the world? I mean, it would be too lazy to supply this village itself. "The joyful grin faded from the snowman, and the elf continued: "Unfortunately, these are also far too few gifts. You would need a million billion times more but it doesn't matter anyway. Christmas is canceled anyway! "When the snowman heard that, he no longer understood the world." Christmas is canceled? The Christmas elf nodded: "And whether that works. Santa Claus got sick and can't give gifts."

"Nazanin" breathed the snowman in astonishment and looked at the elf incredulously. "Santa Claus can't get sick at all." The Christmas elf nodded again: "That's right. Usually not but this year it is so cold that even Christmas elves are too cold for it. "The snowman became nervous:" But Christmas, so Christmas... so, what about Christmas? "He ran around in a hectic circle and spoke to himself:" No, no, no, no, that cannot be. A Christmas without gifts is not a Christmas. "The Christmas elf interrupted the snowman." Christmas is Christmas without gifts. The gifts have always been more and almost too much over the past few years. "The snowman slumped briefly and breathed out." Then he stood up straight and said:" But with gifts, it is a lot more beautiful."

The Christmas elf shook his head: "Christmas is the festival of charity. There is no need for presents. "The snowman spun around and said softly:" Yes, that's right. "Then he took one of his presents and held it up to the Christmas elf:" But look how beautiful the presents are. With a gift like that, I can show my love for my neighbor much better than without. "Then he made the gift disappear behind his back and looked sadly at the Christmas elf." Look, it's gone now. Isn't that sad? Imagine the many little sad googly eyes standing in front of a Christmas tree under which there are no gifts. Now tell the children that we don't need gifts because Christmas is the festival of charity! "The Christmas elf gave in: "Ok, maybe you're right. But what should we do?

It's too cold!" The snowman tossed the gift aside and slid to the Christmas elf: "Ha! Exactly! It's too cold! For Santa Claus. But I'm a snowman!" Then he turned in a circle and began to sing: "I'm never too cold, I will grow old. I can hurry and hurry, hand out gifts to the children. You just have to help me with stuff and team. Take me to Santa Claus quickly. "The Christmas elf covered his ears: "Now just stop singing. I'll take you there. "The snowman jumped in the air with joy:" Yeah! Hey, it almost rhymed. You could also sing a song." Snowman talked for a while on the way to Santa Claus—to the regret of the Christmas elf. Arrived at Santa Claus, he was shocked to see a snowman at home. Usually, there were only Christmas elves there. But Santa Claus loved the idea that Christmas shouldn't cancel.

Because he also thought that Christmas with gifts merely is more beautiful. But how should the snowman distribute so many presents? The snowman chewed nervously on his lips. He was so close to living his most prominent dream. "We don't have to distribute all the presents," he said then. "Everyone gets a little less this year. It's still better than nothing, isn't it? "Santa looked at the snowman:" I don't think the idea is terrible. That should work! But what do you want to drive the gifts with? You can't have my sled!" The snowman was on the verge of despair. "Just solve this one problem, and my dream will come true," the boy thought to himself. Then he said sheepishly: "So, I'm a pretty good sled!" Then the Christmas elf interfered: "Oh, that's all nonsense!

Then you only deliver to the children who live at the bottom of a mountain? Or how should I imagine that? "But Santa Claus raised his hand and moved his fingers as if he were scratching the air. A massive snow slide appeared from nowhere under the snowman. Then Santa said: "You're such a good sled tobogganer. This snow mountain will accompany you. It is a never-ending snow slope. So, you can sled anywhere quickly. "The snowman looked at the vast snow mountain and said: "That Is "then he suddenly jumped in the air and shouted: "yes, the hammer! Tobogganing forever! That's not how I imagined it in my wildest dreams. "

The snowman was happy, like never before. But Santa Claus raised his index finger again and said warningly: "But watch out for the fireplaces! I've already burned my bottom!" But the snowman was cold: "Oh, I have so much snow with me, if I burn my bottom, I'll just make myself a new one—ha-ha." Then he grinned at Santa, jumped on his sled and he was gone. The snowman saved Christmas, that was too cold, but just right for the snowman!

Chapter 8: The Oldest Unicorn

On the tallest hill in the magical land lived the oldest of all the unicorns. Nobody ever came to visit him, and he had lived so long that most had forgotten he was even up there. His only friend was the witch, but even she was too busy to visit him.

One day Spring woke up and found there was something wrong with her horn. It didn't want to glow, and it wouldn't sparkle. Its color was dim, and she couldn't feel any magic in it. Spring quickly visited all her friends but none of them knew what to do.

"I'm sorry, I'm not sure why this is happening," Fay told her.

"It's never happened to me," Cosmic said.

"Perhaps it was something you ate last night," Crystal suggested.

"I hope it's not contagious," Spring said.

"You should go see the witch and ask her," Odd told her.

Spring did what he said, and she went to go see the witch. She was so sad without her magical horn. A unicorn can't just have a normal horn. Every unicorn needs to have a magical horn that glows brightly, and glitters and sparkles.

When Spring got to the witch's garden, she was sure that the witch would be able to help using her magic.

"I'm sorry Spring, but I'm not sure why your horn isn't working," the witch told her. "I don't think I've ever seen this happen before, but I think I know someone who has."

"Who?" Spring asked with a slight smile.

"The oldest unicorn," the witch answered. "He lives up on the tallest hill in the magical land. He is so old that he has probably seen something like this happen before. You should go visit and ask him. Remember to bring him a gift when you do."

Spring thanked the witch and started her long journey to the tallest hill in the magical land. She didn't even know that someone lived up there until now. She was hoping that the oldest unicorn would be kind and help her.

On the way she stopped to pick some flowers and fruit as a gift for the oldest unicorn. It was hard to carry them all because she couldn't use her magic horn. She met some fairies along the way and asked them kindly to make her a basket out of wood and string. They did this for her, and she was able to carry the flowers and fruits up the hill in the basket.

It was the middle of the day when she finally reached the top of the hill. She was surprised by what she saw. There was a small, but lovely house right at the top. There was a garden filled with flowers and a big tree that dropped fruit to the floor.

Spring walked up to the house and knocked on the front door. She put the basket down and waited for the oldest unicorn to answer.

"Go away!" she heard the oldest unicorn yell from inside the house.

Spring was shocked at first, but she knocked again and said, "Oldest unicorn, I need your help."

"I don't care, go away."

"But I brought you a gift."

It was silent for a moment then the oldest unicorn opened the door and looked down at the basket of fruit and flowers. He looked up at Spring.

"What do you want?" He asked.

"I need your help; my horn isn't magical anymore and no one knows what's wrong with it."

"What makes you think I can help?"

"You're the oldest unicorn and the witch said you might have seen this happen before. Can you please help me?"

The oldest unicorn frowned, then sighed and said, "Okay, I will help you, but you have to do exactly as I say."

"Oh, I will!"

For the rest of the day Spring did everything the old unicorn asked her to. She tended to his garden for him, picked the fruit off the ground, and cleaned his house for him. Spring wasn't sure why she was doing all this, but she hoped it would help fix her horn. It was getting late and Spring had done all that the oldest unicorn had asked, but her horn still didn't have any magic.

"What's the big idea?" Spring asked. "I've done all the chores you asked me to, and my horn isn't fixed yet."

"You're not done, there is still more you need to do."

"I think you're wrong. I think you just wanted to get me to do all the chores you were too lazy to do and you weren't going to help me at all."

The oldest unicorn gasped and frowned at Spring, "How dare you? Do you think I would just help you for free? You must first do things for me and then I will reward you."

"But I brought you a gift!"

"It is good manners to bring someone a gift when visiting their home, especially if they are your elder. That does not mean I will help you. First you do something for me and then I help you. Now go over there and eat the fruit that falls from the tree. That will fix your horn."

Spring was angry but she did as he said. She ate the fruit and it worked. She felt all the magic come back to her horn and it started to glow once again. She jumped for joy and cheered, but then she spotted the oldest unicorn, still angry with her.

She bowed her head to him and said, "I'm sorry, oldest unicorn. You were right and I should have respected you more."

"It's alright," he said. "You are young, and too impulsive. You still need to learn how to slow down and wait for things that life will bring you. Just remember from now on to always respect your elders and use good manners. If you can respect others, then they will respect you too. Now go home quick before it gets too dark. If you or any of your friends ever have a problem with your horn, you know where to find me. Remember to bring a gift."

Spring said goodbye and ran home to show her friends her new magical horn.

Chapter 9: Brindle is Scared

Brindle was a beautiful and magical unicorn. Before she went to bed each night, she would brush her long silky mane a thousand times. Her mother would help her, and it was Brindle's favorite time of the day. She would talk about her day, and her mother would listen.

"I played soccer today," said Brindle.

"Did you score any goals?" asked her mother.

"I scored one, but that was all." Brindle polished her golden horn until it was extra-shiny.

"Well, did you try your hardest?" asked her mother.

"I always try my hardest," said Brindle with pride.

"Then that is all that matters," said her mother. "If you try your hardest, then you can do nothing more."

"Can I tell you all about my adventures in the glade?" asked Brindle.

"How about in the morning?" asked her mother. "Look at how late it is? The sun went down a long time ago, and the moon is high in the sky."

"I am tired," said a sleepy Brindle.

Brindle finished polishing her golden horn, and she got into her bed. Her mother read her a bedtime story and tucked her in, giving Brindle a kiss on the head. The light was turned off, but the room still had a glow in it, partly from the small nightlight, and partly from the moon.

It had been a long, fun day for Brindle, and she was excited to rest and dream. She had almost fallen asleep when a noise woke her.

"Hello," said Brindle.

The room was silent. Brindle looked around, but the room was exactly how it had been when she had fallen asleep. She lay there for a moment, scanning the room. It was full of shadows, and that made Brindle a little afraid.

"Mom!" shouted Brindle.

There was soon a clip-clopping noise as her mother came up the stairs and into her room.

"What is the matter?" asked her mother.

"I thought that I heard a noise," said Brindle.

"Hmm," said her mother. "It must have been the wind. Noises sound different at night, but they are no different from the noises that come during the day."

"I think that it is gone now," said Brindle. "I should go back to sleep."

"Goodnight," said her mother.

Brindle soon fell asleep, but, again, she was woken.

She was sure that she had heard a noise, and this time, it had come from the closet. She lay in bed and stared at the closet, convinced that something was in there. Perhaps it was a goblin.

Brindle did not like feeling afraid. She wished that she could be brave and have no fear.

"Mom!" shouted Brindle again.

There was a clip-clopping sound again, and soon her mother was in the room. This made her feel less afraid.

"I felt scared," said Brindle. "I thought that there might be a goblin in the closet, but that's stupid. I wish that I were not so afraid."

"You cannot help being afraid," said her mother.

"But I want to be brave," said Brindle.

"Being scared does not mean that you are not brave," said her mother.

"It doesn't?"

"Of course not. Being brave is about accepting your fear. I have been scared and afraid many times," said her mother with a smile.

"You have?" Brindle was excited to hear more.

"I was afraid when you went out by yourself for the first time. I was afraid when I moved here to start a new life. I was afraid when I had to walk home in the dark one time. But I was brave because I accepted my fear and did not let it control me," said her mother.

"How do I accept my fear?" asked Brindle.

"Well, that takes practice. You have to let your fear be your friend. It has to live inside of you, and then you have to do things anyway. That is how you become brave and courageous. That is how you face your fears."

"Face my fears?" Brindle did not like the sound of that.

"If you can make friends with your fear, you will see that you can control it. Look at the closet over there. You think that there might be a goblin inside. That is the fear inside trying to control you. Come on, let's face it together," said her mother.

Brindle was still scared, but she felt braver with her mother beside her. The two unicorns walked over to the closet, and Brindle opened the door.

It was empty.

“Where else do you want to look?” asked her mother.

“How about under the bed?” Brindle was feeling a little braver now.

“Let’s go and take a look,” said her mother.

The two unicorns clopped over to the bed and looked under. It was a little scary and dark, but there was no goblin under there.

“I feel a little silly now,” said Brindle. “There was nothing there all along.”

“That does not make you silly, Brindle. It only shows that your fear is inside of you and not in your outside world. If your fear is inside of you, you can accept it and control it. That is what bravery is all about, and you have been a very brave unicorn tonight,” said her mother.

“I have?” Brindle was prouder than she had ever been.

“I think that you are brave enough to sleep,” said her mother. “Now that you have made friends with your fear, you are in control.”

“Thank you, Mother,” said Brindle. “Goodnight.”

“Goodnight,” said her mother as she turned off the light.

Brindle was still a little scared, but the fear was her friend now. She soon fell asleep and had wonderful dreams of meadows and rainbows.

Chapter 10: Honesty is the Key

In one of the old villages there was a unicorn called Jack who lived with his mother in a small house after the death of his father, who passed away when Jack was young with a small horn due to his severe illness.

Jack's mother used to take care of her son very seriously, and this care was not limited to caring for food, drink and clothing, but his mother was interested in teaching her child the good morals, such as sincerity and to be kind to those he meets in his life, and that these morals can help him to contribute in his community leaving a good impact in the hearts of all people.

His will is to be a perfect unicorn, and possesses all their beautiful attributes, because they are known for their attractive and valued personalities.

They are an example of goodness, kindness and love. His mother wanted Jack to be the symbol of these qualities among his townspeople, and she made a great effort towards that.

Jack had an uncle working in trade between unicorn countries, Jack went with him on some commercial trips in order to be able to bear responsibility, as these trips needed patience and seriousness, in which the traveler travelled long distances.

They reached remote cities in order to be supplied with goods and resell them for the unicorn in the village where Jack and his mother lived, and in the villages next to it.

Jack was learning from his uncle the concepts of selling and trading, and how to be an expert in the process of buying and selling through clarity with others and not deceiving them, and his main rule was to avoid lying, Jack learned these principles well from his uncle before being allowed to travel with him.

During this trip, Jack dealt with a short but very important story. While he was with the caravan on their way to trade, a group of thieving wolves attacked them, surrounded the convoy including with the ones in it, seized the goods they carried, and took their food and money.

When one of the wolves arrived at Jack, the wolf asked him in a threatening tone: You little boy, how many golden coins do you carry? All of this is now ours.

He answered steadfastly: I carry thirty pieces of gold

Here, this wolf drowned in a wave of laughter, and ridiculed Jack's answer to him saying: You are very funny, boy, you are too young to bear this amount, do not pretend that you are rich, this is funny.

Then another wolf came from the gang members who cut off the road and asked him the same question. He answered the same answer, and the other wolf mocked him, saying: Our leader must see this himself and laugh, come with me.

They took him to the leader of the gang. When Jack reached the leader, he quietly asked him: Tell me how much coins you have, and do not cheat, because I will know right away.

He replied: I am not bluffing, I really told them that I had thirty pieces of gold

So, he asked him: Why do you stick to this excessive honesty and not evade the correct answer, as did the other unicorns in the convoy with this gang to preserve their money?

So, Jack brought out the thirty pieces he owned and told the gang leader: I promised my mother that I would not lie, and I would not betray my mother and my promise to her no matter what might cause me to hide the truth.

Here the gang leader was surprised, and he remembered that in his robbery of this convoy, he had betrayed his father's past command not to follow the path of evil.

At that point, the gang leader did not take control of himself and wept, affected by what Jack said to him, and told Jack: You did not betray your mother's promise and I will not betray my father's promise as well.

The gang leader ordered the release of all members of the convoy and returned to them all what were taken from them, and worked to serve and guard the commercial convoy until they reached the city they intended.

He thanked Jack in particular saying: I really thank you for this honesty and courage that awoke the goodness and extinguished the evil inside me, if you need him at any time I will help you.

Jack bid farewell to the former gang leader and left in peace with his family.

This gang stopped cutting people off and taking their money by force due to Jack's honesty, telling the truth, and keeping his promise to his mother.

Jack found his uncle coming to him with pride, he hugged him happily before his mother came to do the same, everyone was proud of him and the news spread among his town and friends.

He became an example of honesty and trust, and many merchants asked Jack to work with them for their confidence in his morals.

They also showed their great admiration for his mother and for the ideal education methods that she applied, and they praised her for bearing hardships and looking after her son alone after the death of her husband.

Chapter 11: Mary and the Unicorn

A long time ago, there was a little girl named Mary. She was the only daughter in a rich family with a strong reputation in her country.

Her father was one of the richest, wisest and most intelligent men in the city. As for her mother, she was a big fan of fairy tales, she owned a very huge library full of fairy tales and ancient legendary stories, she was also writing some of them and reading them to her daughter Mary, who unfortunately did not like these stories and never believed in them.

One day Mary was sad and sitting alone in her room, she was always missing the magic touch in her life, she needed some surprise and imagination, but she did not allow anyone to help her, she kept her mother and friends away from her most of the time.

Her mother came that day to her room and said: Mary, my dear, do you want me to tell a story? I will not read stories that you did not like before, I will read a new and funny one.

Mary looked at her mother sadly and said with an unhappy voice: No, I do not want to hear anything.

The mother was a little disappointed that her daughter refused her help, she went to her library to return the story back to its place and then went to sleep wishing that she would wake up to find Mary in a better condition.

After the mother left the library, that story that she was going to read to her daughter fell to the ground, she had not put it on the shelf properly.

While the poor mother was asleep, Mary felt in her room a bit of regret, she felt that she was rude and impatient with her mother while all what she was trying to do is helping her.

Mary knew that her mother was in pain when she saw her only daughter isolated, lonely and sad, but Mary did not know what to do, she did not like those stories of unicorns, Santa Claus or other fairy tales.

Mary always said to herself and her mother: I do not know why you believe the existence of these beings, what is the use of loving something that does not even exist, you are all liars and I do not like talking to you.

And when one of her friends said to her: Mary, the unicorns are real, we all know that even if we do not see them.

Mary replied to her: Of course not, I have never seen a unicorn before, not even in my dreams, as long as I have not seen one of them, they do not exist for me.

Then she turned her face and went away to go home and stopped playing with them.

Suddenly Mary decided to give an opportunity that might change her mind, perhaps her mother knows more than her, and maybe she has already seen a unicorn before, but she cannot reveal it.

She rose from her bed and left the room with courageous steps; she quietly closed the door so that her mother would not wake up as she was sleeping in the room next to her.

She thought about going back and sticking to her thoughts, but she was very sad when she saw her mother's face and her disappointed expressions, she continued walking until she entered the library.

Mary was confused; she did not know what to read from this huge number of stories.

She thought, I can read about Cinderella.

She looked a little about her stories and then said: No, I want something more interesting. My mom has read this story to me many times before, so I think I saved it.

On her way, she found books for Santa Claus as well, but she said: We are still in the middle of the year, I will try to read it before Christmas.

Then she found a book on the ground, it's the book that her mother wanted to read to her, she took it and looked at it and said: A unicorn story, maybe this is what I'm searching for, I have always loved these creatures but I have hidden these feelings because I have not seen them before, I have decided, I will read it and give it chance.

She took the book with her and went back to the room, she liked the unicorn drawings so much, and she loved their wings and colorful horns as she liked their cheerful and courageous characters.

She read the story in amazement and great admiration, she even read it three times in a row, but she was not completely happy yet; she said to herself: I loved them very much, but I still cannot see them and this makes me very upset whenever I hear about them. If only I could see one of them, I would go and read all the books in the library, but my feeling that they are not real prevents me from that.

She put the book on her table heavily and sat next to the window watching trees and birds until she slept in peace, and suddenly she heard knockings on the window, Mary woke up to find what made her heart dance from the intensity of joy, it was a unicorn! He was flying his wings in front of the window while smiling at her.

Mary opened the window happily and said to him: You are real! I am very happy, but I want to apologize as well because I doubted you, I really needed to see you.

Unicorn said to her: No need to apologize, my dear, but even if you cannot see things, this does not mean that they are not real. For example, you cannot see the love that your mother and father hold for you, but it certainly exists and you certainly believe in it, I do not have to live with you at home to be real, I live in your imagination and in your little mind, you can talk to me at any time and make sure that I hear you and if you want to tell me something write it on a paper and put it in front of your window and I will read it.

Mary said in astonishment: You are very kind, I promise to become like you and show my love for my mother and father, and even my friends, I will go to play with them when I have the opportunity

The unicorn said to her: I knew you were a kind and beautiful girl, you have a lot of love inside your heart, so go now and spread it to the world.

The unicorn turned around to leave after changing this girl's life, possibly forever.

The mother woke up to find her daughter busy in one of the drawings. Mary was holding her pen and drawing with it on a paper on her desk while she was charmingly smiling.

When Mary saw her mother, she took the paper and presented it to her, it was a drawing of the unicorn who visited her. The mother was very happy of her daughter and sat next to her while she was completing the drawing.

Mary hugged her mother and said to her: My mother, I love you.

Mary’s mother was so happy and said: Me too, my dear, me too.

Chapter 12: White Sands, Blue Water and Dragons

Tommy Robinson was born and raised on the beautiful Caribbean Ocean. He was only a young boy when his Dad took him fishing out on the clear blue ocean. The family lived in Palmas Bellas, Panama, and Tommy was just 9 years old. Tommy's Dad was a priest, and the family had lived in the country of Panama for centuries. The Robinson lineage was heralded as one of honor and nobility. Tommy was psychic, and his Dad did not like it!

Tommy had learned about his gifts when he was a toddler and had been able to move things around in his bedroom from his crib. At first, he was afraid to tell anyone because even he was scared by his own abilities. He just knew it was not normal. One night, Tommy's Dad walked in while he was levitating his Teddy Bear, which was in his toy box and trying to bring it to him in his crib. The door opened, and there was the Teddy, floating in the air and Tommy standing up in his crib, holding the top rail with a look on his face that his Father had never seen before. The Teddy dropped to the floor suddenly, and Tommy started to cry. He always remembered that his Dad didn't say anything to him about it then or any time after, but he knew his Dad was not happy about his only son being what he thought of as a freak.

On the day of the fishing outing, Tommy asked his Dad about the Caribbean Sea, and if there were any strange creatures living in it. Of course, his Dad did not like this question and was not interested in the subject. Since it was to be a fishing trip, Tommy's Dad wanted to get him interested in the sport and had bought a rod and reel for both of them and some fishing gear for the outing. The big fishing boat rocked and rolled in the waves when they reached the open ocean.

Tommy liked the feeling; his Dad hated it and got seasick. Eventually, the captain called out that they were coming up on the fishing spot, and the boat began to slow down, and finally, the motors could be heard powering down. The huge anchor splashed down into the ocean, and everyone started fiddling with their fishing gear.

Everyone found a spot and set up some deck chairs with their snacks and coffee thermoses nearby. Tommy and his Dad did the same, but Tommy wanted to stand. He kept peering down over the side of the boat into the dark and foreboding looking water. "Hey, Dad, you can't see down into the water," Tommy exclaimed. His Dad didn't answer as he was busy trying to put the live bait on his hook. Tommy said, "here, let me help you, Pop." And Mr. Robinson stopped what he was doing and froze for the moment while he considered his son's offer. "Okay, boy, you show me you can do it better than I can then," he said, handing Tommy the rod and the bait can. Tommy grabbed up one of the squirming worms, and to his Dad's surprise, the thing went completely still, as though it was actually helping Tommy to hook itself. "How did you do that so easily?" his Dad asked with a very puzzled look on his face. "I dunno," Tommy answered.

Tommy handed the rod back to his Dad and baited his own rod, and they both cast out their lines. Somebody, a few people down the row, got a big bite. Everyone turned their attention to the man as he reeled in a large fish that looked like it should be good eating. That got everyone excited, and soon, just about all of them had caught something. Some caught more big fish, and some caught sharks and other fish that had to be cut loose.

Then Tommy felt a tug on his line. It was strong, and little Tommy stood up and grabbed his pole with both hands. His Dad watched him with admiration and thought to himself that he had never seen his son take charge like this. New territory for sure. When Tommy got the catch pulled almost up to the surface, it really started to fight. He fought back and eventually stepped back as he reeled and reeled, giving the catch no slack at all. His father was amazed. It looked to him as though Tommy had done this many times, but he knew for a fact that this was Tommy's first-time fishing.

Then, as everyone watched, Tommy snagged the catch up out of the water and flipped it into the boat. The only sound that could be heard was that of the waves lapping up against the side of the boat. Nobody could believe their eyes in what they saw. It looked like it had legs instead of fins, and it had a head like a tiny horse. The thing whipped its head around, pulled out the hook, which oddly was attached to its tail and ran down the deck and bounded up onto the railing just like a little monkey would have. It sat upon the railing for a good minute or so and turned around to look back at all the gawking fishermen. Everyone knew what it looked like, but still, nobody spoke. Then Tommy did!

"It's a baby dragon," he said to much noise and disagreement on the part of some of the other fishermen. "It is," he said again and began to walk slowly towards the little thing. "Don't be afraid," he said, and then in his mind, he heard distinct words and had to assume they came from the little creature. "Why would I be afraid of the likes of you lot?" were the words he heard. He remembered his gifts and stilled his mind. Tommy had been practicing something called mindfulness, and it was easy for him to clear his mind so he could answer the little beast. "Are you a dragon?" Tommy mentally asked the creature. "Well, what else would I be? I'd like to know now, wouldn't I," the beast answered. A moment, and then Tommy thought back to answer again, "my name is Tommy, what is your name?" he asked.

"I am Drake!" the baby dragon replied. "So, you are a dragon, then?" Tommy asked once more. "Are you blind? Of course, I am, I thought we already had that established." Said the young dragon. By this time, some of the other fishermen were becoming antsy, and Tommy could hear some shuffling around, and some of them talking with a low voice amongst themselves. Tommy's Dad, on the other hand, was speechless. He sensed that his son had something going on with the amazing little creature but didn't want to believe what he now found obvious. Watching his son staring at the Dragon and the baby staring right back at him told him there could only be one possible answer. They were communicating.

"I have many questions," Tommy mentally asked the dragon. "Then why don't you ask them instead of staring at me like a moron," the baby said. "You're a cheeky little dragon, aren't you?" Tommy fired back. "Okay, this conversation is over," the dragon spat. "No, wait, I'm sorry then if I offended you. Look, it isn't every day that I get to talk to a dragon, so where can I find you so we can talk later?" Tommy asked. "If you are serious, I will meet you at noon tomorrow at Lighthouse Point, but you must come alone!" the baby said to Tommy. "I will be there," Tommy said, and with that, the little dragon plunged back into the depths and disappeared.

When Tommy turned around to face the crowd, every one of them stared at him speechlessly. His Dad just looked down at his feet and then took up his rod like nothing had happened and returned to his fishing activities. A few of the other fishermen grumbled and then followed suit.

Needless to say, the rest of the days outing was quiet at best, and Tommy wondered how they would all handle the fact that they had not only witnessed a psychic encounter, they had seen a real live dragon with their own eyes.

Tommy's Dad, being a man of the cloth, did not like it at all and wanted to speak to his son about it but somehow never did. Tommy was developing his powers, and nothing could stop it. He never questioned why he had them, but rather just used his mindfulness to access them in a productive manner. He no longer levitated things and kept pretty much to himself for the time being.

The next morning, Tommy arose and went down to eat breakfast with his family. It was summer vacation time, and school was out, so he had a lot of time on his hands. At the table, his Dad said grace as always, and then they ate. When they were done, Tommy's Dad said, "well, what are you up to today, son?" Tommy said, "I'm going to the beach to look for shells." His Father grunted his approval, and that was it for morning conversation.

Tommy finished his breakfast, and then went back up to his room to change into his swim trunks. Then, down the stairs and out the door he went, pulled out his bike, and started to peddle madly towards the beach. He hadn't realized it, but he was excited. Very excited, actually, and he wondered why the little dragon had become snagged in his line. Could it have been intentional? He let that thought dangle, as he reached the cove, and hid his bike in the rocks.

Chapter 13: The Unicorn and The Devilish Dragon

Brindle and her new monster friends wandered down and around and all about. Everyone was getting very tired and even though Zesty kept feeding them delicious things; they were starting to grow tired.

Skeleton kept out front, stopping continuously and looking around. He would nod and see that he had turned the wrong way and sometimes everyone had to backtrack.

This made everyone a little upset at times, but they had faith in their friend that he would get them all to the Dragon.

They rounded a curve, and then a corner, and then... there he was! Brindle had never seen a dragon before. This monster was huge!

He was also so beautiful. It looked like he was made of metal. So shiny, with the sun glinting off of all the armored scales. He was a very intimidating beast indeed. However, Brindle was over all her fear of monsters and was ready to help her new friend, Medusa... whatever it took.

Brindle approached, getting closer and closer. She realized her first impression of this monster being huge was greatly underestimated. It was gigantic. Brindle stopped for a moment.

"No, courage is best," Brindle said under her breath and went on. Closer and closer, and then...

"Stop right there, little unicorn," the beast had a very deep voice that matched his size. "What do you want?"

"Hi... my name is Brindle. My friends over there said you might be able to help our new friend," said Brindle, only a little afraid. "I know we just met. I want you to be honest when I ask for help. I will help you in return if you need. Or maybe I can owe you a favor. I don't know. We just need help?"

Brindle realized that that was not the best introduction she had ever done, but she was very nervous. She stopped rattling on and let the dragon speak. And he did.

"Hmm..." He said slowly. "It does depend on what kind of help you are asking for. You tell me what you want and then I will tell you whether I can help you or not."

"Fair enough," Brindle nodded. "My friend Medusa, over there... well... she has this thing she does that she does not want to do."

Brindle took a deep breath and said, "She looks at someone and then they turn to stone."

The old, metallic Dragon waited what felt like a lifetime to reply.

"Hmmm..." He said at last. "I have heard of this. Medusas are very rare. And they do turn anyone or anything they look at into stone. Including you and me, Brindle. This is a very dangerous friend you have. Are you sure you want to help her?"

"Oh yes I do!" said Brindle.

"Well, I may have a solution. Miss Medusa..."

"Yes?" asked Brindle's hooded friend.

"You have snakes on your head. How many snakes are there?" the Dragon asked.

"Ummm... Ten? Wait... one, two, three, four, five..." Medusa was counting her snakes. "Twelve... Yes... Twelve snakes."

"And your eyes, assuming they turn individuals to stone, makes thirteen sets of stone making eyes."

"I think I have a solution," Dragon nodded. "I will help you, Brindle. But when I am done, I will need you to do something for me. Are you prepared to exchange help for each other?"

Brindle thought for a moment. "Yes. We can do that. I adventure all the time. Another adventure would be a pleasure!"

"I like that attitude," said Dragon. "I need to forge some metal things for your new friend. So, everyone please stand back."

Brindle stepped back to her friends. Dragon saw they were at a safe distance and reached over to some metal rock and ripped a big chunk into its claws.

Then the Dragon began to bellow. Hotter and hotter his chest got. Finally, he coughed a bright flame into his hands where that metal was. Then Brindle saw the most amazing thing. Those huge clawed hands started to tinker and work with that hot metal. Brindle was amazed at how those big hands were making something so small!

Pounding and pounding. Working and working, that old Dragon forged and forged.

Finally, the Dragon breathed out some cold mist to cool down the metal.

"Done," the Dragon was all worked out. "Oh, by the way. I am the Devilish Dragon. Forge expert and maker of many things."

Brindle could have sworn that the Dragon was grinning.

Devilish Dragon took Medusa's hand and led her over to the new things he had created. Brindle and her friends were very curious but stayed back.

Dragon and Medusa talked and talked. Brindle watched Medusa pick up those little shiny things and stuff them under her hood.

Dragon and Medusa kept talking and Brindle overheard them trying to think about how they would know if it worked without trying it out.

It seemed that they were both very nervous about that.

Finally, Dragon decided to test his new things on himself and had Medusa look right at him. And...

He didn't turn to stone.

Brindle could feel how happy Medusa was. Dragon called them all over.

"Take a look at our new friend, Medusa," the Dragon said with a tired voice.

Brindle and all her friends saw Medusa for the first time. She definitely had snakes for hair. And...

"You put sunglasses on all her snake eyes and her eyes as well... Ingenious!" exclaimed Savvy Skeleton.

"Now why didn't I think of that?" Zombie asked, admiring Dragon's work.

"She looks ridiculous. Glasses are ridiculous!" said Rat.

"I don't think she looks ridiculous," said Brindle. "I think she looks really beautiful with her new glasses."

Medusa looked at her new friends.

And she cried. But Brindle could tell that they were happy tears. Medusa could see them, and they could see her, and she was no longer alone.

"Thank you so much!"

Everyone was very happy for her.

“Well, Brindle,” the Dragon waited until everyone’s excitement for Medusa settled down. “There is something that I have wanted to do for a long, long, long time. And it may be a very difficult journey. I hate to cut the party short, but it is time for you to help me.”

“I want a tea party,” he finally announced.

Chapter 14: Danny's Dinosaurs

Danny was sitting on his bedroom floor, playing with his toy dinosaurs. His favorite dinosaur toy was the brontosaurus. Danny liked his long neck and the fact that he only ate plants. Danny said his favorite dinosaur couldn't be one that would eat him!

Danny loved playing with his dinosaurs. Every evening, after dinner, Danny would sit on his floor and play with his pile of dinosaurs. Many nights, Danny's mom would come up to his room to tuck him in and find him sound asleep, his special brontosaurus tucked in his hand.

Tonight, was no different. Danny's mom carefully picked him up and tucked him in bed. Danny never even woke up. Danny was sound asleep, dreaming of dinosaurs. In his dreams, Danny wasn't holding a toy dinosaur he was riding a real live dinosaur.

Danny felt amazing riding on top of his favorite brontosaurus. Who, by the way, was named Diego? Diego carried Danny across rivers and valleys. They walked past mountains and waterfalls. There were many dinosaurs roaming around below them, but Danny felt safe upon Diego's back.

Danny even saw a scary Tyrannosaurus Rex. It had a thick body with little tiny arms. It also had a scary mouthful of sharp, jagged teeth. Diego just laughed when Danny told him that the T. Rex scared him. "Don't worry about him. He has been to the dentist. He doesn't have teeth anymore and it's not a he, it's a she. Her name is Tina." Danny started laughing. He thought Tina was pretty funny.

They walked by a Triceratops. It was a short dinosaur with a wide body. It had three huge horns on its head. “Who is that?”, Danny asked Diego. Diego looked to see who Danny was pointing at. “Oh, that’s Tim. He is a triceratops”, Diego added. Danny thought Tim was pretty cool, especially with his spiky tail. Danny decided that he would definitely stay on Tim’s good size.

Pterodactyls flew overhead and one dipped down and flew alongside Danny and Diego. “Hello, Diego! It is I, Pete the Pterodactyl”, the bird said. “Hello Pete”, Diego boomed. My name is Diego the Brontosaurus. This is my good friend, Danny”, Diego said. “Nice to meet you”, Pete called. “Nice to meet you too!”, Danny yelled as Pete flew away in the distance.

Diego walked over near a river and leaned down to get a drink. Danny slid down his giant neck and began to splash in the water. There were all sorts of interesting fish and turtles that Danny enjoyed watching. Diego and Danny played in the water for a bit and then Diego lifted Danny back up onto his neck. “Almost time for you to wake up”, Diego said.

“Oh no! We haven’t seen the volcano yet! Can you take me to see the volcano before I wake up?” Danny cried. Diego thought about it for a minute and then agreed to take Danny to see the volcano. “Yay!”, shouted Danny. The two of them walked over to the Volcano. Danny waved goodbye to Phil and Tim too. He wasn’t sure the next time he would dream about them.

When they got to the volcano, Danny looked at it in amazement. It was a huge mountain with a hole at the top. He could see the lava bubbling and oozing. He was very careful to hold onto Diego, but suddenly he was falling...falling towards the volcano. “AAAH!” yelled Danny and then...

He woke up! It had all been a dream! Danny was happy that he had such a wonderful dream. He looked down at the little toy dinosaur that he was holding and whispered, “See you soon, Diego”, and Danny fell right back to sleep.

Chapter 15: The Horse that Wanted to Be a Unicorn

In a land where there were pots of gold at the end of every rainbow and where a wish upon a shooting star came true, there lived a horse called Lucky. Lucky was a big light-brown horse with big eyes, white hooves, and a beautiful black mane and tail. He was a happy horse because he had a nice pen, many other horses to play with, and a little girl who loved him very much. Lucky loved the girl very much, too, and he always tried his very best to make her smile. It was a very pretty smile. The little girl always smiled when she went to ride with Lucky or when she was cleaning and taking care of him. They always played and laughed together, and they were the best friends ever. The little girl always made sure that spirit had enough food and his pen was always warm and full of fresh hay, and even if she wasn't really supposed to, the little girl always gave him an extra apple. Lucky really liked eating apples.

The little girl was always so nice to Lucky that he decided he wanted to do something nice for her. But Lucky didn't know what to do for her. There were a lot of things she wanted but none that a horse could do. Lucky went to ask his other horse friends, but they didn't know what Lucky could do for his little girl either. He asked the birds and mice and all the other animals he knew, but none had any good ideas.

One day, a little bird flew by and saw that Lucky was sad. It went over to him and asked why he was so upset. Lucky liked the bird and told him all about his worries. The bird knew the little girl. She always gave the bird food when it flew to her window, so it really wanted to help Lucky. The bird thought about what they could do and got an idea.

"I know how you can do something nice for your little girl," the bird said. "You can become a unicorn."

"A unicorn?" Lucky asked. He didn't know what a unicorn was, but if the bird thought his little girl would like it, he would try.

"Yes," the bird chirped. "A unicorn is a magical white horse with a sparkly mane and a big horn on its forehead. It can run on rainbows and do all kinds of other magical things." The bird had seen a lot of pictures of unicorns all over the little girl's room, and it knew the girl would be really happy if she could have a real one. Lucky liked the bird's idea. He really wanted to try it, but Lucky had no idea how he could become a unicorn. The little bird didn't know either, and Lucky became sad again.

"Maybe you can try a rainbow," the bird said hopefully. "They say that if you run under a rainbow, the leprechauns will change you. Maybe they can change you into a unicorn if you ask them nicely." Lucky wasn't sure if that would work, but neither of them knew what else they could try. Lucky knew that if he wanted to find a rainbow, he had to wait for a very special day when it was raining but he could still see the sun. Lucky didn't know when a day like that would come, so he would have to wait. He asked the bird to help him try to find out about other things he could do to become a unicorn. The bird flew all over the town, asking other birds if they knew anything and looking at books. He went to visit the little girl a lot, too, and sometimes she was looking at a big box with moving pictures. It also made sounds, and a lot of times, the pictures were about unicorns. The bird spent a lot of time looking at the strange box, hoping one of the pictures would show him something.

The box gave the bird three ideas, and it flew off to tell Lucky.

The first idea they tried was to try pixie dust. This was a special world, and it had many different types of pixies, but the pixies didn't like to share their dust. Lucky and his new friend talked to all the pixies they could find. There were green pixies, blue pixies, and even a few little red ones. Many of the pixies were pink or purple, and there were more yellow and orange ones than Lucky could count. There was even a white pixie, and those are very, very hard to find.

Every time Lucky talked to one of the pixies, he had to do something for them before they would give him some of their pixie dust. For some pixies, he had to do little tricks and jump over fences while they watched. Other pixies said their wings were tired, and Lucky had to carry them around all day. There were a few pixies who just wanted to play a little, and they would give him a bit after he let them braid the hair in his mane and tail. The white pixie was the only one who didn't ask Lucky for anything, and she was happy to give Lucky as much pixie dust as he wanted. The little bird took some pixie dust and sprinkled it all over Lucky. They used one color of pixie dust at a time, but all it did was change Lucky's color for a short while. Even mixing the colors didn't help. Only the white dust did something different. It made Lucky fly a little bit above the ground, but he could only do it for one minute.

The next idea Lucky and the bird tried was a magic spell. The bird flew from house to house, taking all the little pieces of chalk and crayon that no one wanted anymore, and Lucky went into the field to collect flowers and herbs. The bird had told him to get special plants but not which ones, so Lucky picked up any flower that looked special or magical and brought them all back to his pen. When Lucky's little girl saw all the flowers when she came to visit him, she laughed and put the flowers in his hair. The little girl liked the flowers, and Lucky decided he would give them all to her once the spell was done. Because the spell had to happen on a full moon, Lucky and the bird had to wait a few days. All that time, Lucky hoped it would rain so that he could find a rainbow, but there wasn't a cloud in the sky.

On the night when they wanted to try the spell, the bird came to Lucky's pen and started drawing special pictures all over the floor. The bird saw the pictures in that strange box and tried its best to make them look just right. The bird then spread the flowers everywhere. When the moon was high and made the night look pretty and light, the bird began to say the magical words that would turn Lucky into a unicorn. When they were done, they waited for the spell to work, but nothing happened. They tried the spell five times, but at the end, Lucky was still just a normal brown horse. Lucky was very disappointed, but the bird told him that they still had another plan. This was a very easy plan. All Lucky had to do was make a wish on a shooting star. Lucky spent the rest of that night looking at the sky, hoping he would see a star fly by, but all the stars stayed right where they were.

For many weeks, Lucky waited. In the daytime, he waited for the rain to come, and at night, he watched the stars. There were never any shooting stars, so Lucky couldn't make his wish. And the few times it rained, there weren't any rainbows.

Lucky became very sad because he couldn't become a unicorn and do something special for his little girl. The bird always tried to cheer him up and tell him that their plan would work if he waited a little longer, but Lucky didn't think it would. Even if he did find a rainbow or a shooting star, Lucky was beginning to think that maybe nothing would happen, just like the other two times they tried. Even his little girl noticed how sad Lucky was, and she didn't know how to make him happy again. She gave him more apples and took him out to ride more. Being with the girl made Lucky happy for a while, but he became sad again as soon as she had to go home again. Lucky didn't like making his girl worry like that, but there was nothing he could do.

One day, while Lucky and his girl were riding, it began to rain a little, but it didn't become as dark as usual. Lucky's bird friend came flying out of nowhere and told Lucky to hurry up. Lucky didn't know what the bird meant until it showed him that there, far away, was a rainbow.

Lucky began to hope. Maybe the rainbow could work after all. It wouldn't hurt to try. Without waiting for his girl to climb off his back, he began to run. He jumped over all the fences and around every tree that was in his way as he tried to reach the rainbow. The girl didn't know what was going on, and she tried to stop Lucky, but he just kept running. He ran and ran until his legs were sore and it was hard to breathe, but he finally made it to the rainbow. Lucky was nervous and a little scared as he looked at where he had to walk under the rainbow. He'd never thought about what a big change it would be to become a unicorn. But then he remembered his little girl and took the last few steps. As soon as he passed under the rainbow, he changed. He became as white as snow. Then he had hundreds of different colors in his mane and tail, and he had a huge horn on his forehead. Lucky was so happy that he began to dance. His little girl was so surprised and amazed, and she laughed.

"I'm so glad you like my gift," Lucky said.

"This is a gift?" Lucky and the girl were both surprised when the girl understood what Lucky had said. The girl could never understand him before, but they were both glad about it. Lucky finally got to tell his girl how much he loved and how long he wanted to do something special for her. This made the little girl feel warm and fuzzy inside, and she hugged Lucky's neck.

"Silly horse," she said. "You didn't have to do all this. Letting me ride you is the most special thing you could ever do for me." This made Lucky feel very loved.

Lucky saw that his girl was getting sleepy and turned around to bring her home. However, when he walked under the rainbow again, he changed back into a normal horse, and his girl couldn't hear his words anymore. It was a big surprise for Lucky, but it didn't make him sad because he got to let his girl know how much he cared, and he knew she would always love him even if he wasn't a unicorn.

Chapter 16: The Last Thousand Dragons

There was once a brave knight named Sir Emile who was very famous for finishing off the last one thousand dinosaurs. Many legends had tried to deal with the dragons, all hoping to live a legacy for being the great heroes who removed all the dragons from existing on earth with human beings. However, they had not succeeded entirely until Sir Emile stepped in.

Sir Emile had spent so many years studying about the dragon behaviors and all the cruelty they had on human beings. But what made him more successful than the rest was his conclusion on the study. They were quite unique and unusual compared to the others before him. He concluded that dragons lived in anger always, and this is what made fire come from their mouths due to the constant rage.

Therefore, when the time came, he decided to finish up all the dragons. He was going to use a very simple strategy; he was going to swap the regular weapons used by the knights for jokes and a cart of ice creams. So, when the first dragon came to eat him, he shouted a joke at the dragon. It was a very great joke that it made the dragon laugh out so loudly. He already knew what was going to happen after the joke, and it sure did work. Immediately the dragon laughed; his fire went off. Next, the knight offered the dragon an ice cream; he was still laughing at the joke he had been told.

The dragon hadn't felt this happy in so many years. The ice cream, on the other hand, refreshed his throat, which had held fire for so many years. Sir Emile wasn't done yet; he was going to take full advantage of the situation. So, when he saw that the dragon was very calm, he offered him some fruit, and the dragon could not refuse it because he was already so happy and refreshed. The fruit was very sweet when the dragon took a bite.

It was very uncommon for dragons to eat fruits and vegetables because the fire in their throats burned them and left them tasteless. That is why the preferred eating animals like cows and human beings were burned by the fire and tasted like roasted meat. But when the dragon tasted the fruit that day, he was so happy that he did not even notice the taste of the fruit in his mouth. He went on eating the fruits because they did not feel as awful as he had been told, plus he was so happy it was impossible to feel anything else but joy.

This continued for a week, and the dragon became so healthy because of eating a good diet. His body transformed, and he was now looking very good. When he was very healthy, he disappeared at night, and what was left of him was a beautiful butterfly that had very large colored wings.

When Sir Emile saw that his strategy had worked, he was very happy with himself. He had just made the first dragon disappear, and he was going to keep doing that with all the dragons until the method stopped working. Fortunately, all the dragons fell in his trap, and he was successful in making all the dragons disappear. He was now left with one thousand very beautiful butterflies that were originally the dragons. People were very happy with him because it meant that the dragons would no longer bother humans again. Everyone was now free to walk deep in the forests without being attacked by dragons. Even the legends who had been there before admitted that Sir Emile was the true Legend.

Chapter 17: The One Green Dinosaur

There were once ten dinosaurs who lined up in a queue preparing to enter their class.

All their frontal teeth were arranged up straight, and so were their back legs.

This was a daily routine for the dinosaurs; it's how they started their day in school every day.

Every dinosaur was blue in color.

Every dinosaur stood on the same height as the others at 35 feet tall.

But that was just how all the dinosaurs looked like. They were all very tall, blue, and had yellow horns.

But one wasn't. He was called Rock.

Yes, Rock was tall, blue and also had yellow horns, but he wasn't like the other dinosaurs.

He wanted to be a different dinosaur. He hated being told that all the dinosaurs were the same.

He wanted to look just like his name, a rock. This was undoubtedly going to make him look very different.

So, he made it a habit that every day just before school, he would paint himself in green.

He would also set himself up in a pair of stilts.

He never forgot about his yellow horn; with this, he would make sure to cover it in a very black wig.

So, every time Rock got to school, he was already looking very different. His body was green, his height was much than the rest at 42 feet tall, and he was the only one who had black hair.

He would also refuse to stand up straight in the classroom queue.

“Rock! Not again! Go get cleaned up and come back looking like the rest of your classmates,” his teacher, who was also standing at 35 feet like the other students called out. “only then can you get back in line,” he exclaimed.

“No, Sir! For today, I just want to look like this,” Rock said to his teacher and joined the rest of his classmates in line.

“That is not possible, Rock! I cannot teach with you looking like that! I will be too confused, looking at you that I will not be able to teach properly. Go clean up, and your classmates and I will wait for you to clean up before starting the classes.”

“But Sir, isn’t this the easiest way for you to know me? When I look different? Plus, I am not hurting anyone when I am looking different.”

“Yes, but you are green,” the teacher started.

But Rock was already in line, along with his classmates. But he was very taller than all his classmates, was green and did not have a yellow horn like the rest.

He was also speaking more than any of his classmates had ever been.

But there was something that had not changed. He still felt the same as he always had. He was still feeling like the rest of his classmates.

“Yes, Sir! My looks are different, but I am still the same on the inside as I always have been.”

The other 100 dinosaurs were now started to feel fear as they queued.

But they were getting excited about the talk Rock was having with the teacher of being different.

“It does not matter, Rock! We still have rules that need to be followed. We all have to look the same,” said the teacher.

“But I don’t mind being a little pinker and less blue,” said a blue dinosaur as he stepped out of the line.

Just as the blue dinosaur finished talked, another blue dinosaur stepped backward from the line.

Then another dinosaur stepped out to the side.

And another just wanted to sit down on the ground and so he did.

“So, am guessing that you all want to be the dinosaurs you very well aren’t?” the teacher asked the group.

This time, Rock felt very brave and was going to answer for the group that had chosen to be different.

“Actually, you are wrong, Sir. All we want is to be the dinosaurs we really are.”

“are you, therefore, agreeing to stick being blue, with yellow horns and 35 feet?” asked the teacher.

“No, Sir, that’s not what we are saying. We know that we are all the same even when we are different,” Rock answered.

And this was very true.

Some dinosaurs were different from the others. They loved to crush on small rocks.

But other dinosaurs just liked to juggle on the small rocks.

Some of the dinosaurs liked so much to swim in blue waters.

But other dinosaurs simply liked their water on balloons which they would play on.

"I believe that you, Sir, also have something different about you. I am sure there is something you like better than being a blue, yellow horned 35 feet dinosaur."

This shocked the teacher, who stood and thought.

"Well, I think there is one thing I have always wanted...a nose with a brown patch."

"but nothing stops you from having your brown patch, Sir! Get one"

So, Rock went inside the classroom and got a marker, a brown one.

He handed the brown marker over to his teacher.

So, the teacher made a brown patch on his nose. Then he looked at Rock and other students and smiled.

That was a very special day for everyone. They never went into the classroom that day.

They had all gotten the perfect opportunity to be what they secretly admired.

So, the only time they made it to the class that day was to go get markers of different shades that they would on themselves to get the colors they desired.

Some painted themselves in patches, while others made full-body paintings. They all looked very colorful. Some went for pink, others red, and all the other colors that they all had deep down wanted to have but were too scared to. They were very happy! They had dared to be different.

But they were gladder that the one green dinosaur had been so brave. It was because of him that they were all happy and going for what they had been so terrified of.

Chapter 18: Grandfather on the Pirate Island

Once upon a time, there was an old grandfather who was called Ronny. He was a very organized old man and one day, he made plans to go camping, and after organizing it, he called his grandchildren to join him. His two grandchildren were Michael and Jess, and they were both very excited about the camp. Jess was even more excited because she had never been camping before. She could not wait for the day to finally come.

“Hey, bro, do you have an idea of where we are going camping with grandpa?” she asked excitedly.

“We are going to a very beautiful island!” her brother Michael answered.

This made the little girl even more excited! She was going to an island! She was so happy that she started jumping up and down. The day of their departure was soon approaching.

So, Jess and Michael got into packing. They had to be sure that they packed everything they would need during the camping and so they decided to park earlier. Their grandfather Ronny also packed his stuff. Soon the day came when they were going to leave for the island, and so they left.

They reached the island after a few hours and began their camping activities. They were not going to camp for long; they were just going to be there for the day since they were only two little children, an old man, and so they couldn’t risk sleeping overnight. When it was time for them to leave for home, they couldn’t because they had a small problem. Jess had eaten too much, and they had to wait for her to get comfortable before leaving.

They waited for so long that it now it became too late for them to leave that late. They were therefore forced to spend the night on the island. But they had not brought with them a tent and therefore had nowhere to sleep. Michael and Jess got leaves and made a bed, which was very comfortable, and they slept. Well, throughout the night.

The next morning, they woke up very early because they wanted to leave for home, but something happened that prevented them from leaving. A pirate appeared before them and stopped them from leaving because they had spent the night on his island. He told them that whoever slept there had to wait until they were rescued before they could go.

The grandfather was confused and worried about his grandchildren. He did not understand why the pirate was telling them that. Instead of explaining to Ronny, the pirate repeated the same sentence.

"Because you spent the night on my island, you cannot leave until someone rescues you."

Then the pirate assigned each one of them with a chore they were supposed to do. Michael and Jess were told to tidy up the place they had slept, removing all the leaves since the island was supposed to be clean always. Ronny, on the other hand, was instructed to remove all the bread crusts they had left on the ground during lunchtime.

Ronny, Michael, and Jess were busy working on the chores they had been given when a peasant came. The peasant approached the pirate and asked him why he was making them work like that. The pirate repeated the same thing that the three had spent the night on his island, and they, therefore, had to wait until someone rescued them. He went on to tell the peasant that while the three were waiting on someone to come help them, they had to work by cleaning up since they had found the island very clean. So, the peasant told the pirate that he was there to help the three hostages. This is what the pirate had been waiting for, and so he let the three go. So, Ronny, Michael, and

Jess left the island and were very grateful to the peasant. They then narrated to him how they had ended up sleeping on the island. But one thing they did not understand was why the peasant had rescued them.

The peasant told them that he was from a town where they had a good education and that the one thing, he had learned was to help people in need. He went on to explain how all peasants were nice and how they all helped people in trouble. He taught them the importance of helping people in need because someday you may need the same people to help you. The three were so happy that they had met the peasant. He was a very nice guy, and they wished he would be their friend. However, it was now time to bid each other farewell as the three were taking a different direction from the peasant.

"I'm glad I helped you, but I have to leave now. Remember what I taught you. You have to always help people in need. Now I have to go since my mother is waiting for me at home." So, the peasant left, and the three went on with their journey back home. They had had a beautiful adventure that they would remember forever.

Chapter 19: Daisy and the Butterfly

Daisy, the fairy, could hop across lily pads and climb up snake grass.

She could paint pictures of ladybugs and summersault across the grass.

She could even create small sculptures out of clay that she found by the side of the creek.

One thing Daisy could not do, though, was fly.

When Daisy was born, her wings were broken and so she could not use them.

As she grew older, her wings grew more mangled and twisted and it became even more obvious that she would never be able to fly like the other fairies.

While Daisy had great fun enjoying her life, she always wished that she could fly as the other fairies did.

Sometimes, she would sit by herself and feel sad that while everyone else was playing tag in the air, she was left on the ground, unable to play with the others.

Daisy's family felt sad that she could not play with her friends all the time, so they did their best to always keep her company and help her have a great time.

One day, Daisy was making a sculpture by the Creekside when a giant butterfly landed nearby.

Enchanted by the beauty of this butterfly, Daisy walked right up to it and started looking at its big beautiful wings.

Daisy was surprised by how still and kind the butterfly seemed as she gazed at its beauty.

Most times, if Daisy walked up to them, butterflies would simply fly away and leave her by herself, wondering about their beauty.

This butterfly, though, was different.

As Daisy gazed at it and walked closer and closer, the butterfly's wings stopped moving, and it seemed as though the butterfly was nodding its head at her.

Curious, Daisy walked closer.

The butterfly again nodded its head as if it was inviting Daisy to sit on its back.

Slowly, Daisy climbed up onto the butterfly and sat on its back, wrapping her arms and legs around its body for support.

Once she was on the butterfly, the butterfly took off flying!

Daisy was surprised: she had never been in flight before.

When she was just a baby, her mom and dad would often fly around with her on their backs, but as she got older, Daisy got too heavy for them to carry.

This was Daisy's first time flying since she was so small!

At first, Daisy was scared, so she clung tight to the butterfly and closed her eyes.

She could feel the rush of cool air blowing against her face as they flew all around the forest.

After a few moments, though, Daisy relaxed and realized how fun it was to be flying.

She opened her eyes and watched as the trees, frogs, and flowers of the forest all floated by while they flew around the forest by the creek.

First, the butterfly simply flew around as if she was playing in the sunlight and dancing in the breeze that swept across the forest.

Soon, though, the butterfly seemed as if she was on a mission.

She started by going to a beautiful meadow filled with wildflowers.

There, the butterfly landed on each one and began drinking in the sweet nectar from the plants.

Daisy watched, surprised at how impressive it was to watch such a beautiful creature enjoying a delicious treat from a flower.

When she was done drinking, the butterfly flew to another flower, and then another one.

All around, bees were floating from flower to flower, too.

Daisy could also see many of her friends playing a game of tag in the distance.

For once, she knew what it felt like to be up in the air with them, even if she was not playing tag with her friends.

Daisy hugged the butterfly tighter now because she was so thankful that the butterfly was giving her such a special treat.

After the butterfly drank nectar from the flowers, she left the meadow and went back to the creek.

There, the butterfly began to drink water from the creek.

As she did, Daisy could feel the butterfly's belly swelling with a delicious meal and drink from the forest.

When she was done drinking, the butterfly took Daisy on another trip.

This time, they went high into the trees and landed on a small twig at the end of a long branch.

There, the butterfly rested for several minutes, digesting her meal and taking in the warmth of the sun.

Daisy relaxed and nestled into the back of the butterfly, enjoying a sweet rest with her new flighted friend.

When their rest was done, the butterfly began to go on the move once more.

This time, the butterfly went to a different meadow where they came across many different butterflies.

Some looked like the butterfly Daisy was riding, while others looked completely different.

When they arrived, some of the butterflies moved from flower to flower, gathering nectar just like Daisy's butterfly had done earlier.

Others opted instead to snack on fruits that were growing on trees on the edge of the meadow.

This time, the butterfly went to the trees and started snacking on some of the fruit.

Curious, Daisy reached out and grabbed a handful of fruit and tried some herself.

The fruit tasted sweeter and yummier than the fruits that she and her family usually ate, which were fruits that were connected from lower to the ground.

Daisy knew she was lucky and that this was a special treat that she would remember forever.

When they were done eating the special fruit, the butterfly began to fly back toward the creek where Daisy had been making clay sculptures.

Daisy held tight as they swooped and swirled through the air, enjoying a playful ride on their way back. She was giggling the whole time.

They finally landed back at the creek and Daisy hopped off the back of the butterfly and landed on the ground on her own two feet.

She thanked the butterfly and gave the butterfly a big hug around the neck and asked if she would please come to visit again one day.

The butterfly nodded and smiled before flying off into the distance.

Daisy watched the colors of the enchanting butterfly as the sunlight caught her wings and created a beautiful spectacle for Daisy to watch.

As she got further away, the butterfly turned back and winked at Daisy, as if to thank her for a wonderful day, too.

Daisy was so happy from her day in the sky that she left her clay sculpture so she could finish it another day.

Instead, she happily walked back to her home with her mom and her dad and sat down at the dinner table to eat a snack with her family.

When her parents asked her why she was so happy, Daisy told them about her experience with the butterfly and how she had taken a wonderful flight around the forest.

She told them about the nectar, and the drink from the stream, and the fruits in the sky.

Surprised, Daisy's parents looked at each other and wondered how such a magical thing could possibly happen.

They were happy for their daughter and for her opportunity to fly with the rest of the fairies.

When Daisy went to sleep that night, she dreamt about soaring through the sky and enjoying a delicious sky fruit.

She felt so lucky to meet such a wonderful friend who would help her have a chance to fly in the sky as the other fairies did.

And the butterfly did return many times.

Each time she returned, she would take Daisy on a flight around the forest and show her the new flowers, sky fruits, and bushes growing around the forest.

Daisy would never again be stuck on the ground with her new friend looking out for her.

What a lucky fairy Daisy was!

Chapter 20: The Unicorn and Her Special Day

Brindle was a very special unicorn who loved meeting new people, helping others and learning new things. She was beautiful and white, with a golden horn. Best of all, Brindle was magic!

One day Brindle was walking around, thinking about all the adventures she had recently had, and all the new friends she had made. It had been quite the adventure lately!

It was a bright sunny day, and Brindle paused for a moment to feel the warmth of the sun and feel the fresh breeze in the air. She reached out with the magic of her horn, and she felt... happy! It was strange, but a good feeling. The happy wasn't coming from her, but she could feel a big happy coming from somewhere nearby. Someone was very, very happy. The thought made Brindle smile, and then she laughed with the pure joy of it.

"I love happy!" Brindle said. "Happy is the best thing in the whole world!"

When she opened her eyes, she saw a light flash in the trees. That had to be the will o' wisp. It was fainter right now in the daylight, but she was sure that was him. So, Brindle decided to wander over in his direction.

Just like when she first met him, when she came close to where he was, the light winked off.

"Yay!" Brindle said to herself. "Someone who wants to play! I hope he's keeping true to his word and only taking people to beautiful places."

Brindle saw the light appear again, still faint in the sunlight, but bright enough for her to see.

“Let’s play along,” Brindle said, and she once again followed the will o’ wisp. Brindle was a little excited. “I wonder what beautiful place he is taking me to?”

Brindle followed the will o’ wisp through the trees, blinking first in one place and then turning off and blinking in another place, leading Brindle on a new adventure. She could feel the happy feeling growing, getting closer, and she became even more excited.

Finally, the will o’ wisp took her to the rock she had met before, on the edge of the trees next to the field of flowers.

“Hello, Mr. Rock,” Brindle smiled happily.

“Hello, Brindle!” the rock replied. “It is very nice to see you again.”

“I agree!” Brindle said. “Are you friends with the will o’ wisp? I think he brought me here to see you. Did you need something?”

“The only thing I need from you, Brindle, is for you to step around to the other side of me,” the rock said mysteriously.

“Oh!” Brindle said in surprise. “All right, then that is what I will do.”

Brindle stepped around the other side of the rock, on the side with the field of flowers and she was blasted with the feelings of happiness, coming from all around her, and even coming now from her.

Sitting in the field of flowers were almost all the friends that she had recently met and shared adventures with...

There was Brup... and his frog brother and sister, Brap and Brop... Cal the caterpillar now turned butterfly... Mari the horse... Benni the beaver... Elli the eagle... Leon the lion... Berri the bear... Sadie the Spider... Fanny the fairy... Toby the troll... the colored unicorns... Red, Blue, Yellow, Green, Purple, and Orange...

Even her monster friends were here... the Zesty Zombie... Savvy Skeleton... Ridiculous Rat... Grinning Ghost... Misunderstood Medusa... Devilish Dragon... and the Sun shined down on top of them all.

There were colors and streamers everywhere, with tables and tables of food and drink of every kind. There was even a big cake with a single candle on top. And the cake had her name on it... it said, Brindle!

"What is all of this?" Brindle said, a little overwhelmed.

"It is your birthday, Brindle!" the Sun said from the sky.

"It is?" Brindle asked. "I didn't know that!"

"It is," the sun said. "I was there, bright and shining in the sky the day that you were born."

"Oh, my!" said Brindle. "Then this is all for me?"

"It is!" all of her friends cried out. "We wanted to show you just how much we love you and are glad to be your friends! You have taught us and helped us so much. We just wanted to show you how special you really are!"

Brindle had never felt so special or happy in her whole life as she went and joined her friends for her party adventure.

Afterward

Thank you for making it through to the end of The Magic Unicorn, let's hope it was enjoyable and fun reading that you can share again and again. Brindle the Magic Unicorn will always be here waiting for you to come back and share in her adventures.

Chapter 21: Dinosaurs in the Bed

Once upon a time, there was a boy named Drew. Drew was in his bed and was scared, there was a storm going on outside. He was wondering when the storm was going to end. His mother said that the storm would pass over their town quickly and that he should get some sleep. Unfortunately, he couldn't get any sleep because of the storm.

Drew kept listening to the tick-tock-tick-tock of the clock. The night seemed to go on forever. Every minute the storm raged on felt like hours and hours to him. He could hear the crashing sound of the thunder outside and the flash of the lightning made him duck under his covers scared. Sometimes, the thunder was so loud it would make his windows shake.

He wondered if he should go to his parent's room, but he was trying to be a big brave boy. He felt that big brave boys wouldn't crawl into their parent's beds because they were afraid of the stormy weather outside. His dad had even helped him to prepare for the weather in case the storm lasted all night.

They had filled a backpack with supplies, games, and toys. He had even snuck some comic books into the bag when his father wasn't looking. The backpack was now hidden under the blankets with him. He clutched on tightly to the Panda bear that he had owned since he was a very young boy.

His mother made sure that Drew had some goodies near his bed. He had a bag of popcorn and some chips to eat in case he got hungry and didn't want to wait for the morning. His mother had told him that sometimes a snack makes her less scared.

He remembered back to the time that his family had gone camping. Even though it was only just last weekend it seemed like it was so far away. He was supposed to be a brave boy that had camping experience. He felt like campers shouldn't be scared of a little storm. But the storm raged on outside.

In his bed, he felt something touch his toes. Then he heard a voice. It whispered under the covers, "Ouch, that hurt." But the noise was drowned out by the noises from outside. Drew looked out the window, but it was dark and the storm clouds in the sky blocked out the stars from the sky.

The sound of thunder and the flashes of lightning stopped for just long enough for Drew to think to himself, "what was that noise from under the covers?"

He rifled through his backpack looking for his flashlight. He couldn't find it. He must have forgotten to pack it when he was trying desperately to hide comic books in his pack. He freaked out for a second and then remembered that he had left it on the dresser in his room. He would be scared to get out of the bed during the storm but knew that the flashlight would help things to be less scary.

He ran over to the dresser and grabbed the flashlight. Just then the crash of thunder was heard from outside and a flash of lightning and without any haste, Drew ran and jumped back into his bed.

He forced his feet into the bed down to the bottom of the sheets and there he felt something rough and sharp at his toes. It seemed to be crawling around his ankles.

"What is in my bed," he wondered aloud.

He knew there was something in his bed, so he peaked inside. Without the flashlight he could barely make anything out, it was so black under the covers, almost as black as the sky looked outside. However, he did see some tiny little spots that looked like eyes.

He heard a roar come from behind one of his legs. Drew was scared so he chewed on his thumbnail but then he had a thought and remembered that he had the flashlight.

He looked under the covers for the sound. In his bed was a bunch of little tiny dinosaurs. But dinosaurs were big and extinct he thought to himself.

But obviously, he was wrong because there it was a tiny little stegosaurus. It was eating one of his rippled potato chips from one of the bags he had opened hoping that the snack would help him feel less afraid as his mother had suggested.

Drew was confused but then he said, “Get out of here.”

The animal began to say something and then he heard more noises. He used the flashlight to look around underneath his covers. He saw more shadows and looked for them. First, he saw a triceratops, then a pterodactyl, and then a tyrannosaurus rex. Drew wondered how many tiny dinosaurs were in this bed with him.

Drew wanted to run away; he was scared but also a little curious. He wondered how there were so many dinosaurs in his bed and where had they come from.

He looked under his bed with his flashlight and thought he could see for miles. He thought about hiding but then thought that maybe he should explore this grand land under his covers.

It looked like a different world under his covers and he was frozen in place with amazement. He felt his heart beating repeatedly. Then he felt a tingle as if lightning had zapped his blanket.

He could see the lightning in the sky of the blankets sky. He saw the animals chasing each other. He saw an Apatosaurus chasing a stegosaurus. He wondered what on earth was going on.

The animals were playing with each other it seemed. At least that's what Drew thought because plant-eaters were chasing meat-eaters. Suddenly a big brachiosaurus began to run towards Drew.

He was scared for a minute but then he remembered that long-necked dinosaurs like the brachiosaur were plant eaters and there was no way he would hurt him. But Andrew didn't want to take any chances. He pulled a fire truck out of his backpack and it grew to a tremendous size. Drew was able to jump into the front seat and turn on the siren. But the sound hurt his ears.

Dinosaurs began to follow him in the truck, first a Brontosaurus and a diplodocus in addition to the brachiosaurus that was following him. But they didn't want to hurt him, they were acting just like big friendly dogs that just want to play. But Drew was scared he might be crushed by their big dinosaur feet.

He gave the truck some gas and it sped forward. He followed a path under the bed and it soon led to a forest. Before he got to the forest, he stepped on the brake and parked. He put on his new sneakers from his backpack and got out of the truck.

He began to run away blowing a whistle that was also in his backpack. He could hear the trampling of dinosaur feet from behind him.

He held on to his panda tightly as he ran. As he ran, the wind blew his hat off his head. He ran through the forest and tried to escape the animals that were chasing him, but he couldn't seem to stay too far in front of him.

He was no longer worried about the storm raging outside his bedroom with all this going on deep inside his bed. He wondered how this even happened anyway.

He could hear the growls of the dinosaurs and heard their speeding thumping feet from behind him. He reached into his backpack. Inside his pack was a pair of roller skates. He decided to stop for a second and put the skates on, he'd definitely be able to get away from these dinosaurs if he was skating, he was a fast skater.

But he didn't get too far before he hit a tree root and fell headfirst into the mud. He quickly took off the skates and began to climb the tree. He wondered where his mom and dad were.

He scrambled up the tree trunk. He began to bound from branch to branch until he was almost going to another branch when a brontosaurus came from out of nowhere eating a mouthful of leaves. The brontosaurus looked at him.

Suddenly, from out of nowhere, he heard someone calling his name. He couldn't figure out where the sound was coming from. He raced back to the opening of the bed and threw off the blankets.

It was his mom and dad. It was morning outside; the sun was shining out from the window. His panda was still tucked securely underneath his arm.

"I see you found the surprises we left in your bed, we left those toy dinosaurs for you to find in the dark, figured it would take your mind off the storm," said his father.

"Toys," Drew said confused. They had seemed so real in the dark.

"And I'm very proud of you for stacking them neatly on your dresser," said his mother.

Drew didn't remember placing any dinosaurs on the table. There were all the dinosaurs that he saw in the land underneath his covers.

The end.

Sweet dreams, little one.

Chapter 22: Growing Up a Wizard

Ever since Janie was young, she knew she had special powers deep with her. She did not know what it meant, but she knew she was not like other people. This doesn't bother her much. She is comfortable with herself.

Janie attended school with her siblings and came home for school each day to help her mother with the chores until her father came home and they would eat dinner, do homework and watch TV. This was all normal for Janie. If it wasn't exciting, it was at least predictable. Her days did not vary much and that was fine.

Janie was in 1st grade when a teacher began to pay special attention to her. This had never happened before. The teacher taught music, and this was not a good subject of Janie. Janie had no real sense of beat and her singing voice was miserable. Janie enjoyed music but that was about as much as Janie was involved in music.

When Janie tried to learn an instrument, terrible sounds came from her direction. She tried to play the violin but there was a scratchy sound that started cats howling. Then she tried the clarinet. She was never able to hit the right notes and her classmates covered their ears whenever she played.

In the end, the teacher, Ms. V, handed her a triangle but never gave her any music. Janie didn't feel bad. She knew she was better at listening to music than playing music.

Even though Ms. V did not appreciate her music, she paid a lot of attention to Janie. Janie would catch Ms. V staring at her sometimes. Janie would even look behind her to see if there was a cat or something walking past. Janie isn't sure why she thought of a cat, it was just the way Ms. V would look at her. She actually looked sort of like a cat.

Either way, Janie didn't know why Ms. V stared and gave her very good marks in music class. Janie knows that in 1st grade, it's about participating more than anything, but Janie didn't really take part. The triangle was always silent, and she couldn't sing. It was a mystery.

Ms. V noticed Janie right away. She had the aura surrounding her that indicated wizardry and magic. Ms. V could tell that Janie was not aware of her power. Janie is too shy and unsure of herself to know that she holds wields true power. Then again. Janie is young.

She isn't thinking about power. Janie will be a good project. She hasn't sensed such raw talent is quite some time. It's obvious no one has taken her into the fold. She will be the one to do it. In order for it to happen, Ms. V will have to cast a spell. The girl has no sense of rhythm or timing or anything that would make music pleasant. It's a shame.

One day as Janie walked past the teacher's desk on her way to her seat in music class, Janie was dusted with a fine sheen of sparkling powder. She didn't even notice it was so fine. Ms. V had begun to make a musician out of Janie with a little sprinkle in Janie's path.

That day, Janie felt the music inside her. She could sing like an angel and Ms. V even gave her a part to play the triangle. She also felt great. She had more energy than usual, and it was just a really good day. At the end of the day, Ms. V was the bus monitor for Janie's bus. Janie arrived at the bus stop early and Ms. V chatted with her while she waited. It turns out that Ms. V teaches piano out of her home. She lives near Janie as well.

Janie explained that she does not have a piano at her house. Ms. V said she would talk to her mom and see if Janie would be allowed to practice 30 minutes a day at Ms. V's. Janie's mom had to say okay anyway, so Janie agreed to ask her mom after school. Ms. V said she would call her that night. Ms. V is sure that there is not a lot of money for piano lessons, so she will set her price low.

She will also have to have some other students, so it isn't weird. She likes Janie and she'd like to get her started on her training as a wizard.

Janie was able to talk her mom into the piano lessons. Her mom thinks it will be a good way to get out of the house herself. Ms. V lives close enough to walk every day. They decided on the time. Monday through Friday between school and dinner. It will only take an hour out of her day. She will just rearrange her chores.

Ms. V is glad the girl will be at her house every day. The mother stays for the first week, but then she starts to drive Janie and drop her off returning to pick her up in thirty or forty-five minutes. Janie practices, for twenty minutes, but then Ms. V asks if she wants a drink or a snack. It is during snack time that Janie confesses does magic and she knows Ms. V is a wizard. Ms. V is surprised.

Janie, even though she doesn't know how much power she has, knows that she has some. She found a strange book when she was still a toddler. It was high on a shelf in her closet. She never saw the book, but she could feel it was there. Even at that young age, she was able to move the book from the shelf to her lap with her mind. Then she opened the book.

She could not read it but when she touched the pages, she knew what they said. She doesn't understand a lot of what is in the book. That is why she got her mom to agree to the piano lessons and practice. Janie wants to use the time to learn the craft.

There was a wand next to the book. Janie brought it with her today and Ms. V is very happy. They can begin the right way to charge the wand and learn a few incantations. The piano is abandoned. Whenever Janie needs to play, she casts a spell and her fingers pluck out the appropriate tune. In fact, at her first piano recital, Janie is discovered as a phenomenon. There will need to be longer lessons and more practice. Janie's mom starts talking about buying a piano.

Janie stops her and says she's not sure how long she will be interested in playing and there is no room for a piano in the house. Janie needs to be at Ms. V's house to continue her quest to be the best wizard on the planet.

The piano lesson arrangement continues for many years. Janie learns how to attract animals to her and repel animals from her. Janie learns how to move objects with her mind. She started out by moving the book of magic, but now she can rearrange furniture and she has even stopped a few car accidents by stopping the cars in the nick of time.

Janie has become a master at using her wand and Ms. V gave her a looking glass for her tenth birthday that she uses to see the past, present, and future. She loves learning and she is becoming a very good wizard.

One day, Ms. V asked what she planned to do with all the wizardry she was learning. Janie had never really thought about it. She is just about to become a teenager. Janie has become a self-reliant girl who, like most people her age, does not know what she wants to be when she grows up. She is almost annoyed with Ms. V for asking such a question. Janie is just a kid. Why does she need to decide now what she wants to do in five or ten years?

Ms. V understands that Janie thinks she has lots of time for decisions like what to do as an adult. What Janie doesn't realize is that she already has adult powers and she needs to be responsible with them.

Ms. V reminds Janie that five years ago, she couldn't sing, she couldn't play an instrument, she could only move the book of magic back and forth between the closet and herself. She has learned so much. She can control animals and people. Ms. V knows that Janie once locked a boy inside a locker because he was picking on a younger girl. Ms. V saw an image of the boy being flung inside the locker when she was walking past it.

She could feel the boy in the locker even though he had fallen asleep on top of a thick winter coat. There was no harm done to the boy, but Ms. V had to use magic to unlock the locker. Janie thinks herself very powerful. Janie is powerful, but Ms. V has much more power than Janie realizes. At the same time, Janie does not realize the limits of her own power.

Janie takes time every day to be a kid. When she was first studying wizardry, she didn't take as much time. Now, she plays games with her little brother and still manages to help her mother with chores every day. Janie's little brother likes to play with his big red ball.

They kick the ball around in the grass outside. He pretends he is a star goaltender and jumps round blocking Janie's kicks and running around in circles. He finds it fun. Janie likes it, but she gets tired. It's a lot of running.

One day, Janie and her brother were kicking the ball around when suddenly he stopped and was swiping at his legs furiously. He started to scream as Janie ran towards him. Fire ants were all over his bare legs they were stinging him and crawling all over.

Janie was in shock. She stood there paralyzed with fear. Suddenly, Ms. V came around the corner of the house and chanted a few words and the ants started marching away. There were a few stings, but Janie's mother was coming to the rescue with antihistamine and a cool cloth. Her mom took her brother into the house and for a cool bath.

He wasn't crying anymore, but Janie could not forget his screams. The sound would not leave her head. Ms. V was still in the yard with her.

"How did you know to come here?" asked Janie. She knew Ms. V didn't just happen to be passing by. She came ready to stop something and knew what was happening before she even got into the yard.

"Janie, I always leave a part of my mind open for the people I care about. When I check my looking glass each morning, I store the glass in my mind. Things that don't make sense at 7 am often become clear by 7 pm.

This morning I saw a red ball covered in ants. Janie looked over at the red ball. It was covered in ants. I was actually coming over to tell you of my vision. I texted you but you didn't answer, so I thought I would come by. I could feel your tension as I pulled up."

Ms. V's explanation made perfect sense. She had been trying to tell Janie that she had a lot to learn but Janie didn't believe her. When it came time for Janie to really help her own brother, she was frozen. This was deeply troubling to Janie. She could have easily controlled the ants.

To prove it to herself, she directed the ants back into the hole. Then she put a rock on top of the hole. It won't get rid of them, but her dad can take care of them when he gets home.

Janie thought about how cocky she had become. Ms. V was trying to tell her that she needed to think about what she will do with her power and with her life. Yes, she has a lot of power now. But she must learn to control herself and when to use the power she has.

Five years ago, she didn't know anything. She couldn't even carry a tune. In five more years, she can double the power she has now. But does she need that much power? Spells and magic wands will only get her so far in life. She will need to decide what she wants to do.

On Janie's eighteenth birthday, she announced her plans at a party in her honor. Janie would study early childhood education at university with plans to become a teacher. Janie had informed Ms. V of her plans and she was happy to turn over the reins to Janie. Janie loved kids and would be great at teaching young wizards how to grow and love their special gifts.

To finance her schooling, Janie opened a gourmet food truck with the help of her older sister. It was called “Love Machine.” The food truck parked outside date venues on weekend nights: Movies, parks, bowling alleys, etc.

The food contains a special blend of “spices” that are known to make the diner more attractive to others. Love Machine has been in operation for six months and there has been more than ten engagement between people who have eaten from their food truck.

Though it took a decade, Janie learned how to be the best possible Janie Wizard. She combined her skills as a wizard with a sound business plan to move from playing at being a wizard to making magic work in her favor.

Janie really was able to go from novice to professional and she will eventually move from professional to a teacher. She loves her magic and she can’t wait to pass on what she knows to someone in the next generation of wizards.

Chapter 23: The Daughter of the Sun and the Moon

Once upon a time there was a woman who had only one child who wanted a soul good.

One day the young man decided to go hunting and his worried mother advised him not to go to the mountain, where a powerful and ferocious dragon was raging that had already killed young people in the village. Many brave men had already entered his territories with the intention of fighting him, but none had ever managed to go back.

The young man, however, paid no attention to his mother, but listened to the invitation of his beloved who urged him to show his courage, saying:

- You must go to fight the dragon because you are the strongest and the bravest. If you don't go, there will never be peace in our village, for us and for our children.

The young man, who loved the girl very much, went on a journey. He climbed the mountain and found himself in front of a gigantic cave full of shadows and scary ravines.

The ground began to tremble, and a frightening creature emerged from the darkness. He had seven heads, his eyes shone like fire and

tongues of fire came out of the gigantic jaws. The flames burned the grass, the flowers and the trees.

The terrible creature slammed its tail three times and the ground shook. The young hero was not afraid.

He grasped the spear and hurled it against the dragon, but it did not hit him. Then, with great caution and speed, he grabbed the sword, but once again the dragon threw it to the ground with a blow of the tail.

The monster began to laugh and scream in a terrifying voice:

- Now I will devour you because you set foot on my mountain. So many others like you came here to kill me, but no one has ever come back. Get ready!

The boy did not lose heart and proposed a pact to the dragon:

- You really are the strongest and I ask you a favor: let me go and say goodbye to my mother and my beloved, then I will come back here and do what you want with me.

- What will you give me if I let you go?

- I'll give you my word.

Defeated, the young man came down the mountain and went home.

There he found his mother and said to her: -I went hunting on the mount of the dragon and the monster took me prisoner. I only came here to hug you because I gave my word and I must go back.

The mother began to cry:

- Why didn't you listen to me? Why did you go there? I beg you: don't come back there!

- No, said the young man, I will go back because I have given my word.

He kissed his mother's hand and went to his beloved.

- I just came to say goodbye, I was defeated, and I have to go back to the mountain. The sword did nothing to him and neither did the spear and so he took me prisoner. I gave him my word that I will come back,

so goodbye!

The girl then proposed to him:

- Wait for me, I'll go with you. Maybe together we can destroy the monster!

The girl got on the white horse and he rode the black one. She looked like she was dressed in light, her face and hair shone like gold.

The boy looked at her and thought: “How can I endanger the life of this girl? I would give the dragon three lives, not one, if they were to save her! "

As they approached, the mountain began to tremble. Suddenly the dragon came out of the cave and began to sing: - Blessed me; lucky me: I had one and now I have two.

The maiden replied to him:

- Poor you, poor you, you had one and now you won't have any!

The girl and the young man approached, and the monster started to throw flames from the mouth. The girl, just with a glance, he immobilized him, and the frightened monster began to back away.

- Who are you, the only creature who can scare me? What is this light shining on your face? What burns me like this?

-I am the daughter of the sun and the moon, the drop of water that falls from the sky to the mountains and meadows for the good and life of men.

- Who is he? Said the dragon trembling.

"He is the companion of my life," said the triumphant girl.

- You defeated me. I have no more space in this world. I will go underground and will never return.

The dragon disappeared and never showed up again. From that moment the villagers went free everywhere. The mountain was populated again with many animals and the beautiful girl and the young hero lived happily ever after.

Chapter 24: The Rolling Pumpkin

For a long time, a woman had no news of her daughter, who lived on the other side of the forest. She was worried and was no longer sleeping at night at the thought of what might have happened to the girl.

So, one day he decided to go and see her, defying the dangers, the ferocious animals, the heat of the day and the darkness of the night. He took some water, some rice with him and went on a journey.

Walk, walk, met a lion, who began to roar:

- Here is finally the meal I was waiting for!

- Signor Leone, the woman prayed, you see it too: they are all skin and bones. I'm going to visit my daughter and I'll put on some weight there; you can eat me on my return in a week.

To the lion this proposal seemed advantageous and allowed the journey to continue.

Walk, walk, the woman met a wolf, who began to howl:

- Uh, uh, here's the meal I was waiting for!

- Mr. wolf, the woman prayed, you see it too: they are all skin and bones. I'm going to visit my daughter and I'll put on some weight there; you can eat me on my return in a week.

Even to the wolf this proposal seemed beneficial and let the journey continue.

Walk, walk, the woman met a tiger, who began to roar:

- How hungry! Here is the meal I was waiting for!

- Lady tiger, the woman prayed, you see it too: they are all skin and bones. I'm going to visit my daughter and I'll put on some weight there; you can eat me on my return in a week.

The tiger also accepted this covenant and let the journey continue.

Finally, the woman arrived at her daughter's house and, with relief, saw that she was fine. Quiet now, she spent all the time talking and

to tell the facts of life. He could rest, eat and drink to satiety.

When it was time to leave, the woman asked her daughter to look for a big pumpkin, but big enough to hide inside.

They found the pumpkin and the woman managed with difficulty to enter it. Her daughter gave her a small push down the hill and the pumpkin began to roll gently through the forest.

He rolled, rolled and stopped right next to the tiger who was meanwhile hungrier.

- Have you seen a woman returning home?

asked the pumpkin tiger.

- No, I haven't seen anyone. Please, can you give me a push? said the woman from the inside.

And the tiger did so.

The pumpkin rolled and rolled over and stood next to the wolf, who had grown thinner and skinny.

- Have you seen a woman returning home?

asked the pumpkin wolf.

- I think it's coming, it's behind me. Please, can you give me a push?

said the woman from inside the pumpkin.

And the wolf did so.

The pumpkin rolled and rolled right in front of the lion, who, now without strength from hunger, was lying all day.

- Have you seen a woman returning home?

asked the lion.

- Yes, yes, it is coming, soon it will be here. Please, can you give me a push?

said the woman well hidden inside the pumpkin.

And the lion did so.

The squash rolled to the woman's house and the three animals remained on an empty stomach.

Chapter 25: History of Colors

A long time ago, Guacamaya was ugly and gray like a plucked hen.

Now, however, he is an all-colored parrot. At that time, the whole world was black or white, with only a few gray shades. There was no other color.

Everyone was sad. The gods, men, animals and plants were even bored to live because wherever they turned, they saw nothing but those two colors.

One day, all the gods gathered in assembly and decided to leave in search of other colors. They left, each one on his own way, with the commitment to find himself in the place of the assembly if someone had found a new color.

One of the gods had gone for a walk. He was so concentrated in his thoughts that, while walking, he hit his head against a stone.

Blood came out of him and he cried for a long time in pain. When he saw the blood, he noticed that there was another color. He immediately went to report it to the others and all the gods decided together to call Red the third color.

A goddess had also left, looking for something to color the feeling of hope.

After a long time, he found a new color and together they decided to call the fourth color Green.

Another goddess had started digging a very deep hole because she wanted to find the heart of the earth. Finally, she found it and together they decided to call Marrone the fifth color.

A god went up to the top of a very high mountain: he wanted to see the color of the world from above. And he saw it. However, he didn't know how to bring it down to show it to others.

He stood on the top of the mountain watching it for a very long time, until he went blind.

When he finally managed to return to the others, he said to them: "The color of the world has stuck to my eyes". All the gods saw the color that remained in their eyes and called Azzurro the sixth color.

Another god had approached a laughing child. He had stolen his smile and the boy had started to cry.

It is for this reason that babies go from rice to crying so easily! When that god came to the assembly wearing the boy's smile, they all decided to call the seventh color Yellow

When the gods were tired, they went to sleep a little drunk.

But first they put all the colors they had found inside a box, under the shadow of their big sacred tree.

Since the box was not properly closed, the colors began to come out and mix with each other, giving birth to many other colors.

The sacred tree, when he saw what was going on, sheltered all the colors and saved them from the rain that could erase them.

When the gods woke up, they saw that the colors were many, many more than the seven that they had found and said to the sacred tree: "Since you have done all the colors, you will have the task of protecting the world, we instead We will paint ". The gods began to randomly cast colors everywhere.

Yellow colored the sun, green painted the grass and leaves, blue ended up in the sky and the sea, brown covered the earth, red colored the men and animals inside because they had eaten it, the white and black was there before.

Some sketches also hit men fully and it is for this reason that men have different colors and thoughts.

The gods, tired and happy to have colored the whole world, began to think of a way to preserve the colors: they feared to forget them.

But here, just then, the Guacamaya passed by. The gods took her and stretched her feathers, then stuck all the colors that were successful on her.

Guacamaya is still proud to be able to show men, when they forget them, that there are many colors and thoughts and that they go very well together when each of them has a right place.

Chapter 26: The Story of the Magic Mirror

Once upon a time, in the beautiful streets of Granada, everyone was chitchatting about the same thing: who was the right woman for the king of Granada? When would he marry her?

That was indeed the question that concerned everybody in Granada:

Your majesty, any girl would be lucky to have you as her groom. – said his servant.

I do not want a girl who is lucky. The girl I shall marry will be the queen of Granada. She needs to have a strong personality. She must have enough love for herself and my entire kingdom. She has to be sweet and kind. – explained the king.

But, your majesty, how will we know if the girl has all these qualities? – asked the servant politely. Hmm ... that is the problem. I will only marry a girl that has no secrets and has a pure heart. – said the king.

Hmm ...we can ask a doctor for help. – said the servant.

Duncan, what are you trying to say? What I meant is that the girl must be kind and generous. explained the king.

Oh, yes, of course, I knew that ... Hmm, I think I will need something magical to help us out here. – said the servant.

The king seemed to be very distressed about it; he could not stop thinking about what his servant had previously said to him. He made up his mind and the next day, he decided to call his trusted barber Emilio and invite him over to his palace:

Emilio, I need your help. – said the king.

Huh? How can I possibly help you, your majesty? – asked the barber surprised.

I know that, a few years ago, you found this magic mirror in a cave. I want you to use this special mirror to help me to find the perfect bride. This magic mirror is the solution to my problem; it will show us the true personality of the person looking into it. If the girl doesn't have a pure heart, then as soon as she looks in the mirror, her face will show some dark spots. The perfect girl will be the one who looks into the magic mirror without getting any spots on her face. – explained the king.

Yes, your majesty! Your wish is my command. – said the barber as he left the palace.

Soon the news spread like wildfire. Every day, women would gather outside the barber's shop, just to see which girl dared to look in the magic mirror.

A few days went by, but nobody entered the barber's shop. Women grew their hair longer and longer just to avoid having to look in the magic mirror. The fathers in Granada were unhappy with their daughters:

Mary, why don't you try? – asked a father.

And have dark spots all over my beautiful face? No can do, father. – replied his daughter.

So, you do not think you have a pure heart? – asked her father.

Hmm, no... I mean yes. I mean ... oh, father, I have decided to never get married. – replied Mary.

What? Why? What are you saying? – asked Mary's father surprised.

That's right! I will live with you for the rest of my life. Oh, I love you, dad. – said Mary

Much to everyone's surprise, Mary was not the only one to have suddenly taken an oath to never get married. It seemed like all the girls in Granada would rather stay single for the rest of their lives than look in the mirror. Some girls were so scared that they refused to look in their normal mirrors too; they even stopped using spoons, because they did not want to risk seeing the reflection of their face in them.

Since women never stepped into barber's shop, he only cut men's hair now. The barber, then went to visit the king to inform him about the situation:

This is terrible! Are these qualities so hard to find? I think I will never find a bride. – said the king sadly.

Hmm ... your majesty, there is actually a girl I know who, I am pretty sure, will not be afraid to look in the magic mirror. But she is a.... – said the barber

What? Who? Tell me! – asked the king, curiously.

She is a shepherdess. – said the barber.

A shepherdess? Are you out of your mind? Do you think a shepherdess could be queen of Granada? How dare you. – warned the king´s servant.

- Why can´t a shepherdess be a queen? If she has the right qualities to be a queen, then her being born in a shepherd's family should not stop her. Remember, Duncan, true leaders often come from humble backgrounds. Emilio go find her and bring her to me. – said the king.

The next day, everybody knew about the shepherdess. All the people went to the palace because they wanted to see her. When she arrived, the shepherdess entered cautiously; she felt scared and nervous to see so many people gathered in the palace:

Please, do not worry about them, my lady. Tell me ... aren't you scared to look into the magic mirror? Are you aware of what could happen? ... if you made mistakes in your past and you do not have a pure heart, your face will be full of spots. – said the king, politely.

Hmm … I understand, your majesty, but I do believe that it is normal for human beings to make mistakes. We all make mistakes. I am pretty sure I have made a lot of mistakes and made some terrible decisions, but I have learnt from my mistakes. I am still learning and always will. I am not ashamed of my flaws, I accept them; they make me stronger. – said the shepherdess, wisely.

As she said this, the shepherdess bowed in front of the king and walked towards the magic mirror. Her blue eyes and her fair skin looked absolutely flawless in the reflection. Then she stepped away to look at the king, who in turn stared lovingly at her:

Granada has finally found its queen. – announced the king while he kept looking at the beautiful shepherdess.

Everyone in the palace was rejoicing when suddenly a girl started shouting: Wait a second! I want to look in the mirror as well. I can prove that there has never been any magic in it at all. It's just a big lie! – shouted the girl as she stepped forward from the crowd.

You could have done so if you had wanted to. We gave everyone a fair chance to look in the mirror, but none of you had enough confidence to do so. Whether the mirror had magical powers or not is not important anymore. You should have looked in it when you had the chance – replied the king wisely.

You are right, your majesty. I apologize on my daughter's behalf. – said the father of the girl – my queen, I will never forget what you said earlier. We should not hide our mistakes; we should accept them and learn from them. If we can forgive ourselves, then, we are able to accept other people's mistakes and forgive them too. Only then will we have a pure heart. Your heart is the purest of all and my lovely town is honored to have you as its queen.

After waiting for a very long time, the king found his queen and was finally happy with her right by his side. Their wedding ceremony was one of the greatest Granada had ever seen. People danced and celebrated for days. They were happy to have finally found a strong and generous queen. No one would ever know if the mirror was really magical or not, but what counted was the magic in their hearts.

Chapter 27: The Story of Mr. Wolf and the Little Lamb

Once upon a time, there was a naughty little lamb that got in trouble in some way every single day:

Oh, no! I'm all dirty and smelly. Mummy won't be happy! - Said the worried little lamb as he lay in a puddle of mud.

After a while, his mum arrived, saw the little lamb and got angry:

You never listen to me, do you? How many times have I told you not to jump from such a height? - Said his mum, furiously. But I also told you that it's fun. You don't listen to me either. - said the little lamb with confidence.

His mum couldn't hold a grudge and started laughing and hugging her son:

Come now, let me clean you up. - said his mum with a smile.

The little lamb´s mother was always worried about her son and always repeated: Be careful, my son! Do not go to the forest; wild animals live there. They could hurt you and even eat you. - warned his mother.

You worry too much, Mummy. - said the little lamb, bravely.

Despite the warnings of his mother, the naughty little lamb often played in the forest till late in the evening.

One day, the little lamb went deep into the forest and found a beautiful spring: A spring! Just in time, I'm very thirsty. - said the little lamb, anxiously.

In order to calm his thirst, he decided to drink the water from the spring. While the little lamb drank, a scary wolf watched him from behind a tree: Ha, ha, ha! Today is my lucky day! I see a delicious and appetizing little lamb. - said the hungry wolf.

Little by little, the wolf approached the lamb. As no one was there to save the poor little lamb the wolf said:

Why are you drinking water from this wellspring? Don't you know that wild animals, like me, live in the forest? – said the wolf with an evil smile. The little lamb was surprised to see the scary wolf. He knew that wolves could be dangerous. My mom warned me about the wolves and I'm sure that this ferocious animal wants to eat me for dinner. I need to run away as fast as I can! - thought the scared little lamb to himself.

Apologies mighty, Mr. wolf. I'm just a little lamb who doesn't know much. - he said.

You've also polluted the water. How can I drink it now? - Said the wolf.

Forgive me again mighty, Mr. wolf, but on your side, the water is not polluted. The water flows from where you are standing, sir. – replied the little lamb, politely.

The wolf was amazed by the intelligent response given by the little lamb, but that did not change the fact that he just wanted to eat him.

How dare you argue with me? I think you are the same little lamb that mistreated me last year! - said the wolf, furiously. But mighty Mr. wolf, I was not even born then. – said the frightened little lamb.

The little lamb realized that the wolf was trying to trick him so both the lamb and the wolf used words and gestures, wisely. Suddenly, from where he was standing, the little lamb saw some lumbermen coming towards him. He thought:

If I keep talking to the wolf, I´ll buy some time for those lumbermen to come and chase the wolf away. - thought the little lamb to himself. Mighty Mr. wolf, you are right. I've polluted the water, but it wasn't my intention to make you angry. - said the little lamb, wisely. But I'm already unsettled. - replied the wolf.

Oh, let me make it up to you by telling you a story. – said the little lamb, pretending not to fear the wolf.

A story? Argh, what a waste of time! But I will listen and slowly get close to him, so I don't have get tired chasing him around. – thought the wolf sneakily to himself.

Once upon a time.... - started the little lamb. By telling the story, the little lamb kept the wolf at bay while the lumbermen got closer until they saw them: Look! A wolf! They are so dangerous. - pointed out the lumbermen. The lumbermen stopped the wolf from eating the lamb. The little lamb was very relieved. Today I was very lucky; this could have ended in a very different way. That wolf could have eaten me. - thought the little lamb about the risk he had taken. He quickly ran home to his mother to tell her what had happened in the forest with the wolf and the lumbermen. Then, he promised his mum that he would never go into the forest again and his mother felt relieved: Oh yes, mother, now I understand. I should never go again to dangerous places where fierce and wild animals could eat me.

Chapter 28: The Princess Under the Sea

There once was a lovely young woman who lived in the sea. She was born in the sea and knew only of its properties and its abundance. Her father was the King of the Realm, and guarded her aggressively, as he loved her more than life itself.

Her name was Ari, and she was a mermaid. Ari often swam close to the land and then popped up to the surface to watch the men on the beach and in the neighboring town. She was lonely and had begun to feel restless with her life under the sea. She wanted so very badly to walk like the land women she saw on the beach and to find a landman who would love her and want to take care of her forevermore.

One day, she went to see her Fathers Sorcerer and told him about her dreams and her desires. The Sorcerer was aware that the King had bid her never to even speak of the land species, and that to ever leave the safety of the water was never going to be allowed. He knew that, and she knew that, but nevertheless, he came up with a plan, and on the following week, he called Ari to his chamber.

Ari was intrigued by the Sorcerers plan and became very excited. She had been spending more time watching the people on the beach than ever, and she knew that she would never be happy until she was able to go forth unto the world of the walking and find her mate. She listened carefully, as the wicked Sorcerer outlined his plan and agreed to all its terms. The plan was kept a secret from the King, as she knew her Father would lock her in her chamber for an eternity if he found out. She had the Sorcerer make up a potion that she would drink and would become a landlady, but there was a catch. She would only be able to stay a landlady for a period of one week before she would again turn into a mermaid.

On the day she had set aside to swim to the water's edge and then drink the potion, she made herself look as pretty as she possibly could, and then left the King's domain. As she swam nearer to the water's edge, she became nervous. “What if the potion does not work, and I get stuck on the land forever? What if the potion does not work, and I become old and ugly and stuck on the land forever?” she thought. Then she said to herself, “You are just being silly. The King’s Sorcerer is the finest Sorcerer, and he would never make such a ridiculous mistake.”

Ari swam on her back for some time going over what it would be like to be human, and to walk on two legs, and do human things like fall in love. “Fall in love,” she whispered to herself; “Fall in love?” yes, that is what she wanted, so she would go ahead and drink the potion. With that, she pulled out the vial the Sorcerer had given her and drank the entire thing down. Then, she began to feel very strange but in a very good way. Her vision blurred for the moment, and she felt light-headed and drifty. Then, everything changed, and she felt as though she had been sleeping for all her life and not had woken up. She felt elated, alive, and excited all at the same time.

Ari looked around at the beach again; only this time, the beach looked like where she would have to go if she wanted to go home, and the deep ocean looked like a place to go if she wanted to explore. “The potion has worked beyond all my expectations!” she thought to herself. “And now, for the ultimate test of its power,” she thought as she looked down at her tail. The tail was nowhere to be seen and in its place were two long, slender, and beautiful legs. “This will do nicely!” she exclaimed aloud, “Very nicely.”

She immediately began swimming for the shore, and for the very first time in all of her years, she put her feet down and felt the sandy bottom, the sand between her toes, and the movement of legs and feet. Something she had been dreaming about for so very long. Then another first. Ari was now in the shallow waters near the very edge of the ocean, where it meets the sandy beach. She looked at the beach now only a matter of feet from her and watched as the water lapped up and down on the seashore. It was a beautiful sight to her as she could never have come this close to land before when she had a tail instead of these two wonderful legs, as she could have easily become stranded and then discovered by the humans. Everyone had warned all the children in the realm that if the humans ever caught them, they would poke and prod them and put them in cages and treat them like a freak. “Nobody should ever have to endure such treatment,” the king had taught them.

But now, she could easily just walk out of the water and up the beach and talk to whomever she pleased. Her time had come, and so, for the very first time in her life, she placed her two new feet on the sandy bottom, leaned forward to put all of her body weight over them and pushed up. She was standing. For the very first time in her life, she was actually standing, and she loved this new feeling. “This is great!” she called out aloud. “What is great?” a man’s voice nearby asked. Ari was shocked and stunned. She had never ever heard a real man’s voice spoken over the air of the planet. She turned to see an old man wearing a pair of ugly bathing trunks standing not 20 feet from her. “Oh, hello,” she said. “I was just planning a party for my husband,” she lied, “And I thought of a great way to surprise him.” She continued. “Oh, so it’s a surprise party, eh?” the man muttered. “What? Oh Uh... yes, that’s right. A surprise party for my husband.” And then she turned and walked for the very first time. She walked like a real woman that she indeed was on that day. She walked with confidence. She walked with character and charisma.

“But where was she walking to?” she began to wonder. “Oh no,” she thought. “I did not think this through very well. Now, what do I do?” she asked herself.

She saw a small building with a palm leaf roof and noticed that there were a lot of people sitting on highchairs and leaning on a long platform. They were all facing the same way and laughing and talking, and most were men. “Right.” She said to herself. “I’ll go there and join them.”

As she approached the shack, most of the men suddenly became all in a bother and began shuffling around to look at her. One of them let out a strange whistling sound that came from his mouth. “Well, hello there, sweetheart!” the closest one said. “Hey, there, honey. There’s an open seat here by me. And it’s open forever for you, baby!” another one claimed. She noticed all the men were asking for her company with the exception of one. As it happened, he was way down at the other end of the platform and was very handsome. She headed towards him and was in luck. There was an open seat on the very end of the platform on the other side of the man. She walked right up to it across the sandy beach and climbed up into that highchair.

There was another man whom she had not noticed on the other side of the platform, and he had on a funny outfit. It was not a bathing suit like all the men on her side had, on but had bright red and white colors on it and was quite ugly. She tensed when she saw the strange man behind the platform walking straight towards her. “What’ll it be, miss?” the man asked her. She froze. She had no idea what he was asking her or why he was even talking to her.

She just stared at him for a moment and then said, “I don’t know,” which was the truth. He thought she meant she didn’t know what she wanted and said, “Okay, miss, I’ll check back with you in a few minutes.” And went back to fiddling with his glasses and bottles. The gentleman whom she had sat beside turned to look at her, and she found herself hypnotized by his bright blue eyes, his dark curly hair, and his smile.

Then he spoke. “I’m John Blake,” he said, and then he waited. She knew she was supposed to say something, but she didn’t know what. Her name! That was it; he wanted to meet her. Of course! “I’m Ari,” she said finally and then turned to face forward again. He did not stop looking at her, and in fact, he held out his hand in a way she had never seen. His thumb was facing up, and his little finger down, and his hand was stiff like a knife. She turned and made her hand into the same gesture. He looked down at both of them, holding their hands out in a ridiculous fashion and quickly took her hand with his and bobbed their hands up and down a few times and then let go of it. “How strange,” she thought.

A little more time passed, and then the handsome Mr. Blake turned towards her again and said, “I was wondering if you would like to join me for a walk on the beach?” Ari’s face lit up because this was something she did understand, and she liked this man very much. “I would love to,” she answered with a smile. The two slid off their barstools and walked down towards the water and then down the beach. They walked and talked for over an hour and became good friends. Then, she noticed that he was a little bit nervous, and she guessed that she was too. This was wonderful. She had walked out of the water and into the life of a tall, handsome stranger.

Then suddenly, out of the blue, John asked her, “May I buy you dinner tonight?” Before she knew what, she was doing, she agreed, but there was a problem. The Sorcerer had forgotten to provide her with the whole story. She needed clothes and money and who knew what else to function on the dry land world. Realizing that she was in a bit of a jam, she quickly made up a story about how she had been on vacation with some girlfriends and had become separated from them.

That day, they were scheduled to board a bus somewhere and get to the airport, and now all she had were the clothes on her back and nowhere to stay. He bought the story and took care of everything. They went to the clothing store and bought some fine items for her and then went to dinner. After dinner, she went home with him, and he let her stay on his couch, but before long, they fell in love, and he wanted her to stay forever. Of course, she couldn’t do that but continued to make up stories about why.

Eventually, they became very happy together, and he began asking questions she had no answers for. This made her very uncomfortable, so she decided to tell him the truth. "You're a Mermaid?" he said with an astonished look on his face. Ari was amazed at how well he took this incredible information and was then even more in love with him. How would they do it? What could they do to make it work now that he knew her complete truth? Then John had an idea. He told her that he was a scuba diver, and he asked her what she thought of him coming out into the water for some visits, and then she comes up on land like she was then on other visits.

That plan seemed like the only one that could possibly work. "I'll buy a sailboat," he said. "And I can pick you up, and you can be yourself and be with me on the boat. We can sail around and have lunch, and well, what do you think?" he asked. She was overjoyed at the thought of having truth between them and agreed.

In the months that followed, John and Ari spend every spare moment together. Sometimes swimming together and playing in the ocean and sometimes sailing which as it happened, she loved. She had never been on a real sailboat, and John was a great sailor. Then, one day, she went to the Sorcerer and asked him if he could change her permanently into a land walker. He was very worried about what the king would think but then figured out a way to make it, so she had control over her body. She could be herself in the water and share precious moments with her father, and she could be the land girl and be with her man whenever she liked.

Soon, John asked her to marry him, and after learning what marriage meant, she was very happy to marry him. As time went on, Ari spent most of her time with John, but just enough time with her father, so he did not suspect anything or get angry because she was spending so much time away. That was how our story went, and anyone who read it was charmed by the little girl who grew up as a Mermaid and one day actually did meet her prince charming.

In the end, she had three wonderful children, and to her relief, they all had human legs and were perfect babies. She was sad that she could not tell her Father but happy that she had achieved her dreams beyond what she had ever thought possible.

Never ever let go of your dreams!

Chapter 29: A Mermaid's Song

The sea of Urania has a secret passage that leads to the big ocean in the other world. Marina is a mermaid who has a cousin, Coralina, who lives on the other side.

One day, Marina decided to visit her cousin Coralina in the big ocean. She remembered there were many fish and colorful corals in the big ocean.

When she passed the cave passage, she was surprised to see many floating things in the water. It tasted different too. It wasn't easy to breathe and there was oil sticking to her skin. It made her skin itchy and she couldn't see well in front of her.

She took out the big shell Coralina gave to her. She blew on it to call for her cousin. She waited and waited but Coralina did not come.

She was all alone in the dark and dirty ocean. She was about to go home to Urania's green sea when she heard someone calling for help.

"Please help me, anyone. Please, I'm stuck!" She swam towards the voice and saw a turtle with something wrapped around its neck.

"Master Turtle, what is that on your neck?" Marina asked.

"It's plastic. I was swimming and could not see it. My head went through the circle, but my body could not. Now it's stuck on my neck like a necklace. Help me take it off." Marina didn't know what **plastic** was. They did not have such things in Urania. But she had a feeling it might be a bad thing because it was attacking turtles.

She tried to cut the plastic with a sharp flat rock she had with her. The turtle had a red mark on its neck after the plastic was removed. “Master Turtle, is plastic a bad creature that lives in the big ocean?”

“It’s not alive. It’s trash. Don’t you know what plastic is?” The turtle seemed surprised that she did not know.

“I’m sorry, Master Turtle. I am Marina from Urania. I live in the Green Sea. I don’t live in these waters.”

“Well, all the merfolk left these waters last year. They had to leave because they kept getting hurt and people kept throwing trash into the ocean. The waves bring them from islands, big and small. They couldn’t stop them anymore.”

“That’s so bad. Why are people throwing evil things into the ocean?”

“The plastic is not evil. It’s just a thing people made. But many fish eat them because they think they are jellyfish. Before they know it, they are sick for eating the wrong thing.”

“Master Turtle, where are the merfolk now?”

“They are in the big hidden cove that can’t be reached by humans. But I don’t know who can help you find them. They must have left some markers, but you can’t see them in these dark waters.”

“I have to find my cousin and help her go to Urania. The big ocean is not good for mermaids anymore.”

“When the merfolk finally leaves, then the whole ocean will die. That’s why they are staying even if it is dangerous for them.”

“Why didn’t Coralina tell me what was happening?” Marina always told Coralina her problems through the magical mirror they shared. She was hurt that Coralina never asked her for help.

“Coralina? She is not here.” The turtle looked concerned. “She came to the surface to tell the people to stop putting trash into the big ocean. She hasn’t been back in years.”

Marina took out her magical mirror and tried to reach Coralina. “Coralina, come and talk to me.”

“Marina! How are you?” Coralina greeted her sweetly.

“Where are you right now?” Marina frowned.

“I am in the big ocean, silly. Where else would I be?” Coralina laughed nervously.

“Master Turtle said you are in the surface!”

Coralina looked shocked. “Are you in the big ocean right now? No, Marina! You should go home. It’s not safe in the big ocean!”

“I saw it. I saved a turtle from that evil plastic.” Marina was really angry. “Why are you in the surface? Do you want to become bubbles too?” There was a sad story about a mermaid who became bubbles. They were not allowed to go to the surface at all.

“I have to come here. People are destroying our home. They don’t listen to our kind because they think mermaids are story characters. In Urania it’s different. Your king is wise and good. Here, the kings worship gold.”

“I’ll come and help you.” Marina knew that Coralina would do things that were dangerous if she was all alone.

“It’s too hard to pretend to be human, Marina. You don’t have to come. It’s my ocean to protect.”

“I am going to help you because I want to see the big ocean be clean again.”

Marina went to the surface and took out a pearl necklace her mother gave to her. She was to use it only when she had to go to the surface during a storm. But now she was using it to become a human. She swallowed and said, "To a human." Her beautiful pink tail became legs. It was hard to walk for a few steps but when she got used to it, she skipped and ran.

"What a wonderful feeling, sand on my feet and the sky in my hands." The sky was something she always longed to see. Even in Urania, it was hard for her to come to the surface to take a look. Now, she was going to help Coralina and see the sky as much as she could.

Coralina was waiting for her near the breakwater. "Marina, you really came!"

"I always do what I promise to do." The two mermaids hugged each other. "I have missed you so much."

"I have missed you a lot too." Coralina looked like a mermaid even in her human clothes. She had black flowing hair and her dress was shiny like scales. "You can take the mermaid out of the big ocean, but you can't take her scales off." Coralina laughed and showed off her clothes. "I was supposed to be doing a show for children when you called for me. I had to come to you, or you would have been as lost as I was when I first came here."

"You are lucky a fisherman didn't catch you!"

Coralina smiled and hugged her cousin some more. "I was lucky. A boat of big ocean lovers found me and helped me with my goal."

"What is your goal anyway?" Marina knew mermaids had magic that could control people but outside of the water, that power was weaker.

"I helped take videos of the bad things that happened in the big ocean. I can go to places where people can't normally go. This way, we are able to show the people just how bad the situation is."

"Why didn't you just go to the cove with the others?"

"I am not afraid to do something that can help us all. I won't be happy just praying to the ocean god for protection." Coralina was always a fighter. She does everything very well and does what she thinks is best for everyone.

"How can I help you?" Coralina looked like she was thinking very hard.

"You can sing!" Marina did love singing but it was always just to her family. She never sang in front of strangers.

"I am not sure if people would like my singing here." Coralina took out something from her bag.

"This is called a video camera. We can take a video of your singing and people can watch it and be inspired to help. We can sing the songs we sing in the big ocean and in Urania!"

"Would people like those songs?" Marina didn't know if humans like merfolk songs.

"Our songs are about the beauty of the ocean and the creatures that live in the water. It's a world they don't know but if we sing about it, they can come to care for it more." Coralina was very excited.

Marina began to sing and Coralina took a video of it. Many people heard Marina sing that day. They stopped in the beach and took out their cameras and mobile phones. Marina's song was about Master Turtle's painful encounter with plastic.

People clapped after hearing her song. Coralina was very happy. "Do you really think my song can help?"

"Every little thing can help. If we can tell one person about how beautiful the ocean and the creatures living in it are, then that is one less person who would throw bad things into the ocean."

Marina looked at the big ocean and heard the waves crying. "The big ocean is asking for us to help it. She feels like she has so many things she has to carry."

"I listen to the ocean every day too. I just hope someday, she can sing happy songs again." Coralina smiled a sad smile.

"Humans are gifted with so many things. I hope they learn that the ocean is someone's home too."

"Now **that** is something we can sing about!" Coralina and Marina looked at the ocean and prayed for the day when the ocean can sing happy songs again.

Chapter 30: The Humble Herd of Elephants

It's time to take a bath," says Mama Elephant to her baby.

Baby Elephant is young and has learned how to take a shower with his own trunk.

He can spray water all over his own back and spray water all over Mama Elephant, too.

She laughs when he does this.

The elephant herd has come to the watering hole to drink and wash before they are going to find their place of rest for the night. The elephants are always close together.

They never leave anyone behind, and they are always walking all over the African savanna in search of water, food, and a place to take rest, whether it is for an afternoon nap, leaning up against a tree for support, or in a warm, safe place to lie down and huddle together as a family. Close your eyes and imagine the African savanna. It is vast and wide and carries on for many hundreds of miles. The trees are scattered across the land, not too densely, and are food and shade for many animals. The rainy season has come, and all the wildlife is here to drink and eat and prepare for more challenging days ahead. Take a deep breath in as you imagine this wild world of animal life.

The ebb and flow of this majestic world are untouched by civilization, and you can see all of the animals taking part in the great relief of water that comes at this time of year in the savanna.

The elephant herd has the work cut out for them, finding everything they need to survive.

Mama Elephant encourages Baby Elephant to climb out of the watering hole and come together with the pack. They are all washed and watered and ready to rest.

Baby Elephant is tired from the long hot day, walking for miles and miles to find the watering hole.

His family has crossed vast land and desert to come to the savanna for a cool, fresh drink, and a soothing, refreshing bath.

Baby Elephant follows the herd, walking to-and-fro underneath the giant legs of the elephant herd. The sun has begun to set, and the sky id colorful with oranges, reds, pinks, and golds.

The land has turned the color of the setting sun, and all the animals are looking for the place of rest for the night. Mama Elephant comes to a grove of trees and begins to lie down with the other elephants. Just as they are finding their comfort and rest, a pack of hungry hyenas comes over to their quiet place for the night, surrounding them and showing their teeth.

"You cannot sleep here," one growls through his snarl. "This is our turf. We hunt here at night. You had better find another place to sleep."

The hyenas all snarled in agreement. Mama Elephant clambered to her feet.

"We elephants are humble and will not fight with you. We will move on and find another place to rest for the night."

Mama Elephant helped Baby and all the other Elephants up as they moved along, away from the Hyenas, and onto another place of rest. The humble herd found another place near the hilly, mountain ridge, where the rains brought soft green grasses for them to lie upon. The herd huddled together and found themselves exhausted and greatly appreciative of such a welcoming place to camp for the night, the grasses falling on and around them as they laid down on the Earth .Just as they were feeling comforted by the promise of sleep, a pride of lions emerged silently and gracefully from the tall grasses.

The elephants woke up suddenly and stood up, knowing that it would not be safe for them to stay within the territory of the pride of lions.

“These are our grasses for the night. Lucky for you, we are full of our feast from our afternoon hunt.”

The lions were clear with their message. The elephants were all standing on foot once again; Baby Elephant huddled behind his mother. “We elephants are humble and will not fight with you. We will move on and find another place to rest for the night.” Mama Elephant led the humble herd away from the lion pride and off to another place where they could finally be at peace for the night. They arrived at a giant pool of water being fed by a waterfall.

The elephants gathered around the pool and prepared to lie down for their night of rest.

No sooner had they arrived than a flock of flamingos landed all around the elephants and began to perch on top of them and claim their territory.

“This is our pool!” squawked a Flamingo.

“You can’t stay here unless you want to be up all night at our Rain Dance Party!”

All the flamingos squawked at the sound of a party about to unfold. The elephants were not interested in trying to sleep through a wild flamingo party, so they decided to move on... “We elephants are humble and will not fight with you. We will move on and find another place to rest for the night.” The elephants were already tired, and now they felt so sleepy from having to move around and find a place to rest that they could have just leaned up against some trees for a nap. Just then, a pack of tall giraffes wandered near the elephant herd. They were also sleepy and looking for a place to relax.

"Hello there!" called out the leader of the giraffe pack.

"Nice night for a stroll, wouldn't you say?"

Of all the animals that the humble herd of elephants had encountered, the giraffes had been the politest and kind in their greeting.

"Hello to you!" Mama Elephant replied.

"We are strolling around looking for a place to rest and sleep.

The sun has already gone down, and we are tired from our long journey.

Everywhere we have gone, we have been turned out by those who are already there." The elephant herd was close together, their giant ears flapping and listening as Mama Elephant explained.

Baby Elephant came forward to look at the tallest giraffe. "Do you know where we can sleep tonight?

We would be so grateful if you could let us know.

You are taller than all other animals and can see great distances.

Perhaps you can spot a place with that we can humbly call home for the night."

Baby Elephant appealed to the kindness of the giraffes. The tallest giraffe listened to the words of the small elephant and looked far and wide across the vast savanna.

"There are many animals here tonight since the rains have come back to fill our watering holes and turn our grasses green once more.

You are humble and kind, and we trust you.

You can stay with us, and we will share the space together.

Safety in numbers," the giraffe explained.

"Thank you for your kindness tonight," replied Mama Elephant.

"We humbly accept your offer."

The elephants wandered off in their herd, side by side with the pack of giraffes, toward a grassy area near a copse of trees and shrubs. It was the perfect place to dwell for the evening, and there were already other giraffes there, standing tall in their sleep, yawning and snoring away.

The giraffes gathered around the elephant herd and prepared to shut their eyes and rest, never lying down, only standing tall. The elephants found great comfort in this protection from the giraffes and finally felt ready to fall deeply into sleep.

They snuggled together in their huddle and began to drift off into sweet dreams, until...

Baby elephant remembered the journey of their day as he was falling asleep.

Do you ever like to do that when you are falling asleep at night? Looking back on your day today, what did you enjoy the most?

What was the most exciting and fun?

What were some things you might have done differently?

Were you humble and kind, like the herd of elephants and the tall giraffes?

Or did you feel more like a lion, hyena, or flamingo? At the end of the day, when you finally get tucked into bed, and you are in a soft, soothing, warm, and comfortable place, you can really enjoy letting yourself fall into your dreams, like Baby Elephant and Mama Elephant and the whole herd.

It feels so good to find a place to rest for the night, to feel safe and secure, and to know that tomorrow when you wake up, you will have your family, your friends, and all kinds of new adventures to explore.

And if you want to picture yourself asleep with the humble elephants, you can imagine their large bodies all around you, their giant ears lying flat, their tails twitching, and their trunks curled.

Imagine the giraffes standing tall around you, guarding you while you sleep, seeing far ahead into the night sky.

Take a deep breath in and let yourself fall more deeply into a restful state, along with the elephants and all the animals of the savanna.

You are just where you ought to be, and now, after a long day of working hard, or playing hard, or finding what you need, you can just let your body sink into your mattress, underneath your covers, like the elephants lying on the tall grass Sweet Dreams...from all of the animals, and all of the land...sweet dreams to you from the Humble Herd of Elephants...

Chapter 31: The Eagle and the Crescent Moon

Your daylight journey is ending, and you may be wondering how you will drift off into sleep.

Tonight, as you snuggle in deep, prepare yourself for a calming and soothing ride on the feather back of a Giant Eagle who will take you a breath-taking visual journey through your imagination and carry you over the Crescent Moon and into the world of your dreams.

Are you under the covers? Are you warm and cozy?

Take a deep breath and inhale a feeling of peace and relaxation.

Let your breath out and exhale slowly, letting your body feel more relaxed now.

Try it again! Inhale and breathe in a feeling of peacefulness, and exhale the day away, for it is now night when you are under the covers and tucked in tight. Close your eyes and begin a new adventure. You can keep enjoying your relaxing breaths as much as you like, as long as you feel comfortable, cozy, and warm in your bed. Now, imagine that you are standing outside in your backyard or in front of your house. It is nighttime, and the stars have come out. It is a clear night, and you can see lots of stars. Use your imagination to picture a starry night. Now, imagine that you can see the moon in the sky and that it is in a crescent shape.

This moon is a special way for you to see in the nighttime. Could you imagine flying all the way up to the crescent moon? How would you even get there? Now imagine, as you are standing outside under the stars that a gigantic Eagle comes floating down and lands right in front of you. This Eagle is big enough to carry you on its back and would like to take you on a relaxing ride tonight. Use your imagination to climb on top of the Eagle's back and find a way to hold on tight! As soon as you ready, the Eagle takes flight, swooping off the ground with a sweeping flap of its wings, taking you higher and higher into the sky. Eagles are excellent fliers, and their specialty is soaring. Have you ever seen an Eagle or a large bird soaring through the sky? It is so calm and peaceful, barely moving, its wings outstretched, riding the wind. You are going to soar on your friend Eagle's back and feel the relaxing sensation of gliding through the air. The night air is warm and pleasant. Imagine being able to see all around you from up high in the sky.

The night world is peaceful and pleasant, and all the lights are turning off in people's houses as they get ready for bed. You can feel the soft silkiness of the Eagle's feathers and feel comforted and warmed by them. You can feel safe and relaxed up here. There is no way you could fall with such a big bird friend to carry you into your dreams. You are getting higher up in the sky, and you can take a deep breath right now to help yourself feel calmer and more peaceful as you soar. Exhale slowly and let yourself feel even more relaxed. Use your imagination to picture what the world looks like now, high up on the Eagle's back. It is very quiet up here in the sky.

When you look down below, what do you see? Is there a forest or a creek? Do you see any nocturnal animals roaming around? Are you near an ocean or a lake or some mountains? Use your imagination to picture the view from your friend Eagle's back. Take another soothing breath in...and let it out.

Soaring is so calming and serene, and as you continue up and up, you feel so much closer to the moon than you ever have before. It is a yellow-orange tonight, and it looks like a banana lying on its side. You are going to get even closer to it now. The Eagle is taking you higher and higher, and as you get closer to the moon, you realize that it is close enough and small enough for you to stand on it if you want. Your friend Eagle is heading straight for it and is preparing to land.

The Eagle lands on the very point of the crescent, holding onto the point of it with its feet. You are free to climb down and stand on the glowing yellow-orange moon now. When you climb off, you feel yourself step down on the smooth surface. It is so bright and shining you can barely see your feet when you look down. You can hold onto the Eagle for comfort if you like, or you can walk around a little. It's almost like you are standing on top of a shelf that is just hanging magically in the sky, and you and your Eagle can sit here calmly and look at the world down below. You can see all the lights that are still left on in the night. Perhaps you see the distant lights of a city or the lights of cars driving tiny little roads down below.

Take a few moments to breathe and calmly imagine sitting up here on the crescent moon with your friend Eagle perched by your side It is a beautiful view, and nothing feels more peaceful than seeing a bigger picture. Your Eagle friend nods to you and lets you know that after some quiet time way up high, it is time to climb back on and take a ride back down to the ground. You can use your imagination to climb back on the Eagle's back now. As soon as you are ready, the Eagle flaps its wings and begins to soar, letting the air carry you both in the direction you need to go to get back home.

Your journey back to your bedroom is not far, but you can take your time and enjoy the pleasure of this soothing flight.

Standing on the moon was refreshing and made you feel at home and at peace with yourself.

You are going to carry that feeling all the way back home to your bed tonight and feel the soft, warm glow of the crescent moon filling you up with wonderful golden light.

As you steadily soar back down to your house, you appreciate the softness and silkiness of the Eagle's feathers. You caress them with your hands and feel the gracefulness of this warm, feathered friend in flight. You can see your neighborhood a little more clearly in the distance as you pass over the landscape you had flown over on your way up to the moon.

Everything looks so peaceful and serene. All the forest creatures are nestled into their dens and tree hollows. All the people are in their homes, safe and sound, and breathing deeply, calmly relaxing before a good night's rest. As the Eagle approaches the ground for a landing, you are already dreaming of your next flight on its back, up and up, and up to the moon for a relaxing journey, soaring through the starry night sky. You land softly and can feel the quietness of the earth with your feet as you climb off the Eagle's back. The Eagle nods to you and assures you that you will see each other again.

You can walk back into your house now and return to your bed. Your bed is even cozier and comforting after your journey with the Eagle to the crescent moon.

You have found a deeper sense of calm and inner peace. You have found comfort in a restful state and are now more ready than ever to drift off to sleep now. Take a nice, full deep breath in...and let it out slowly. Again, take a soothing breath in...and let it out gently. Your Eagle friend will meet you again and take you as high as the moon. And tomorrow will bring whatever you need before your rest will come again soon. May you sleep softly with the warm glow of the crescent moon inside of you, and with the friendship of Eagle to carry you into your night, soaring into Dreamtime.

Pleasant dreams!

Chapter 32: The Three Princesses and the Magic

Anne, Kate, and Trisha were lovely daughters of a powerful king, the king loved his little daughters. In the palace, the little princesses shared a giant bedroom; they had their own bathroom, living room and a giant library. The princesses had it all, and they were very talented girls; they dance, and sing, they can also draw while riding their horses. But in the night, the girls had a secret. In their huge dressing room, through a magical wardrobe, lay a small hidden candy village. Every night, they never went to sleep, they travel to the candy village and ate as much as they could.

One night, the girls ventured on another sweet adventure and left their beds empty. At the same time, the king couldn't sleep and decided to see his daughters, but as he opened the door, his daughters were missing! He called all the guards and sent them away to find the princesses, all night long he was so worried. The king didn't sleep and stayed by the palace door, waiting for his daughters to come back home. Meanwhile, in the candy village, the princesses were having a great time. They swam in the chocolate fountain and slid down the gummy slide. They all ate as they played, and once they were full, they came back to their room.

In the morning, the guards were back but without the princesses, the king was in panic and was very worried. In his despair, he came back to his daughters' room, suddenly his worry went away when he saw his daughters sleeping peacefully in their beds. When they woke up, they had lunch with their father, unlike other days, he was angry this time and asked, "tell me, where were you last night?" he asked. But the girls remained silent, they feared that when their father knew, he wouldn't let them go to the village again. So, the eldest daughter lied, "we were asleep, father, didn't you see us?" Anne asked, seeming innocent. The king let it go and went on to eat his lunch with his daughters.

The next night, it happened again. This time, the king ordered the guards to search the whole palace. This time, the king stayed at the girls' room and didn't sleep, he waited for them to come back in the morning. Meanwhile, the girls were having fun in the candy village, "I wish we wouldn't have to go back! Why should we go back when we can stay here forever?" asked Trisha.

"Because father wouldn't like it if we don't come back, speaking of, we should head back," Kate said. The girls returned the door and went back to their room. To their surprise, they saw their father by their beds. He was in disbelief to find his daughters coming out of the dressing room, "where did you go? What were you doing there?" asked the king. But the girls were afraid they will get scolded, so they remained silent. Suddenly, the girls felt their stomachs grumble, suddenly, they were on the floor. The king panicked and called the royal doctor. The doctor soon came and said, "they had too much candy, the pain will soon fade." But the king was confused, "I never gave them candy, how is it possible?"

The doctor left and the king stayed by his daughters' side, "now tell me the truth, where have you been going?"

Anne felt bad for lying to his dad, so she decided to tell the truth, she told how they found the magic wardrobe and said they'll never come back again. The king forgave his daughters and decided to get rid of the magic wardrobe.

The girls were sad at losing their magic place, but it was better than having stomach aches.

-END-

Chapter 33: The Unicorn and His Rabbit Friends

Once upon a time, there lived a Unicorn who had a wife and a son, which he named Pear. The Pear was very dear to his parents and they did everything to protect him from hunters. Whenever they are going out, he usually puts him at his back while he flies, and his son usually enjoys himself behind his father's back. His father even taught him how to fly.

One day, the father and mother decided to go and look for food while Pear was sleeping but some hunters caught both of them. They were so sad that their son would have been looking for them and they made up their minds to escape but despite all they did, they couldn't escape. When Pear woke up, he began to look for his parents in the forest. He checked everywhere but didn't find them. He began to cry because he was seriously missing them.

Two Rabbits were living beside a lake. These have lost their parents, but they enjoy each other's company. They made a beautiful house for themselves. In the evening, they go to the lakeside to behold its beauty and also, play. When they are done, they would lie on their neatly made bed.

Pear had lost his way in the forest and was moving from one place to another looking for her mother. One night, he got to the lake. He stood at one side of the lake but one of the rabbits saw him from afar and he said to the other, "See that handsome unicorn. I love him already. I can't wait to make friends with him". The other one replied to him and said, "making friends with him will be very beautiful. It looks like he is sad. Let's go over to his side to say hello and ask what's wrong with him". They quickly ran to where he was and both of them greeted him and introduced themselves. They asked him what happened that made his face so unfriendly. He then, told them that he is looking for his parents. They felt so sorry for him and invited him to come and spend the time in their place. He agreed. When they got inside, they tried to cheer him up and they told him that he should relax as they are the owners of the place and they would take care of him. He was so grateful for the comforting words they spoke to him.

When they woke up the next morning and they said they said their good mornings. They told him that he can stay with them as long as he wants and that they would even help in search of his parents. He was very grateful for his newfound friends. The three of them started living together. Since his father had taught him how to fly, he usually carries each of them on his back and they would play around the forest close to their house. They also eat and drink together. They were so in love with one another. They also helped him to look for his parents but didn't find them, but they assured him that he would find his parents.

One day, while they were playing beside the lake, two hunters came to that side of the lake to rest after hunting for a long time. As they sat down, they saw Unicorn and two rabbits. They were so fascinated by the beautiful appearance and they planned to catch him and take him home. When they saw that the three animals were not looking at their direction, they went quietly and caught the unicorn unaware. The rabbits couldn't do anything at that point as the hunters were armed. They were so sad that they couldn't help their friend. They made up their minds to rescue Pear. They quickly followed the hunters from afar. They walked deeper into the forest and when they got to a place, they saw the hunters enter a hut. Then, the rabbits decided to stay in a place not too far from the hut to watch the hunters and also, be able to rescue their friend. They missed him.

The second day, after the hunters had gone out, they entered inside the hut and they found the unicorn inside a cage. They were so happy to see him but sad that he was put in a cage. They talked to him quietly and he was so happy to see them. He said to them, "Thank you for everything. A friend in need is a true friend". They promised him that they would get him out of that place. As they wanted to ask him if he has an idea of where they kept the keys to the cage, they heard the hunters' voices outside and so, they quickly went out through the back door before the hunters entered. They kept on coming to see their friend whenever the hunters are out. The unicorn was able to discover where they usually keep the key to the cage, and he told his friends. Then, they planned what to do.

The following day, they hid behind the kitchen where the hunters usually cook their food and when they saw that the two of them had left what they were cooking on the fire, they sneaked in and put sleeping pills in their food and went out quietly so that the hunters won't notice. After the hunters finished eating, they slept off almost immediately. The rabbits were proud of themselves and they entered, as one of them dipped his hands in one of the hunter's pocket, the man did as if he was going to wake but slept again because of the drug he had taken. They quickly went to open the cage. The noise of the cage woke the hunters and by the time they got out, the unicorn had carried the two rabbits on his back and was about flying. The hunters were too weak to catch up with them and that was how the three of them escaped. The hunters were very sad but there was nothing they could do.

The three friends went to look for another place and this time, they made up their minds to stay together forever.

Chapter 34: The Obedient Boy and The Magic Drum

My name is Richard. The names of my parents are Mr. & Mrs. Jackson. Right from the time my mother became pregnant with me, they made up their minds to train me well so that I can be useful to myself, them as my parents and even, my society at large. When I was born, my parents were happy to have me, and they gave me the best care you can ever think of. They made sure everything I needed was adequately provided. As a boy-child, they began to instill values in me by teaching me to say my greetings when I wake up, do house chores, help my friends, respect my teachers and everyone that comes across my path. They didn't only teach me, they did it and I learned it from them.

Everyone in my neighborhood loved my parents because they are respectful, and they were happy to know they are my parents. All the parents in my area wanted me to be a friend to their children because knew that I was well-trained.

When I started school, at first, my teachers never knew me but before the end of the second week, they started noticing me and before you know it, all the teachers in the school knew me. I made a lot of friends. My parents taught me to influence my friends positively and not, they influence me negatively. So, this has always kept me in all the things I do. My teachers were always amazed at the way I handled my studies.

Though my parents were not rich, yet we were content. So many times, we get to buy on foods on credit yet, my parents believed that with time, things would change. Whenever my teachers gave us assignments, I was always the first to submit even among my friends. One day, our class teacher gave us a project. Nobody knew why they gave us the project and because they didn't tell us that marks will be awarded, almost all my classmates didn't take it seriously. When I got home, I showed my father and he helped me. Through his help, I was able to do it and submitted it before the deadline. After the project was marked, I did well, and the School Authority rewarded me by giving me cash gifts. Some of my friends were jealous and some of them made up their minds to develop the right attitude. The money was used to pay part of our debts.

My Province that time was not a safe place as we usually experience armed robbery attacks, kidnapping and all sorts and the level of security was very poor. Parents try to lock up their doors very early so that these evil people will not gain entrance into their homes although, sometimes these people break doors especially armed robbers. So many of us lived in fear. After some time, the cases subsided, and we were happy about that as we could go ahead with our normal activities.

One day, one of my parents' friends told them that there was a menial job in one of the towns in my province. He told them that if my parents could come and do it together, it would help them to finish in a day and they would be able to come back home. My parents were not willing to go as they didn't want to leave me behind but there was lots of debt to pay and they saw that as an opportunity to make money. They also thought of taking me along, but the friend told them it won't be possible as there was nowhere to sleep. Reluctantly, they agreed to go for the day and come back the next day. They called me and told me about it, and I told them to go. They now told me that once I get back from school, I mustn't go out with anyone, not even visit a friend. I should just stay indoors. I promised them I was going to do as they had said.

I left for school while they left for the town. When I got to school, I told a few of my friends that I would be at home alone till the next day. They asked if I could stay alone and I said: "why not?". After the school closed, we all went to our different homes. I got home, ate, washed my clothes, had my siesta and after that, I started doing my assignments. As I finished with the last one, my friends came, and they told me that they had come to call me to join and play football. It was close to the evening at the time. I was tempted to go out, but I remembered I had assured my parents that I won't go against their instructions. Though my friends did all they could to convince me, yet I didn't budge.

They left for the field without me. I stayed back at home and slept. I dressed up the following morning and went to school. New got to me in school that as they were on the field the previous day, kidnappers came again and kidnapped all of them. I was sad and at the same time, happy that I heeded my parents' instruction. Though their parents did all they could to get the boys up till now, they haven't seen them. I feel so sorry for them.

Life continued. One day, my Mum sent me to the market to buy some food. As I was getting close to the market, I saw an old man who was ahead of me. As I was getting close to him, he fell, and I quickly ran to help him up. I got water to clean his bruises and asked him to sit down for some time before he continues walking. I asked him where he was going and he described his house, I offered to help him home and he agreed. When we got to his house, he thanked me. As I was about leaving, he asked me what my name is, and I told him. He said he is so grateful for what I did, and he was going to reward me. He went inside and brought out a small drum and called it a "magic drum". He said his father gave him and he was also going to give me. He told me that when I get home, I should lock the doors and windows and tell the magic drum to do its work and I will see for myself.

I was surprised but I hid it and I thanked him. I quickly rushed to the market and bought what my mum sent and ran home. When I got home, I told my dad and mum everything that happened. They were so surprised, and they decided that we gave it a trial. We close our doors and windows and my Dad asked me to speak to it. I then said, "Magic drum, do your work". Right in our presence, the drum began to roll out money. We were all shocked that we almost ran out. After some time, it stopped.

The following day, I ran to the man and told him what happened, he smiled and said, "Son, it's all yours. It's a reward for helping and honoring me". I thanked him and left. With that money, we paid our debts. I am the only one who could talk to the magic drum, I called the drum again and it brought out a lot of money and my Dad and Mum started their businesses with the money.

In a little time, the businesses grew, and we moved out of our province to another city. My parents built our house and bought cars and I am still in school. Till now, whenever we need money, I just call the magic drum and it will do its work. Obedience paid off for me and my family.

Chapter 35: The Cruel Prince

Once upon a time, there was a prince named William. The prince was notorious throughout the entire region for his cruelty. He had no love, affection, or sympathy for anyone-- not even for blood relatives. To him, there was no value in humanity. He believed that because he had wealth and power, he was superior to all the people in the region. He treated others as being inferior to him.

Everyone in the region was scared of Prince William. No one even dared to say no to the orders of the prince. If someone tried to disobey his rules, the prince would order his soldiers to kill him in front of the public. The prince would threaten innocent people and snatch their houses and lands. He loved to execute his power and use it to abuse and torture the common people. He always wanted people to be at his service. Those who refused faced great consequences.

One day, the prince came to learn about a person who lived a few miles away from the castle. The prince was being told that the man owned a great part of the land in the region. The prince made his mind up that somehow, as prince, will take possession of that land. Prince William thought of different ways. After contemplating for a while, he decided to go there himself with his soldiers and threaten the person to give the land to him. After a couple of days, the prince went to the person's home with hundreds of soldiers following him. They entered the person's house forcefully.

The prince ordered his soldiers to call the house owner. The soldiers complied with his order. They went inside and brought the house owner out. The owner was trembling. He had no idea why the prince and his soldiers were there. For a minute, he stood still in front of the prince and then dared to ask what his fault was. To this, one of the soldiers replied that the prince wanted all his land. The landowner said that the only source of his living was his land. He earns money by selling the crops. If the land is snatched from him, he could not care for his family. He further said that he had six sons and three daughters. The prince was enraged to listen to the man's excuses. The prince drew closer to the man and said directly to his face, that he was not there to listen to any excuses. The angry prince further said, "Whatever I say, you have to obey."

The man started begging, telling the prince that his family would die of hunger. He started crying. The prince was so enraged that he took out his sword and killed him. The man's family was watching the scene from inside. The moment they saw this, they all cried and rushed outside. They were really disheartened. They lost their breadwinner in a single moment.

The prince announced that, "from today onwards, I will be the owner of all the land." He then left with his soldiers. The poor family was left in a state of despair. They all cursed the prince and prayed to God for his downfall. It was really hard for them to bear their loss.

Days went by, but the family was unable to forget how cruelly the prince had killed their husband and father in front of their eyes. They were all upset and enraged. They wished that they could get revenge on the cruel prince, but they all knew that it was out of the question.

Three of the man's sons sat together. They were discussing the miserable incident that changed their lives. All of them were equally enraged and furious. They could not think of a way to get even with the prince. They knew that there were thousands of guards and soldiers in the castle, and that it was not possible to reach the prince. So, they decided to play a trick.

The eldest son suggested that after a couple of days, they would send a message to the prince that they want to serve in the castle. Whatever work they would be offered at the castle, then they would do it. In this way, they would be able to reach the prince. The three of them agreed to this plan. They discussed the plan with their mother and their other siblings. Their mother did not agree. She clearly stated that she had lost her husband. Now, she cannot afford to lose her children. To this, the three of them said that nothing will happen to them. They will handle everything so cleverly that no one will be able to even doubt them. Their mother insisted that they forget whatever had happened in the past. She urged them not to think of any revenge. They consoled their mother and made her understand that nothing will happen to them, or to the family. They further said that the prince keeps on killing innocent people every day. They cannot tolerate it anymore. The sons of the man thus made their mind up that they will take revenge of their father's murder from the prince.

They promised their dead father that they will surely avenge him. From that day onwards, their only purpose of living was 'revenge the prince'. They decided that they would follow a proper plan to get their mission accomplished. One of them suggested that first they needed to win the trust of the prince and all the people in the castle. So that if anything happens later on, they would not be doubted. The youngest one suggested that it would be better if just one of them shows the desire of serving the prince. If two or three of the go to the castle, there are chances that they would be doubted. All of them contemplated on it and finally agreed. Although all of them wanted to take revenge from their father's murder, they had to select just one. After discussing the matter, they selected the second oldest son, Wren.

Wren was much bolder and cleverer in comparison to the rest of them. They mutually agreed to the decision and all their plans.

After a couple of days, the three brothers sent a message to the prince through one of their neighbors who already served at the castle. The letter said that their father was the only earning member of their family. And that because their father was no more, and because they had no land of their own to grow crops, they want one of their brothers to serve at the castle. In return, he would get food for the family. Their neighbor took pity on them and told them that he would convey their message to the prince.

The castle members were all happy to listen to Wren's sympathetic words. They waited for their neighbor to return from the castle so that they could ask him about the prince's decision. They did not sleep that night. At around midnight, their neighbor returned from the castle. He came to their home and informed them that the prince had agreed to their request. They were extremely thrilled by the news. Their neighbor further told them that the prince had ordered him to come to the castle tomorrow, and Wren agreed to this.

The next day, Wren got up early in the morning and left for the castle. He was a bit nervous, because it was the first time, he was visiting the palace. Deep down in his heart he was happy, because the days were coming nearer when he would kill the murderer of his father with his own hands. He also promised himself that he would act sharp. He would not ever let anyone doubt him. When he reached the castle, he saw his neighbor there. He was being introduced to the other guards. His neighbor explained Wren's duties to him. Wren took a deep breath and got started with his mission.

He prayed to God to help him succeed. He handled every situation very cleverly. With time, Wren managed to prove himself as the most honest and loyal guard at the castle. He did not miss even a single chance to prove his loyalty. Thus, within a very short span of time, he was able to win the trust of the people in the castle. He was liked and trusted by all. After about a month, his brothers told Wren that now he had to focus on his actual mission. The brother's stressed the importance of their plan. His brothers also told Wren that they did not want to delay it. Wren agreed with them. He told them that the next day, he would find the right moment and would kill the prince.

The next day, Wren went to the castle with a small knife in his pocket. He made a plan that he would attack the prince while the prince was asleep. When Wren reached the castle early in the morning, he discovered that the prince was awake. So, he had to wait until nightfall for the prince to go to sleep.

At around 9:00 pm, the prince had dinner with his family. After a while, Wren saw the prince going back to his room. All the people around them were busy with their work. Wren waited for a few more hours so that the prince would have time to go to sleep. After a while, Wren peeped through a window of the prince's room. He saw that the prince was asleep. He looked around. People were all engaged in some sort of activity. He realized that it was the right time to take his revenge.

Wren somehow managed to enter the prince's room. He locked the door from the inside. He saw that the prince was deep asleep. He went closer, got a pillow, and put it on the prince's mouth to suffocate him. The prince was suddenly awake. He tried to rescue himself, but Wren stabbed him three times. The prince could not scream as his mouth was covered with the pillow. After a while, Wren saw that the prince was dead. He cleaned his hands, put the knife back in his pocket, and left. Luckily, no one saw him. He then left for home.

He told his family about the whole incident. He told them how fearless he was to commit the murder. The whole family was really happy with the news. Wren's brothers appreciated him for his courage and determination. The next morning, Wren went to the castle again as if nothing had happened. The moment he entered the castle, one of the guards informed him about the tragic incident. Wren pretended as if he knew nothing, and as if he were really shocked and sad to hear about the death of the prince. Deep down in heart, he was extremely happy. His greatest mission was accomplished. He was able to take his revenge. Above all, no one in the castle even doubted him because they trusted him a lot.

Chapter 36: The Sorcerer

There was a town called Winter cost. It was a town full of rules and regulations for the natives and strangers. The rules for strangers are quite hard and because of this, strangers find it difficult to live in that town, they rather move to a nearby town where their rules are a bit simpler.

For every child born in Winter cost, there is a fortuneteller who will predict how the future of the child will be. The king had so much trust in the fortuneteller because they believe that whatever he says comes to pass. If you are living in the town, when you give birth, the fortuneteller must predict the future of your child. There is a way they do it. On the day of the delivery of a child, the fortuneteller will take the baby out in the night with his parents. He will then look into the skies and afterward lift the baby towards the sky, then, give his predictions and also give them names according to the predictions. Any family that refuses to give their child for this activity is usually banished from the town as the king considers them a rebel.

Mr. & Mrs. Pehlo were natives of Wintercost. They were given birth to in that land and they grew there. When they met and got married, they decided to settle down there too. After their wedding, they gave birth to a twin boy and like it's their custom in the land, the day the boys were given birth to, the fortuneteller was invited and he came to their house at night. When he got to their house, he carried one of the twins and the husband carried the other while the wife followed closely behind. When they got outside the house, he lifted the child in his hands and gave the following predictions. He said, "how amazing is the smell from thee, oh dear one. You, o boy rule over kingdoms and nations. Men come from far and near to pay tribute. They come to honor you with their gifts. See them bowing low to you". He then named him, Dan. Afterward, he gave the child to the father and collected the second one and also gave the following predictions. He said, "Behold the one who is to serve his brother. He is to always attend to his brother's needs. This one shall be a servant!". He went ahead to name him Paulo.

When the parents heard the predictions, they weren't happy because they couldn't imagine that a son will be a king and the other, a servant. They kept what they heard to themselves and they just had to accept their fate because they know that whatever the fortuneteller says must come to pass.

Dan and Paulo began to grow in their father's house. They began to pay attention to the two boys as they grew. The parents began to give preferential treatment to Dan because they know that he will soon be a king and they knew Paulo was going to be his servant. So, they were treating Paulo like a servant. The two children never understood why their parents prefer one of them to the other, but they saw it. Dan was always made to supervise the chores while Paulo did every work at home.

One day, Paulo did what made his father angry and the man shouted angrily, "you this servant of a boy if you ever repeat what you did today, I will send you out of my house". He was so sad but didn't understand what his father meant. He cried and cried. He later went to his mother and asked her questions. He wanted to know why his father said that. The mother didn't want to tell him but when he pleaded with his mother, she told him what the fortuneteller told them many years back.

Paulo decided to leave home and he went to a thick forest. He made up his mind and said to himself that before he will agree to be a servant everyone will see that he has done his best in this life to be a success. He left the house with a sharp cutlass. He got inside the forest and cleared large hectares of land and started farming. He planted so many crops. Dan decided to live a wayward life because he believed that one day, he was going to be a king. He was very lazy.

Years after, there was a great famine in the land of Wintercost and they didn't have what to eat. So many people had died because of the famine and when some of the natives couldn't bear the hunger again, they decided to go to another town. As these natives got into the forest, they saw a large farm and they were so happy. They met with the farmer and they bought some food. They now ran back to Wintercost to announce they have seen where to buy food. Then, all the villagers went to the forest to see the farm. When they got there, they asked the farmer to sell crops to them and he said the only condition that will make him sell is if they can make him their king.

The villagers agree because of the level of famine they have gone through. They installed him as king right from the forest and they danced with him to the town. When he got to the palace, he asked that he needs a servant and he asked them to look for Dan Pehlo to become his servant. Everyone was surprised that how did he know Dan. When Dan got to the palace with his parents, king Paulo asked everyone to excuse them and he asked if his parents could recognize him, but they said "no". He then told them he is Paulo. All of them began to cry and beg for forgiveness. He then commanded that from that time, Dan will be his servants.

Mr. & Mrs. Pehlo left the palace angry with themselves for believing the fortuneteller.

Chapter 37: The Unicorn and the Sad Child

Brindle the magic unicorn was a happy little adventurer who loved to make new friends and have adventures, learning new things.

One day, Brindle was walking along the edge of a neighborhood and came across a playground where there were all kinds of things for children to play on and have fun. The thought of children like her friend Hannah playing and having fun made Brindle smile.

Then she felt a sadness coming from someone in the playground. Brindle looked around to see if she could find where the sadness was coming from. And she did. Hiding in one of the playground toys was Hannah, her human child creature friend from the beach. But Hannah looked very, very sad.

Brindle poked her head in through the hidey-hole where Hannah had tucked herself away and blew some sparkles from her horn in Hannah's direction. "Why are you so sad, Hannah?"

"Oh, Brindle!" Hannah cried. She stuck her foot out toward Brindle. "I have something stuck to my foot and I can't get it off!"

Brindle looked closely and saw what the problem was. There was a sticky piece of paper clinging to the bottom of her shoe. Brindle gently touched her horn to the paper and pulled it off from Hannah. The only problem now was that it was stuck to Brindle's horn!

"Oh, Brindle!" Hannah laughed and crawled out of her hidey-hole. She reached out and grabbed the piece of paper off of Brindle's horn. "Thank you, Brindle. I have missed you."

"I was just thinking about you, Hannah," Brindle said with a smile. "Here, let me make that go away with my magic."

"Silly," Hannah said. "That is a wonderful thing, but you don't have to be magic to take care of this."

Hannah took the piece of paper, crumpled it up and walked over to a garbage can on the playground and threw the paper in.

"You're right!" Brindle said. "You don't have to be magic to do that!"

Brindle looked around the playground, noticing the garbage all over the place. Pieces of paper, wrappers, plastic, and soda cans were crumpled all over, making the playground look not so fun after all.

"Is the trash the reason that kids don't come here to play anymore?" Brindle asked.

"I think so," Hannah said sadly. "I never see kids come here anymore."

"Then maybe we can clean this place up and children can come to find the magic here again!" Brindle offered.

"Really, Brindle?" Hannah asked. "That would be wonderful!"

"Then let's get started!" Brindle laughed.

She and Hannah spent the rest of the afternoon cleaning up all the mess on the playground that careless people had left behind. When they were done, Brindle and Hannah sat together on the merry-go-round, gently turning to see all the cleaning they had done.

"It looks wonderful, Brindle!" Hannah said happily. "Thank you so much!"

"Of course, Hannah!" Brindle smiled. "I love to help my friends. And maybe now you can make some new friends."

Brindle pointed her horn to where some children were coming to look at the now clean playground.

"You go meet them and I will come by again and see you again someday."

"Thank you again, Brindle!" Hannah gave Brindle a quick hug and ran off to make some new friends with the children in her neighborhood.

Brindle smiled and left but checked back every once and a while to watch the children play. It was the kind of magic that was better than any other... the magic of friendship and play!

Chapter 38.
The Princess and The Dragon

Once upon a time in a kingdom far away, there lived a beautiful princess. She was, however, not the regular princess; she did not act or behave like all the princesses around the world do. This greatly angered her mum and dad, who were the King and the Queen of the kingdom. They expected her to behave nor less than a princess should, but she was disappointing them.

She had the habit of keeping her hair unkempt, and soon it was very tangled. To make everything worse, she wore very ragged clothes like a mere peasant, and that made her Nanny feel like crying. The cook was also very frustrated with her. He was her personal chef, but he never seemed to make a meal that pleased the princess. She was the most complicated princess to serve, and she was getting on everyone's nerves. No one ever saw the princess smile; the only time she did was when she played a bad trick on the old knight. She became so bad that she eventually became the talk of the whole kingdom. All mothers and all fathers warned their little children not to behave like the princess. They did not want their children to turn up like her, even though she was the princess. Many little girls envy princesses, but no girl in that kingdom wanted to be like the princess of their land, she was that bad.

Then it happened that one day, people spotted a dragon moving on the mountains and then eventually got into a cave there. All mums and dads were scared for their lives and the lives of their little children. So, they ran to the king and queen so that they could be helped. But where they went seeking help was no different because the king and the queen were terrified as well. They were more terrified because they knew that the dragons liked to kidnap little princesses. They couldn't imagine what would happen to them if their little girl were taken away. But of all the most terrified people in the entire kingdom more than all the mums and dads and even more than the king and the queen was the old knight. The old knight was very upset and scared at the same time; it was his job to protect the princess.

The princess heard about the dragon, but unlike everyone else, she was not terrified. Instead of worrying about her dear life, she got terrible ideas on what she was going to do about the whole situation. She had a very bad and mean idea. “Would it not be really awesome to see the old knight fight the dragon?” she thought to herself. This idea made her very happy; she felt very smart that such an idea had crossed her mind.

So that night, when everyone was deep asleep, the princess silently got out of her bed. She tiptoed to the out of the kingdom and went up to the mountains then went inside the dangerous caves. However, when she got inside the cave, she found the dragon comfortably seated and daintily playing the piano. He was not anything like the princess had expected because he did not look as scary as people had said about him. The dragon was also equally surprised what was the princess doing in his cave? Both their expectations about each other turned out to be the complete opposite. While the princess thought the dragon would be fierce, he turned out to be the complete opposite. Then while the dragon expected a fairy princess, this one wasn’t gentle at all, she seemed like a street child.

The princess was very disappointed. How can such a big creature be that soft? If only she were that big like the dragon, she would be very mean. She thought of how she would terrorize all the little humans. Why wasn’t the dragon taking advantage of his big body, she wondered. She would sure do much more than just play the piano and hide inside the cages like this dragon. She would have already gone to the other kingdoms to kidnap more princesses and torture their old knights. She then made up her mind that she would have made a better dragon than the big creature seated there playing the piano.

The dragon, on the other hand, looked at the little girl and wondered what was wrong with her. She could have anything she wanted. All she had to do was ask from the queen and the king, and it would be given to her. If only he were the princess, he thought. He would wear the most dazzling princess dresses and eat all the good foods that would be specially cooked by his personal chef. Why did the princess not see how lucky she was? If he were the princess, he would have been the best princess that ever lived. He would be so happy and would make her hair so pretty. He knew that he would make a much better princess than this little girl standing in front of him.

They were both very deep in their thoughts that they suddenly thought they were thinking alike. They looked at each other and smiled as an idea crossed both their minds. So, they both shook hands as an agreement of their plot, they were going to switch places that same night. So, the dragon went to the kingdom and tiptoed to the girl's bedroom and slept. The princess, on the other hand, was left behind inside the dark cave.

The next morning as was always the routine, the Nanny went to wake up the princess and prepare her before she could go out for breakfast. But she was shocked when she got inside the bedroom and saw the dragon who had transformed into a princess. Instead of being shaggy and rough like the real princess was, the dragon was now wearing a very pretty blue gown. She also seemed to have better manners than the original princess; the dragon made a perfect curtsy and even wanted to put makeup on her face. The Nanny was shocked at the sudden change, but even more shocked was the king and the queen. They were shocked and happy at the same time because their little girl was looking more beautiful than they had ever thought possible. They had been waiting to see her transform for so long that right now, they felt like they had just been given the perfect gift ever.

When the cook joined the royal family in the dining room to serve them breakfast, he was so shocked that he almost dropped his tray. Instead of the usual shaggy girl, he was used to, seated next to the king and the queen was a well-groomed princess and she was even smiling without being mean to anyone. The cook was even more shocked when the little girl cleared everything from her plate and even asked for more. This was the first time this had happened, and he was very happy that finally, she got to appreciate his cooking. That made everyone's work in the palace easier. The mean girl who terrorized everybody had transformed and was treating them better and obeying without asking too many questions.

However, the original princess only made bad pranks at the old knight, who was her bodyguard. The others had been safe from the jokes. But all that had changed now, the dragon was a much gentle princess and was never mean to the old knight. Word spread of the changes in the princess; everyone got to know that she had become a really good girl. And soon, all the mothers and fathers wanted their children to be as well behaved as the princess of their kingdom. Most little girls also started envying their little princess. Nothing was heard of the original princess who had now become the dragon, but the kingdom was now at peace since the king and the queen were happy with their little girl.

Conclusion

Storytelling has existed for centuries. Tales of intrigue and adventure have always captivated the human imagination. It is so important to foster the development of creativity in children; they see the world in such a magical and marvelous way. The most important goal that storytelling serves is to bond us together. You can use those precious moments before your little one falls asleep, to create memories that they cherish forever. I hope that this book has allowed you to create a few of those memories.

Remember: a good night's sleep is an important part of waking up feeling refreshed and ready to have a great day.

You should always practice doing everything you can to help have a wonderful night's sleep every single night.

Through mindfulness meditation, an individual will become aware of what is happening within as well as become more adept at allowing distractions and frustrations to flow leaving the person more peacefully. Letting us know what you think helps other kids find this wonderful book and helps me write more great stories for kids just like yours!

Part 2

BEDTIME STORIES FOR CHILDREN

Original Fun Adventure Stories for Boys and Girls, With Brave Heroes, Pirates, Dragons, Unicorns and Magic Animals to Help Your Kids Fall Asleep Peacefully and Easily

Introduction

Congratulations on your purchase of *BEDTIME STORIES FOR CHILDREN: ORIGINAL FUN ADVENTURE STORIES FOR BOYS AND GIRLS, WITH BRAVE HEROES, PIRATES, DRAGONS, UNICORNS AND MAGIC ANIMALS TO HELP YOUR KIDS FALL ASLEEP PEACEFULLY AND EASILY*

The imagination of a child is an exciting and miraculous world of adventure. I am honored that you have chosen this book to entertain you and your child.

Meditation has been found to be beneficial for both physical and mental health. People who meditate regularly report lower levels of stress, an increased ability to handle the stress in their lives, better sleep quality, and fewer sick days. Meditation benefits everyone and even a simple ten-minutes session at the end of the day is beneficial.

Children who meditate demonstrate greater impulse control, compassion, and empathy. In fact, research shows that meditation practices have benefits for attention deficit hyperactivity disorder, or ADHD, anxiety, depression, sleep behavior issues, eating disorders, and even how well your child does at school.

Introducing your children to meditation will set them on the path towards success. The calming mind and body exercises that they will learn will be able to be recalled at any period of stress in their lives and are often referred to as grounding.

Grounding is a useful tool that settles the nervous system, especially when in distress caused by anything that may cause anxiety and angst for a child. Once your child has learned how to ground themselves, this tool will be available to them during any stressful events in their life, including before taking a difficult test at school or during a stressful dentist visit.

The morals found in this book are both relatable and actionable. Children will relate to the problems their adorable jungle friends are experiencing and will also be able to take the lessons they are learning with them to use in their everyday lives. It is important to expose children to quality content such as the stories that are found in this book.

Fantasy fuels our dreams and imaginations. That fuel is called inspiration. Inspiration is the basis of creativity. Creativity is what invention comes from. All that starts with fantasy and a vivid inner world. The best way to nurture that inner world in children begins with the bedtime story.

These stories will introduce your child to the idea of exploring the world through literature, and that is one of the greatest ways to do that. Exploring the world and everything that it has in store for the people is one of the greatest ways that you can help your child to succeed.

Children are endlessly fascinated with the subject of fantasies. They love that break from realism, and the imagination of a child knows no bounds. The imagination of a child can be endlessly expanded and feature all sorts of different characters; it can involve unicorns and magic; or it could involve time or space travel.

Each of the stories that you find in this book should be fun, exciting, and thought-provoking. They should involve finding great new ways for your children to think about the world and what it entails, and if you can help your child begin to open that door to these sorts of fantastical adventures, you would likely find that you are hard-pressed to ever get them to close that door again. And that's okay—for the world of fantasy and adventure is welcoming to all, young and old.

Chapter 1: The Mountain Giant

Once upon a time, there was a little girl who went camping with her family. She was a very sweet child with bright blue eyes and fiery red hair. And she was brave! Braver than any of her brothers, even the older ones! The little girl was also very curious and loved to wander. Her name was Feyr! It was a name as bright and powerful as she was. One that was as memorable as the child. Feyr meant freedom and passion, bravery, and determination. This was everything that the girl held in her little heart. And that's exactly why the old folks gave their daughter that name.

Feyr was born on a stormy day. Her parents liked to tell her that is where she got her fierce spirit from. On a Sunday, at midnight, the storm rolled in. It was wild. It tore the roof off some folks' homes, it uprooted entire trees, and it turned the streets into waterfalls. Feyr silently wished she had gotten to see that storm with her own eyes, but she was too busy being born. Just as the big grandfather clock struck midnight, a massive bolt of lightning touched down on the earth. It struck the tree outside the family's home and set it on fire. And just as the bolt of lightning struck the earth, Feyr entered the world.

Ever since that day, Feyr has been different from other children. A little weird, some kids would call her. But everyone knows that being weird is the best way to be, and Feyr couldn't help that. She ran faster than all the other kids. She certainly couldn't help that she was stronger than all the little boys and girls, or that she was smart as a whip. Who has control over how a child grows except the heavens? Certainly not Feyr's parents, who were constantly chasing the little girl around the village. She was their little bolt of lightning, that's for sure. Chaos and fire come to life. A storm walking around on two legs. But, despite her wild behavior and all her shenanigans,

Feyr's family loved her. They knew she was special. Even if she was causing trouble.

Speaking of trouble, let's get back to the story. Once upon a time, there was a little girl who went camping with her family. That girl was Feyr, and she was about to get into some more mischiefs. She was brave and fierce, wild and uncontrollable. Feyr was just like the storm she was born in. Feyr's family went camping in the mountains at least four times a year, ever since she was a little girl. They always picked the same area to set up their tents. A beautiful spot beneath the bushy pine trees. Feyr loved this spot because she could gather up some pine needles and throw them into the campfire, which made the camp smell like a fancy candle. But now Feyr was getting older and wanted to see something new. Or maybe she was just restless. While Feyr's family was content to hang out around the campfire for a week and just talk, she wasn't.

So, the little girl hatched a plan. She was wild as the great forest, but she was also bright as a bolt of lightning. Feyr knew her family wouldn't let her just wander off into the woods all by herself. She'd need to sneak away. The little girl did everything as she always did, so nobody got suspicious. She helped set up the tents by hammering stakes into the ground. She collected the rocks and set them up in a circle for the campfire. She sharpened some sticks with her handy swiss army knife that her dad gave her for Christmas. The sticks were supposed to be for roasting marshmallows, not hunting. She threw the tarps over the tents, just in case it rained. The little girl even wandered around the edge of the campsite, gathering sweet berries they could eat later. There were wild blueberries and raspberries, mulberries and strawberries, and even lingonberries! It was all perfectly planned.

During the day, Feyr and her family gathered herbs and berries. Feyr's family wasn't as adventurous as she was. They preferred to stay near the campsite out of fear of getting lost in the woods. So, most of the time, the big family would do simple, peaceful tasks like birdwatching and learning animal tracks. The most adventurous thing the group ever did during the whole day was climbing a tree a few feet to help fix a bird's nest and walk down to the river for a swim.

When night came around, things usually got a little more interesting. Dad would grill some food over the fire. It was almost always hotdogs, sausages, burgers, and cans of beans. The rest of the family complained about this part, but it was Feyr's favorite. Two awesome things coming together! Meat and fire! That was a dream come true in the little girl's book. And after they ate, the family sat around and told one another wild tales of mystery. Some of them were scary, some of them were silly, but all of them were entertaining. While they told their stories, they roasted marshmallows on the sticks Feyr sharpened. And after the burgers and sausages were eaten, the stories were told, and the marshmallows were roasted, the final part of the night came. Dad took out his guitar; Mom took out her violin, the boys took out their drums. They all began to play loud and exciting music together. Finally, it was Feyr's turn. She began to sing.

"Oh Lord of the Wood and Vine. Thank you for bringing us to this home of thine.

Oh, Queen of Leaf and Stars. Thank you for teaching us these lessons of yours.

When the willow shakes and the fern whispers, time is nothing but a mystery to me."

It was a beautiful and haunting song. One that whispered about the wonder of the forest and the welcoming arms it spreads to the visitor. A tale in the form of a tune, if you will. When a girl is born from the very forces of nature, she has an idea for these sorts of things. Feyr's family loved the song, of course. They clapped and cheered as she whirled about, her long red braids leaping like fire from her head. Her Dad got up and began to dance with her. Her Mom took one of Feyr's brothers and danced with him. The night was filled with music and laughter, drifting up towards the starry sky like the embers from the campfire. It went on like that late into the night.

By the time everyone had settled down, the night had turned into dawn. The stars were still bright overhead as everyone climbed into their tents, but the birds were also starting to call out their morning songs. Now, if Feyr was one of the boys, sneaking out would have been very tough. The boys, all four of them, slept in a tent with Dad. And you can imagine sneaking past five people in a cramped tent would have been a difficult feat, even for the lightning smart Feyr. But the girl was lucky. She didn't have to share a tent with her brother and Dad. Instead, Feyr and her mother had a whole tent to themselves. It was big as a small room, which meant Feyr got to sleep on one side of the room while Mom slept on the other. With all that space between them, sneaking out of the tent was easy as blinking an eye. All the little girl had to do was wait until the sounds of her mom's breathing slowed down. That told her that the lady was asleep. And once Mom was asleep nothing could wake her up. Feyr crept out of her sleeping bag, slipped on her hiking boots, grabbed a flashlight and a small backpack she had packed while no one was looking, and whooshed out of the tent like a night-time breeze.

Sneaking out of the camp was even easier. She didn't have anything loud or heavy in her backpack that would rattle and wake her family up. There was one close call, though. As the girl was creeping past the campfire, she accidentally stepped on a branch laying on the ground. The snap was loud enough that it scared Feyr, causing her to jump and bump into Dad's guitar, which was leaning on a log beside the fire. The guitar went tumbling down to the ground in a loud, musical ***TWANG THUMP*** that caused Feyr to gasp. At that moment, the girl was sure the jig was up. Scared and shaking, she turned to look at the tents where her family was sleeping. There was a rustling and fumbling for a few moments. Feyr's heart sat in her throat. Then came a rumbling snore that could have belonged to a grizzly bear.

"Oh, dad." Feyr covered her mouth to stop a laugh, then turned and crept along her merry way.

Once she was far enough away from the camp, the girl began to run along the mountain trails. She was as excited as a child on Christmas Eve. The woods howled with an early morning wind. The darkness was quickly being traded for the grey light of dawn. The beasts and critters of the night were slipping away for a goodnight's sleep. Or more accurately, a good morning's sleep. The owls were being traded for robins; the bats being replaced by starlings. A finch or two flapped its wings with irritation as the girl trampled through a bush, they were resting in. A fox scampered out of a log when Feyr jumped on top of it somewhat rudely.

"Sorry, Mister Fox! Sorry, Finches! I'm just very happy. I've never been this deep in the woods, but I've always wanted to be here. And now I finally have the chance I've been waiting for. To explore! To learn the secrets of the woods. And to go on an adventure! A great and epic adventure! An adventure that I will tell my children a bunch of years from now. If I ever have those. I'm free!" The girl shouted out loud with a happy heart. Her words echoed through the forest and sent birds flying into the morning sky.

"But now that I'm free, what should I do? Where should I go? Where would there be secrets and mysteries on a mountain?" The girl looked about the mountainside, searching for a hint of adventure. "Oh, I know! I'll climb a tree! I'll be able to see everything from up there!"

Looking to her left and right, Feyr climbed up the closest pine tree. It was tall, really tall! But the girl wasn't scared. She wasn't scared of anything. And she knew that climbing to the top was the fastest way of finding her adventure. So, Feyr popped her little redhead out of the top of the tree and turned about like an owl hunting for a mouse. She squinted her blue eyes at the giant forest below her, looking for any hint of adventure. And she found it!

"A cave! That's a great place to start! If there are any secrets on this mountain, they are sure to be in that cave! Oh, I wonder if there is any hidden treasure there."

Feyr slid down the branches of the tree like a little squirrel. Landing down on the ground, the girl lifts her arms over her head and sniffs herself. And then she began to laugh. “I smell like a Christmas Tree! And I’m all sticky! I bet I look like one too.” Running her fingers through her hair, Feyr watched as about a thousand pine needles fell off her head.

So, the quest to reach the top of the mountain began. The family was already camping pretty high up on the mountain, thankfully. But the cave was still at the very top! That meant Feyr had to hike high up into the sky to reach the very top! And even then, she had to find the cave hidden inside! So, the little girl started her hike. As she made her way up the mountain, she made all sorts of new friends! The animals were a lot friendlier and less scared when she wasn’t running and screaming through the woods. There were foxes, rabbits, hawks, skunks, deer, all sorts of birds, and even a bear or two. Of course, Feyr didn’t get too close to the bears. She didn’t want to make them angry or anything. But they seemed nice enough! And with all sorts of new furry friends following her like a game of “Follow the Leader,” Feyr reached the top of the mountain in no time at all.

Normally the top of a mountain would be very cold. Freezing even! But Feyr and her family chose a good time of year to go camping. It was the middle of the summer, some of the hottest months in the year. Thanks to that, even the top of a mountain wasn’t too cold! In fact, it was pretty refreshing. Like standing in front of an air conditioner or a fan turned all the way up. Sitting on a smooth boulder, Feyr took a few minutes to let her sweat dry and drink some water. “Huh, I wonder how close the cave is. It can’t be too far away. I know I saw a trail leading to it from up in the tree.”

Suddenly, one of the baby deer that had been following her tugged on Feyr’s shorts. The little critter couldn’t speak, but it didn’t need to. The girl was connected with nature enough to know that the animal was telling her to follow it.

“What’s up, little guy? Do you know where the cave is?”, asked Feyr.

The deer stamped a hoof on the ground impatiently. Clearly, it didn’t want to wait around for her because without warning the baby deer turned tail and started hopping up the mountain. Feyr gasped and clumsily shoved her water into her pack. She didn’t want to lose her mountain guide, so she began to run after the baby deer with all her speed. But keeping up with a deer isn’t easy, even a baby one. They move fast and can jump over most roadblocks as if they didn’t exist. Still, the redheaded girl managed to keep up. And when the race between the child and the deer ended, the two of them were standing in front of a giant cave!

Standing in the mouth of the giant cave, Feyr was stunned! As a curious girl, she would always explore and look for the coolest places she could find. Not only that, Feyr would read lots of books with stories from around the world. But in her entire life, the girl had never read nor seen a place so beautiful as this cave. It was a magical place, clearly. This redheaded child could see that with just one look. How? Well, the cave was packed top to bottom with crystals! Massive crystals that came in every color you could imagine. Blue crystals and red crystals, crystals of silver and gold. There were even green crystals and purple crystals! And each crystal glowed brightly in the cave. The deepest part of the cave, where no light from the sun could reach, was filled with an explosion of color that made it look like a portal to another realm!

“Hello! Is anyone in there? Does anyone live in this magic cave? Any secrets I can discover?” Feyr called into the cave. There was no answer. Just the howling of the wind and the whispering of water on wet stone. “Well, okay! If there is nobody here, then I’ll just go ahead and wander on in. I hope I’m not bothering anyone!”

Feyr stepped into the cave quietly. She was careful not to kick any stones or make any loud noises. Even though she was screaming just a second ago, now she was trying to be more careful. Thankfully the little girl could see everything so clearly. Those glowing crystals made for a handy source of light. And as she was walking along the narrow path that led between the piles of crystals, her foot bumped into something and sent it rolling across the ground. A piece of crystal! Stunning and beautiful, throwing golden light on Feyr's face. She stopped to pick the little crystal up off the ground and gasped when the colors changed. Starting at the bottom of the crystal, the golden light mixed with a crimson light. The gem started to look like a solid fire in her hands. Pointing the object around, Feyr's realized the stone worked better than a flashlight!

"I'm keeping this!" The girl says, holding the crystal in front of her to help guide the way.

Feyr walked for many minutes. She walked deep into the cave, though the crystals made sure the child could always see. After walking for a long time, she began to wonder if she was wasting her energy. After all, wouldn't she have found something in here by now?

"What type of magical cave doesn't have hidden secrets?"

"Who's in there?!" A voice suddenly boomed. It shook the cave walls, making some of the crystals fall off. The voice sounded like it was coming from all around her.

"Hello? Who's there?", she asked in a loud voice.

"You dare ask me who I am? You're in MY ear!" The voice sounded very old and rough. Like rocks falling down a mountain.

"Your ear? What do you mean? I'm just in a cave!"

"That's no cave, little human. That's my ear! Now get out of my head!" And before Feyr could react, the whole cave began to shake like it was about to collapse. The light from the sun was blocked by something being shoved into the cave. Something gigantic! "Come on, get out of there! You're making the inside of my ear itch!" It was a giant finger! Someone, or something, was shoving a giant finger into the cave!

"Whoa! Whoa! Chill out, dude. Take a chill pill. You're gonna squish me if you aren't be more careful. Just give me a moment, and I'll come out."

The voice grumbled a little bit before pulling out the giant finger. "Fine. Crawl out of my ear so I can go to sleep. I had a very nice dream. My purpose was finally fulfilled."

Feyr quickly ran out of the cave as fast as she could. No way she was going to risk getting squished by a giant finger! But when she ran out, she almost fell right off a cliff! She was so high up. Higher than the clouds. Higher than all the other mountains. In fact, all the little girl could see was an endless sea of clouds and the misty peaks of mountains far below.

"Whoa... Where am I?" The girl whispered to herself.

"Well, you're nowhere special. Just above the clouds."

"But where did the mountain go?" Feyr asked the voice, which sounded like it was all around her.

"Mountain? Mountain! Hohohoho! You thought I was a mountain? There never was a mountain girl. Just me, taking a long nap. Been sleeping a few thousand years or so now." The voice laughed at Feyrin. It made the girl blush.

"What are you talking about? There was totally a mountain here! I saw it! I climbed up it. I walked into that cave on the top of the mountain."

"I told you, child. That was no cave. That was my ear."

"Your ear? What are you? A giant?" Feyr started to walk along the edge of the cliff, looking for where the voice was coming from.

"A giant. An elder. A far walker. We have been called many names. But yes, a giant is the simple way of saying it."

“Pfft. As if. Prove...”

Before the little girl could finish what, she was saying, a massive hand came crashing down over her head. For a moment, there was nothing but darkness. The Feyr could feel herself being swung around, like a ride at an amusement park. She could feel her stomach spinning. But what she saw when the hand opened up was worth the crazy flight. A stoneface the size of a mountain was staring down at her. It had a long beard of moss and trees covering its head like green hair. Feyr’s jaw dropped. The eyes of the giant were two burning orbs. They were full of the same light that was in the cave.

“You were saying, small human?” The giant said, pieces of stone and patches of snow falling off him as granite lips moved.

No way... You really are a... A giant! That’s so cool. I’m sorry, Mister Giant! I was wrong. My mom says I talk before I think sometimes.” The little girl looked down at the giant’s palm in embarrassment.
“It’s okay, little human. That seems to be a common trait of your kind. But there’s no fault in taking action and making mistakes. As long as you are willing to learn from your mistakes.” The giant smiles at the little girl, revealing big golden crystals that look like teeth.

“Oh, okay. I’ll try to remember that! So, are there other giants around here? I always thought that the giants disappeared years ago.”

“Well, they did. A long, long time ago. But when humans filled the world, giants left it. We are very big. We step in the wrong place, and we crush an entire village. We fall asleep for a few hundred centuries and when we wake up for a stretch, we knock a whole town off our shoulders! It’s very troublesome. Especially when so-called ‘Giant Hunters’ come wandering around. They attack us, we attack back, and we look like the bad guys! There just wasn’t enough room for us in the land of humans. So, all the giants went home. Well, all the giants except me. I stayed behind.”

"Why in the world would you do that, sir? Don't you know family is everything?"

"Says the little girl who ran away from her own family just to find a little adventure."

"Okay, fair point!" Feyr said, holding up her hands in the air. "But why didn't you go with them, sir? Don't you miss them."

"Well, of course, I do! But I have a very special job given to me by a very important person!" The giant grumbled, making a noise that sounded a lot like an avalanche.

"Oh. Of course, you do. What's your job, sir? Who gave you the job?"

"My job is to wait for the Prince of Dragons to wake up and become king. I was given this job by the King of the Dragons himself."

"There are dragons too?"

"Of course. The world was once full of dragons, just like it was full of giants. But then humans came along. For a while, humans and dragons lived in harmony. The Dragon King hoped that when his son finally hatched, the world would return to that way. So, I'm here to protect his wish and his egg. To watch over it until the day the Dragon Prince becomes the Dragon King."

Feyr was shocked, silly. She sat down in the giant's hand and stared into his eyes. The flames of the crystalline light behind that gaze... The small girl was sure she was still dreaming, snuggling up peacefully under the blanket. She was still at camp and would wake up at any moment to smell sausages roasting over the fire. But looking at the giant's eyes, so serious and real, she knew this wasn't a dream.

"Can I see it?"

"See what?"

“The egg!”

“I don’t know, little girl. A human hasn’t seen the Dragon Prince in over one thousand years. It could be a disaster.”

“Please, sir! I’m a kid. What could I possibly do? It’s just that an opportunity like this doesn’t happen every day! How many humans have seen a dragon? How many kids have seen a dragon egg? This could change my life forever. This is the adventure I was looking for!”

“Well...”

“I just want to be able to tell my children that dragons do exist. That I saw a real giant and a real dragon. That magic isn’t dead!”

“Alright, alright. Here, child. Take a look at this.” And then the giant reached into his mouth with his other hand and pulled something out of his belly!

The dragon egg looked just like the crystals in the giant’s head. The crystal of the egg glowed a deep blue, like a sapphire, with bolts of light crackling through it. Almost like lightning. Feyr tried to crawl across the giant’s hand to get a closer look. Her eyes glowed with the flash of lightning, and her heart pounded like a thunderstorm. And the moment she did, she saw all of her dreams flash before her eyes. Feyr felt like she was connected to the stormy dragon egg. Maybe it was the fact she was born from a lightning storm? And maybe it was something else entirely.

Chapter 2: The Ugly Duckling

Once upon a time, there was a mother duck that sat on a nest of eggs. She had four little white eggs underneath her and she was very happy to have them. She worked very hard to keep them warm and she tried very hard to make sure that nothing got to the eggs. She knew that sometimes, some animals would try to take them to eat them, but Mother Duck was very good at protecting her eggs. Whenever sneaky Weasel would try, she would chase him off with very loud quacks and big wings. And she usually did keep him away.

She waited many, many nights for her eggs to hatch, but she knew that it would happen soon. She sat atop her nest, waiting patiently for them to start to move. She knew it was soon, for the eggs were starting to move around underneath her. She could feel the baby ducklings moving around! It would be any day! So, Mother Duck continued to wait for them to hatch. After all, everyone knew that babies were always worth the wait!

One beautiful morning, she heard the sound of cracking underneath her. It woke her up from her morning nap. She heard more and more of it. She heard the little tapping sounds of tiny beaks trying to break out of the eggs! So, very excitedly, she hopped off of the nest and looked down at her babies. They would hatch soon enough! She was certain of that much! So, she waited for the nest to hatch.

The first egg to hatch held a little yellow duckling covered in fuzz. She looked up at her mother and quacked quietly. "Why, hello there, darling!" said Mother Duck. "I'm going to name you Dina!" She smiled at the baby duck, and the duckling scooted her way over to her mother to cuddle up. The hatched world was very big and very cold, and she wanted to be comfortable and warm!

The second egg to hatch held another fuzzy yellow duckling. This duckling was just a little bit bigger than the first one, and he looked around curiously. He wanted to see everything there was to see in the wide, wide world. “Hello there, little guy!” said Mother Duck. “I’m going to name you Dave!” And just like Dina, Dave scooted closer to Mother Duck to cuddle and get warm.

Then, the third egg began to crack as well. Soon, out popped the third duckling! This one was fuzzy, yellow, and smaller than Dina. She appeared to be very, very shy and tried to hide right back in her egg. But Mother Duck gently picked her up and sat her next to her siblings. “Hi there, sweetheart!” said Mother Duck. “I am going to name you Debbie!” So, Debbie cuddled up to Dave and Dina, and they all looked at the last egg.

The last egg did not move. It did not move for a long, long time, and Mother Duck was sad. Maybe this egg would not hatch at all. But, a day later, it began to hatch as well. The egg rocked about and finally cracked open, and out tumbled the ugliest duckling Mother Duck had ever seen! The duckling was not little and yellow. Instead, it was long and fat and grey! It looked as if it had rolled around in a pile of dirt!

But Mother Duck did not mind. Just like with her other babies, she pulled the little ugly duckling closer and said, “Nice of you to join us, honey. Your name is Greg!” She cuddled the baby, as mothers do, and did not seem to think anything of the strange look.

“Mama!!” squeaked Dina. “That duck is ugly!”

“Now hush there, Dina!” said Mother Duck. “That duck is your brother, and how he looks is just fine! He looks perfectly like himself!” And with that said, she cuddled up to her baby.

As the ducks all grew, something about Greg was different. The ducklings did not like their brother and they often left him out of all of their games. They would spend all of their time playing by themselves, and whenever Greg would come nearby, they would all swim away as fast as they could.

Sadly, Greg wandered away. He did not want to stay there any longer, so he went off as far away as he could. He swam until he got to the end of the pond, and then he started to walk. He walked until his feet were so tired that they could not walk anymore, and he slept.

But he was very quickly found by a person. The person was very kind and took him home to live on a farm. He did not know what the person was saying, but he felt good with her.

But soon, the cat that lived with the person started to make fun of him, too. “What are you?” asked the cat when he got home.

“I’m a duckling,” said Greg.

And the cat laughed and laughed at him until he felt very, very embarrassed. He did not like the way that the cat looked at him, so he decided to leave again. Greg wandered around and around. He was very sad that he was all alone, lost, and so ugly that no one wanted to see him.

One day, he found a pond that was filled with swan and he thought that the swans were the most beautiful creatures he had ever seen! They had beautiful white feathers and the most graceful long necks. They were so kind looking and so nice to see. So, Greg went over to the swans and jumped into the water. He swam closer and closer to them.

“Please don’t laugh at me!” he squeaked as he got as close as he could to the swans.

The swans all looked at him in surprise. “Who are you?” they asked. The swans all looked at each other.

“I’m Greg the duckling,” he squawked.

The swans all stared at him. They seemed very surprised by his answer. “A duckling?” they all started to laugh and laugh, and

Greg felt very, very sad again. Everyone wanted to laugh at him when they saw him. He wanted to laugh at himself, too. His neck was too long, and his beak was black. His feathers were grey instead of yellow, and he did not look at all like his brothers and sisters.

So, he looked at the swans in embarrassment. “I can’t help it that I’m ugly, but it’s the inside that counts, not the outside!” he announced sadly as he turned away from them. “I can’t help that I was born grey instead of yellow, but that does not mean that you should be so mean! I might be ugly on the outside, but you are all ugly on the inside!” and with that said, Greg began to swim away as fast as he could.

But then, one of the swans stopped him. “Greg!” the swan called out. “You are not a duckling at all!” she said. She pointed to where a bunch of little ugly ducklings was swimming about in the water. They looked just like him. They had grey feathers and they had long necks, and they had black beaks. They were all looking right at him and he looked right back at them and realized something.

He was not a duck. He was a baby swan!

He looked around at all of the beautiful swans that were in front of him.

“You must be the egg that Anna lost!” said one of the swans, and then, another swan came swimming over to him excitedly. This swan had the same little white spot above its beak that Greg did. The swan and Greg looked at each other for a very long while before the swan gave him a big hug with long, white, beautiful wings. “My baby!!” she cried out in joy and she gave him the tightest hug she could, not wanting to let go.

And for the first time, Greg felt like he belonged. He felt like he was in the right place and that he had found his home. He was not a duck at all, and just because he was ugly by duck standards did not mean that he was ugly. He was the perfect baby swan and that was what mattered. It is not fair to judge a swan to be a duck, but when he was home with all of the other swans, he felt much, much better and much, much happier. All he had to do was realize that he needed the time to himself.

And so, Greg grew up to be a beautiful swan that looked just like all the rest. He grew to have beautiful white feathers and long, graceful neck and soft wings just like his mother. And he learned a very valuable lesson—you cannot judge someone else for how they look because you do not know their story.

Chapter 3: The Princess and the Pea

Once upon a time, there was a prince named James. Prince James was told that he could not be king until he married a suitable princess. He had to marry a princess, but every princess that he had ever met was not right for him! Some of them were too loud. Some of them were too rude. Some of them were not smart enough. He had searched far and wide to find someone that could have been a suitable wife and a good queen, but he could not find one anywhere.

"Oh, if only I could find a princess that was as kind as she was beautiful! And as smart as she was sweet! And as caring to everyone as she was for herself! What a queen that would make!" Prince James really wanted to make sure that the queen of their kingdom was a very good one, for they had suffered through bad queens before. He had read stories of queens that were not kind and how they would make everyone work until they fell over. He had read stories of queens that were vain and only cared about keeping their appearance perfect. He had read stories about queens who would throw away the whole kingdom just to make sure that they got what they wanted, and he did not want his kingdom to be ruled like that! Instead, he wanted a kingdom that would be ruled by a kind, fair, just queen that would make sure to take care of everyone that was there. He wanted a queen that would make his people proud and be beloved by all!

One day, Prince James was on his horse-riding home to his castle. It was pouring down rain and it was very, very cold. As he went along his way, he heard the sound of crying nearby. He was not sure that he had heard it at first, but when he stopped riding his horse and listened very, very closely, he heard the sound of crying. So, as all noble princes would do, he went off to investigate! And sure enough, he found a young woman hiding under a tree in the mud, soaking wet. She was crying and shivering as she sat there.

“Ma’am are you okay?” he asked her gently and she seemed surprised that someone had stopped to talk to her. She looked up at him and blinked in surprise.

“I’m very, very cold,” she said, and Prince James believed her. She looked very, very cold, so he took off his coat. The rain was very cold through his clothes without the jacket on, but still, he offered it to her. Then, he invited her back to the castle to dry off, get warm, and wait out the storm.

So, off they went, riding back to the castle as quickly as they could to get out of the rain. When they made it inside, Prince James’ mother came up. “And who is this?” she asked, looking curiously at the new visitor.

“I’m Princess Sasha. I have gotten lost!” she said, and she told a tale of how she was traveling with her family on a journey to meet a prince from a neighboring kingdom. But something terrible had happened and Sasha had gotten lost and could not find her way back home.

The queen looked at the young woman suspiciously, but she had an idea. All royalty knew that princesses were very sensitive. So, she invited Sasha to stay the night. And then, she placed a pea underneath the mattress of the bed that Sasha was going to sleep on.

Sasha was dried up and allowed to change into clean clothes. They fed her a great, big, warm feast. During the feast, Sasha had perfect table manners and was very smart as they talked. She was very kind to everyone that brought the food out and she had talked about how much she loved the people of her kingdom. James really liked her. She was not just pretty on the outside, she was pretty on the inside too, and he really liked that. Then, James’ mother said that it was time for bed. So, the queen showed Sasha where she would be sleeping and said good night with a smile.

Sasha was very grateful to come into the room and get some sleep. She was very glad to be warm and out of the rain. She got onto the bed and tried to get comfortable, but she could not! She rolled to the left, and her back hurt. She rolled to the right, and then her neck hurt. She tried rolling every which way she could to try to find a good, comfortable spot, but nothing was working!

Tired and sad, Sasha began to cry.

The queen heard the crying and was excited. Could it be that she was actually as sensitive as she thought? Or was she only crying because she was not at home with her own family? So, the queen very quietly crept down the hallway before opening the door. She walked in and saw Sasha sitting on the side of the bed. Sasha's legs were hanging off and she was wiping tears from her face.

"What is wrong, my dear?" The queen asked when she heard the crying.

When Sasha heard the queen, she tried very hard to stop crying. She wiped the tears off of her face and took a very big deep breath. "I'm very sorry, ma'am, I don't want to be a bother, but I cannot get comfortable! The bed is hard, and it is hurting me!" said Sasha. "It is okay, I will leave in the morning and try to get home if I can." She sniffled to herself and looked very sad.

But the queen was happy. That was a very good sign after all. "Oh, no worries!" said the queen with a smile. "I can fix the problem! We always want our guests to be comfortable! Please, feel free to tell us anything that you need, and we can help!"

So, the queen had someone come in and bring more mattresses for Sasha to sleep on. They piled a new mattress onto the bed and then helped Sasha up to see if it was any better. But every time they added more mattresses, Sasha was still uncomfortable. By the end of the night, she was very tired, very sad, and she had a curious bruise on her back. She was not happy. She felt like that was a worse night than the one she had spent in the rain! But she did not want to complain to her hosts, because they had been very generous when they let her go and visit.

But the queen was thrilled! The queen clapped her hands. “My dear Sasha, you are a princess!” she declared as she pulled the pea out from underneath the mattress and then asked for Sasha to get back on. The bed was fine then, and she realized that it was much better now than before. Then, James walked into the room. He saw that Sasha was sad, his mother was happy, and there was a strange pile of twenty mattresses piled up on the bed! How absurd! He looked around at everyone. “Mom, what’s going on?” he asked, worried that his mother had done something to upset his guest. He wanted Sasha to be as happy as she could be before he tried to help her home!

“I put a pea under the mattress to make sure you are a real princess!” said the queen with a smile. “You see, my son needs to marry a princess and you are a very good one! Better than all across the land!”

James smiled at Sasha and Sasha smiled at James.

Then, it was decided that there would be a royal wedding for James and Sasha. The wedding was spectacular! There were carriages of horses, and people passing out flowers. There was a cake that was almost the size of a horse for all to share, and everyone was very happy that James had found a Princess.

And from that point on, the kingdom was ruled by King James and Queen Sasha. Queen Sasha was found to be just as kind as she was beautiful, and she would always help those in need, just like James had done for her. She was always helping other people whenever she could. She was found to be wonderful and smart, and she cared about all of her kingdom, and she was very good to everyone she met. Queen Sasha was a true queen, through and through, and her beautiful hearth shone brighter than even her beautiful looks. She was loved by everyone, and she and King James lived happily ever after.

Chapter 4: Peter Rabbit

Once upon a time, there lived a family of rabbits. There was a Mother Rabbit. There was a Flopsy Rabbit. There was a Mopsy Rabbit. There was a Cottontail Rabbit, and there was a Peter Rabbit. All four children lived alone with their mother. Their father had been caught by the farmer named Mr. McGregor that owned the farm that they all lived near. So, their mother always told them that they were not to enter the vegetable garden. If they were to ever go into the vegetable garden, she warned, they would get eaten, just like their father!

Flopsy, Mopsy, and Cottontail were very good at listening. They listened to their mother's warning very carefully, and they never went into the vegetable garden. They knew that their mother only told them to stay out of the garden because she loved them and wanted what was best for them, so they were very glad to listen. But Peter was not very good at listening at all. He did not like being told what to do and he did not like it when his mother tried to say that he should not do anything at all.

Peter would often sneak into the vegetable garden whenever he could. He was not afraid of a farmer! He would go in and eat vegetables as much as he wanted. He was not worried about being caught at all, and even when his siblings would watch him and ask him not to, he would still go in and get some food. He would even try to ask the other bunnies to go in with him, but they always told him no.

One day, Peter decided that he would go into the farm himself. He did not tell anyone that he was going to go. He dug a little hole underneath the fence and squirmed his way into it. He looked around at all of the vegetables that there were in the garden. There were so many that he could not believe it! It looked like many more had been planted since the last time he had gone. He licked his lips hungrily and looked all around. They looked delicious!

Peter could see carrots and lettuce. He could see peas growing on their vines, wrapped around little stakes. He saw big, red tomatoes, hanging heavily from their vines. He saw just about any vegetable he could think of! And seeing them all made him very, very hungry. He was very excited to eat them all.

So, Peter decided to eat a little bit of everything that he could. He grabbed a carrot and chewed away at it. He grabbed some peas to gnaw on, too. He took at least one of each and every fruit and ate exactly half of each one, discarding the rest onto the ground and turning away.

But soon, Peter's tummy began to feel full. It felt very, very full and he felt ill. He had eaten too much food! He knew he had eaten too much, but it did not stop him from wanting more. But he knew that he would need to find some parsley for his tummy ache, so he started to look all around him to find some. He looked to the left and to the right. He looked all around the garden, and then he saw some, far on the other side.

So, off the full little bunny hopped to go get some parsley. His hops were very slow because he felt sick when he moved too much and he did not like how it made him feel. He hopped and hopped and hopped, slowly getting closer to the parsley, and then settled down to nibble at it.

Soon after he nibbled on it, Peter fell asleep, rubbing his poor, full belly and trying to make himself feel better. But he was woken up when he heard something dropped and the sound of a loud voice.

"What do you think you're doing?!" the loud voice boomed over the garden and when Peter looked up, there was Mr. McGregor, staring at him angrily. He was holding a pitchfork in one hand and a basket in another. He must have been coming to pick some vegetables when he found Peter, sleeping in the garden, and all of the food all over the ground!

Peter hopped up as quickly as he could with his still-too-full belly and tried to run away. He tried to squirm underneath the fence through the hole he had dug but could not quite make it through. He pushed and he pushed as hard as he could to get out from the fence, and then, he did it! He popped out of the fence! But his shoes and his jacket were left behind in the yard. He could not stop to go and get them, for he had to run very quickly to avoid the very angry Farmer McGregor.

Off he ran as quickly as he could, but he did not know where he was. He was lost within the farm and could not see where he could go to protect himself! But then, he saw a little shed. He hopped into the shed as quickly as he could and hid underneath the little watering can that was on the floor. He could hear Farmer McGregor coming closer and closer and closer, and he was careful to hide as quietly as he could.

Farmer McGregor did not seem to think about looking inside the watering can, for he kept on walking, mumbling and muttering about the rabbits and how he needed a new pie.

Peter hid very quietly in the can until he no longer heard any footsteps. He very carefully peeked his head out of the can and then saw something horrible! There was an orange cat, sleeping next to the door. He would have to very carefully, very quietly climb out of the watering can without making any noise at all and then sneak past the cat that was sleeping there. It was not going to be easy, but he would have to go and do it!

So, he snuck out, very quietly. He had a very hard time trying not to knock over anything, but he did it! Step by step, little by little, he snuck his way out of the can and out of the room! One time, he saw the cat twitch a little bit and was very afraid that she would get him, but she rolled over and started to snore. He was safe!

He started to hop toward the garden so he could get his clothes before going home. He knew that his mother would be very angry if he lost his clothing again. But then he saw it—there was a great, big scarecrow, decorated with his clothes! It had a silly hat and a corncob pipe, and it had his jacket over its little stick arms that stuck out. He frowned. How was he supposed to get it back? He scooted closer and closer to the scarecrow, wondering if he could climb it.

But then, he saw Farmer McGregor there again and he froze. The farmer saw him and ran right after him again. So, off Peter ran, without any clothes at all, all the way home. He made it all the way back through the farm and home without the farmer catching him. He ran straight into the den and fell on the ground.

His mother looked at him in shock. She looked so surprised to see him there, without his clothes on. “Peter!” she shouted angrily. “Where are your clothes?”

Peter shrugged his shoulders. “I feel ill,” he told his mother.

“Well then. Straight to bed with you!” And then, his mother shooed him into the bedroom and told him to go to sleep.

Peter curled up in his bed and felt very, very sorry for himself. His mother brought him just a little bit of chamomile tea for his tummy. But, Flopsy, Mopsy, and Cottontail, after being so good and listening to their mother, were rewarded with a very yummy dinner. They got to eat blackberries, bread, and milk, and they were very happy. They were glad that they had listened.

Peter, on the other hand, felt very bad about everything. He felt bad that he lost his clothes. He felt bad that his tummy hurt. He felt bad that his sisters had delicious food and all he got was a bit of tea. But Peter learned a very valuable lesson—it is never a good thing to steal from others.

Chapter 5: Stars Like Glass

Each broken bit became a celebrity. The Pieces of crystal swept and collected and glued from the woman to the ceiling of the chamber to become something wondrous, something fresh. Every night, she reached up and touched on what had belonged to her mom. Every night, she cut off her hands onto the shards.

She had bandages. She also had droplets of blood.

One afternoon, she followed up the dried drops throughout the home as though they may lead someplace different. Another evening, she simply sat in her room and observed the other women - the small women, the newest sistergirls - toddle from the lawn beneath.

Are you moping? the stepmother said. Do you think we do not need you?

The woman had informed the stepmother that she had broken the crown accident, cut on her hands by accident. However, she could inform the stepmother suspected in the lie, so she understood the world hadn't any space for these mishaps. Crowns remained on shelves or else they did not. Actual mothers remained with brothers or they did not.

Why does this matter? The woman wanted to state into the stepmother. Why is it that I need to become part of the?

Rather, she said nothing and walked in the area and found her solution into the stepmother's wardrobe. She pulled her off; she smeared blood to the dresses. She cut them and stood beneath the stains and fabrics. Somewhere, she recalled that her mother doing the exact same to her dad's suits. They had been dressed in frills and crowns. They had sung and they had twirled, and her mom had cut herself bled. But this had made them joyful. It was wondrous.

The stepmother pulled on the shards away the ceiling. She also sent the woman to acute guys who talked of healing and loss and used words such as masochism and mechanics as well as malice. They gave her actions to occupy her thoughts and course to civilize her soul. She swept and dusted at the evenings. She sang and recited French played violin in the afternoons. She did not of them well, not one of them right. After her father returned from his company to learn what talents she had discovered -- she had been, as he stated, yanking it together -- that the woman ran out of the den and also up the staircase and bolted herself into her chamber.

She discovered her father's feet following. She discovered him lean in the doorway. “Sweetie”, he explained in that strong voice. “Sweetie, you have to stop this today”.

He remained longer, talked louder, left demands. He desired her to say that she understood her stepmother was something great. He desired her to say that she understood the crown had only been a bowl behind when her mom ran away. “You cannot keep being like that”, her dad said. “Everyone adores you,” he explained.

However, the woman did not reply. She Stood her bed and ran her hands round the 1 sliver of crystal glued to the ceiling. She considered sitting frills and implants at the wreck of her dad's suits. Her mom had run the ribbons round the tops of her wrists along with the bloodstream slid down and then disperse in the carpeting. Her mom laughed. She staged. Tears were in her eyes.

“Make it fresh”, her mom had been sung. “Make it fresh, make it fresh to continue the entire day”.

The woman pushed her thumb from the shard around the ceiling, then felt that the border cut into her skin. She found her father's voice increasing. She discovered her stepmother nearing. She cried for the pain to again proceed throughout her entire body. However, as Much as she attempted, she couldn't locate the miracle in it. She felt Just the damage.

Chapter 6: Princess Peripatetic

Once upon a time, there lived a princess of a small realm who longed to see everything that the world had to offer. While she felt quite lucky that she was a princess, she was very aware that her kingdom was pretty tiny and didn't have a lot to offer in many areas. When she got the chance to talk to princesses from other realms, she found out that they had ever so many more things to do and see: exotic animals in lush natural settings, fun parks with all sorts of rides and games, and elaborate arts and crafts traditions which created all sorts of fascinating and beautiful objects. She would sigh, longingly, when she would hear these stories, and dream about one day being able to travel to all these other, more interesting realms.

Her parents, though, had different ideas: first, the princess needed to be trained in all the customs of the realm, of course, so that she could carry those traditions on when she got to be the queen. Second, she also needed to complete her schoolwork so that she would be both knowledgeable and wise as a ruler someday. Third—and worst of all, according to the princess—she needed to find a suitable match that she would one day marry. Any time the king and queen arranged a social event, Princess Peripatetic would groan she knew it was yet another attempt to get her to like some boy who would be good enough to someday be king.

"I'm not sure I really want to have a king," the princess thought to herself when dressing for yet another ball. "Why can't I just rule the land all by myself? I've sat through all these lessons and I know everything there is to know about my realm. It's not fair that I should have to be ruled over by a king." Because that was the sad fact of the matter: no matter how smart and powerful a queen was, the king still had the final say in important issues of how to rule—at least, that's how it worked with her parents.

So, Princess Peripatetic was not always the most cooperative princess when these social events were arranged. She would, of course, wear her most beautiful gowns—the deep purple one with the gold embroidery on it was her favorite—and loved her sparkly tiara which only highlighted the beauty of her long, curly hair. But she would often wear her heavy black leather traveling boots instead of dainty slippers with her beautiful dresses. Sometimes, she made a point to carry a traveling cloak and knapsack with her to emphasize to her parents that she was very much determined to do some traveling before she settled down in her small kingdom.

In the meantime, though, the princess buckled down at her lessons, especially interested in the studies of geography, history, and politics—she wanted to find out as much about these faraway lands that she longed for as possible. In fact, the princess was quite smart and did really well at all her studies, even if she didn't always enjoy the politeness and restraint that a good princess had to display. And, even though her parents were eager for her to find a good match, they were quite proud that Princess Peripatetic was very smart and, secretly, they kind of liked her mildly rebellious ways. The king, in particular, would often chuckle, seeing Princess Peripatetic in a long, flowing gown and big heavy boots, and say, "Now, isn't she something else?" That was the way he expressed both his confusion—she wasn't like other princesses—and his pride in her uniqueness.

The princess also busied herself with learning methods of fighting and self-defense. When she traveled—she had no doubt that she would, one day—she might as well be prepared for anything out there. But she also knew from all the visiting princesses and other royalty who occasionally passed through her small realm that most people were kind and generous to travelers. At least they were in her world, during her time. It never hurt to be prepared. And, the princess liked being outside, learning to shoot a bow and arrow or practicing sword play. She was quite good at the former, despite not having the best eyesight; she seemed to have a feel for where the arrow would land. With regard to swords, she was okay, but always a little intimidated by the heaviness and sharpness of the weapon. Nevertheless, she excelled at just about everything she did.

Yet, finally, the inevitable happened: at one of the balls, Princess Peripatetic actually met a young man that she quite liked. She had seen him before, of course, hard at his own studies or jousting with other young men on the field. He was the son of a well-liked duke and duchess, so he was appropriate as a match, but he was also a bit of a rough and tumble young man. His breeches would always be smudged with dirt or sporting a small rip about the knees. He liked to chance on his horses and devise new methods with his sword. He wasn't a showoff, by any means; he just enjoyed being active and having fun. Baron von Hoven was his name—a little stuffy sounding, perhaps, but his rumpled hair and easy grin could just as easily have fit a kid from any corner of the kingdom.

Once they hit it off, Princess Peripatetic and Baron von Hoven would spend lots of time together out in the field, practicing shooting and sword play as a team. The king and queen were quite pleased that their rather unique daughter had found an equally unique match—who didn't seem to mind that the princess would rather wear breeches and broad swords than dresses and slippers when they weren't at a formal ball. In fact, he seemed not to be intimidated by her one little bit, just as she wasn't intimidated or meek around him.

"Watch out, you nerd!" Baron would yell as the princess would let fly her arrow just as soon as he put out the target. "You're going to shoot me in the foot!"

"Only if you're lucky," she would laugh, and string another arrow through her bow.

They had fights with snowballs in the winter, gathered flowers and crops for harvest in the spring, set up picnics just for the two of them in the fields in summer, and planned the joyful fall parties for the whole small kingdom. They became best friends. After a decent amount of time had passed, and the king and queen were convinced that this would be a good match, they gathered Baron's family to meet at the castle to discuss the marriage.

Needless to say, it didn't quite go as planned.

"Married! Do you think I want to get married?!" Princess Peripatetic cried in anguish. "I told you my whole life: I want to travel. I don't want to settle down in the castle and be married and have children and stay here, stuck forever!"

The king and queen were surprised and upset. They thought that she had gotten rid of all those old dreams when she might this lovely young man. The king tried to appeal to her better senses, to tell her that she had a duty to fulfill, that her life of privilege had a price that came with it: she must serve her kingdom. The princess fretted and fumed, but knew that they were, in the end, right. And then Baron spoke up, as well.

"I think Princess Peripatetic has a really good point, actually. And I for one don't think that she will be nearly as good a leader if she hasn't seen some of the rest of the world. I love her, yes, and she is my best friend. But I am not going to be the one to hold her back." He stood with his arms crossed, almost as determined as our fierce princess.

All of the adults were a little taken aback, but Princess Peripatetic was beaming she knew there was a reason that she and Baron had become best friends. With the two of them standing strong together, she reasoned rightly, they would both get exactly what they wanted. Baron, too, thought it was a bit early for a marriage; he also wanted to do some things on his own. Ruling a country, however small, is a big job, and it takes time to build up the kind of experience and responsibility that will make you good at such a big job.

So the king and queen talked to the duke and duchess, and finally, all the adults agreed: Princess Peripatetic would be allowed two years for travel and studies in realms as far away as she wanted, while Baron von Hoven would be allowed to undergo some advanced studies in science and some leisure time with friends.

"But," warned the king, especially to the princess, "you realize that you may not feel the same when you return. It is quite possible that you and Baron will grow apart." He shrugged. "You might have to settle on someone quite different. You may not have a choice in it, either, for that is ultimately your duty to fulfill."

Both the princess and Baron were somewhat dismayed at that idea, but not worried enough to want to change their plans. So, an agreement of sorts was drawn up, and Princess Peripatetic began packing her bags that very night, intent on leaving as soon as first light was up. She said a hurried good-bye to Baron and rushed off.

Soon, the princess was in the remote Kingdom of Entwerp, a place where there were moats flowing throughout the city, with a thousand little dams and bridges to connect the winding streets. She met purveyors of the most interesting wares, who offered her perfumes and silks, potions and spices from all over the wide world. Entwerp was one of the wealthiest kingdoms known across the world, dependent on its many merchants to get the best items to trade and sell. From there, she headed south to the Kingdom of Sol, where she learned how to make food from all of the wonderful ingredients that grew well in the south, like bright citrus and big red tomatoes and peppers, with warming honey and spices and the freshest eggs and cheese. Compared to the dull stews and brown bread of her own kingdom, the Kingdom of Sol was a tasty sensation.

She went on to the even more distant shores of the Kingdom of Marruecos, where everyone spoke at least four different languages while she tried to keep up. She learned of great forests and vast deserts and of all the remarkable animals that lived there—magnificent lions and tall giraffes, the oddest of lizards and the largest of insects, the fastest of gazelles and the largest of hippos. It was a wondrous education in the marvels of the world.

After two years, she came home, full of knowledge and respect for the other peoples and environments of the world. She was humbled by her travels, knowing that she loved her own small kingdom, even with all its limitations; in fact, she started to see great value in things that she had once taken for granted. The regular old farm animals seemed noble in their hard work and sacrifice for her kingdom, while that old brown bread tasted familiar and rich to her now. She would, indeed, protect and serve her home with all her heart—even if she did want to take a journey now and again.

The best part of the whole story is that, when Princess Peripatetic returned, she was thrilled to see her youthful companion all grown up, as well. Baron von Hoven had also spent his time wisely, using his studies to invent things to better the kingdom and running around with his friends as he liked. Their reunion was immediate and happy. It was decided—by the princess herself, by Baron himself—that they would one day rule the kingdom together, as equals. And take as many journeys as they could.

Chapter 7:
The Story of the Blue Crabs

There lived two young blue crabs, Nino and Jessi. Nino and Jessi loved adventure so much, even though they were very young. They would spend most of their time hunting treasures; at times, this hunting would take them far, far away from their home. At first, their parents were okay with their adventure missions, but as they spent more and more days away from home, their absence became a significant source of concern for the parents.

"Nino and Jessi, never spend a night again away from home," said both of their parents. They would receive warnings each moment they failed to return home.

"Yes, mum and dad," they would reply cheekily. But the allure of what the world held was irresistible, and the young lads became even more daring, sometimes swimming deep into ocean surfaces where no one had dared to venture into before.

Sometimes, they were lucky to find valuable treasures like gold, bronze, and currencies that fell from moving ships or sunken ones. Sometimes, they were not so fortunate. Once in a while, they would return home empty-handed. And there were days when they would have to flee their location for fear of being mauled by ravenous predators like the sea whale.

One day, they overheard a conversation between the turtle and the frog about a ship that had disappeared several years ago without a trace. The vessel was thought to have carried several tons of treasures. Many believed the vessel encountered rough waters and had sunk.

"My friend, I tell you, no one has ever seen the ship ever since," the turtle told his friend, the frog.

"I also heard it had tons of gold on board. Anyone who can find it will become wealthy and filthy rich," his friend retorted.

"Oh, yeah. He will be the richest person in our kingdom. Wealthier than the king" confirmed the turtle. He seemed to know too many things that no other animal knew.

"And perhaps, that lucky person will be installed as the new king," the frog interjected wisely.

"Of course, with so much wealth, you can simply run a smooth campaign, and before you know, you'll be controlling this vast kingdom," the frog seemed to agree.

Now, to the two adventurous kids, once they heard of the sunken ship with immense treasures that could make them wealthy and famous, their curiosity was instantly aroused. They had to find the missing ship by all means.

"But where do we start?" Wondered Nino. They sat down and thought for a long time. But still, they couldn't think of any place where the ship was probably located.

"Perhaps if we swim toward the island with big, tall buildings, we may be lucky to see the missing ship," Jessi offered.

He was referring to the inland port where large vessels customarily docked.

"But we will never get permission from our parents' to venture that far," Nino replied, concern written all over his face.

"Don't be silly. No one will know, and besides, we will be back before anyone starts missing us," Jessi replied. He knew they were risking a lot.

It may take them several days to arrive at the dock. And he feared there might even be more dangerous predators waiting to swallow them up. But the thought of all that treasure lying somewhere was an encouragement worthy enough for them.

After arguing among themselves for long, they agreed to set off in search of the missing ship with the treasure. They would go off without informing anyone. The following day, as agreed, they quickly set off toward the island. It was a long journey, so they started quite early.

"We will survey the depth of the sea for any sign of the treasure once we arrive there," an excited Nino informed his friend.

"And what do we do next after locating it?" asked his friend.

"Relax, my friend, relax; you know me. I'm a genius. I will think of something. How we will haul the treasure and sell it off to make tons of cash."

Meanwhile, near the island, a small vessel was preparing to set off into the deep sea on its way to another continent. The ship was massive with all kinds of merchandise, including a large number of heavy drums full of oil. You know the nature of men; some are too careless. And so, it happened that two or three of these drums were not fastened securely. As the ship moved, the drums became too loose that it started hanging dangerously on the rails of the ship.

Soon, the ship encountered rough waters, and the drums fell into the ocean, one after the other.

Meanwhile, Nino and Jessi kept swimming; they were quite sure they were not far off their destination. And so, their excitement rose so much that they did not notice the two dark figures moving at a dangerous speed toward them. The first drum missed Nino by a whisker. Jessi was not so lucky, and he was carried off by the second drum, which hit him at full force, rendering him unconscious instantly.

Nino, once he had recovered from the initial shock, cried out to his friend.

"Jessi, hold on; I am coming for you," he said in a terrified voice. He swam back and started chasing the drum, which was carrying off Jessi. He was struggling to catch up with the rolling monster, and luckily, it started slowing down once it encountered opposing sea currents. Nino took the opportunity to grab Jessi off the imposing drum.

When they were safe, Jessi realized he was in so much pain. But he was relieved to see the familiar face of his friend again. For a moment, he had thought he was in heaven.

Nino assisted his friend to get back home, where a doctor was promptly called to examine him. Apart from minor injuries, Jessi was lucky not to suffer any serious life-threatening injuries. The two boys promised never to venture into the unknown again.

However, Jessi and Nino had severe psychological issues triggered by the incident. They couldn't sleep alone in their rooms again. Every time they fell asleep, they would wake up, screaming and sweating. They were having severe nightmares of the rolling drums. But if they were sleeping in the company of their parents or siblings, they had the most beautiful rest.

This problem went on for a while until their parents decided to seek help. They were tired of babysitting the two boys all night. They needed help desperately, and there was nowhere to start but at Mermaid's clinic. She was the best therapist around, and many people had found treatments for their psychological issues.

Together with the kids, they left for Mermaid's clinic. Luckily, she was in, attending her patients. They were welcomed warmly by the friendly receptionist. After waiting for a few minutes, it was their turn to see the therapist. They were promptly ushered into the cozy office of Mermaid.

"Welcome, and what can I do for you?" Mermaid asked them once they had settled.

"Well, it is about our sons. They had a traumatic experience recently, and since then, they find it hard spending time alone in their rooms," replied Jessi's father.

"And we are tired of babysitting them, sometimes throughout the whole night," Nino's mother added.

"Well, first of all, I must thank you for taking the initiative to come and see me. It shows you have a genuine concern for the welfare of your kids," Mermaid started. Then she continued talking.

"This phobia of loneliness affects several people, and as you have rightly put it, it is caused by a major traumatic experience you might have undergone in the past."

"Is there a cure for the problem?" Jessi's mother wanted to know.

"Well, there is always a solution. You should encourage your sons to expose themselves to a low-rank fear. At first, they may feel incredibly nervous and anxious. This is normal, and they shouldn't worry. In time, their body will relax after a few miserable attempts. When you expose yourself to your fears, you begin to think more deeply about the fears behind your initial panic," answered the Mermaid.

With the help of their parents, Jessi and Nino exposed themselves to their fears. At first, they did it gradually and then did it more. They would spend a few minutes alone each day. And as the days passed by, they gradually increased the moments they stayed alone until, finally, they were able to stay and sleep soundly alone in their rooms. They had successfully overcome their fear of being alone.

Chapter 8: Elijah Has a Sleepover

Elijah and Benjamin had been friends since before they could even walk.

Their moms were friends from high school, and that meant that Elijah and Benjamin had spent their whole lives together.

They learned to crawl together, talk together, walk together, run together, and play together.

They were so close that they even got to spend dinners together and go to movies together with their families.

Whenever they did something, they always did it together, and it made Elijah and Benjamin very happy.

One day, Elijah's mom had gotten pregnant with Elijah's little brother.

For nine months, Elijah watched as his mom grew bigger and bigger, while his little brother grew inside of her belly.

He also went to the doctors with her and watched his baby brother kicking around on the sonogram.

It was a very cool experience to get to watch his little brother growing up inside of his mom's tummy.

After school one day, Elijah was on his way to go find his mom when Benjamin's mom came to his class and picked him up instead.

She told him that his mom was getting ready to go have his little brother, so Elijah was going to stay with her and Benjamin.

He was going to have a sleepover with them until his mom and dad could come home from the hospital with his baby brother.

This all made Elijah very excited.

Elijah and Benjamin got in Benjamin's car and went back to his house.

When they got there, they had a snack of apples and juice.

Then, they went to Benjamin's room to play with his toys.

Elijah knew Benjamin's house very well and felt at home there, but this was their first time having a sleepover.

At first, everything seemed the same as any other day that they hung out at each other's house.

They played cars, airplanes, and action figures.

Then, they went out in the yard and played on Benjamin's jungle gym and swing set.

They kept playing all the way until it was time to have dinner.

When they went inside, the table was full of plates of chicken, rice, potatoes, and cheese.

It looked so delicious; Elijah was excited about dinner.

He and Benjamin filled their plates with the food and then sat down at the table to eat it with Benjamin's family.

While they ate, Elijah asked questions about his baby brother.

"How long does it take for my baby brother to come?" Elijah asked.

"Well, that's hard to say. It could take a few hours, or it could take more." Benjamin's mom asked.

"Once he's here, can I go see him?" Elijah asked.

"Soon, but your mom and dad need to make sure that he comes safely and that the doctors are happy with his progress before we can go see him." Benjamin's mom smiled.

"Is he sick?" Elijah asked.

"That's a good question. No, he is not sick, but babies do need to be monitored by doctors to make sure that they are growing well. The doctors want to make sure your brother and your mother are happy and healthy before they go home." Benjamin's mom answered.

"Oh, okay," Elijah said.

Elijah ate the rest of his dinner quietly, as he thought about what it would be like to have a little brother.

Benjamin wondered, too.

"Am I going to have a little brother?" Benjamin asked.

"No, not right now." his mom answered.

"Why not? Elijah is getting one!" Benjamin complained.

"Well, it's just not the right time." his mom smiled.

"That's not fair." Benjamin frowned.

"It's okay; you can share my little brother," Elijah said, smiling.

Benjamin smiled too, and together they talked about what it would be like to have a little brother to play with.

After dinner, Elijah and Benjamin helped clean up the dishes and put away the leftovers.

Then, they went back to Benjamin's room to play again.

This time, they played board games and card games, and they talked about what Elijah's little brother would be like.

They wondered if he would want to play when he got home, or if he would be too tired to play at first.

Elijah told Benjamin about how his mom and dad said that his little brother would be too small to play at first and that he would need to grow.

Benjamin was surprised, and they wondered how small Elijah's little brother would be.

Soon, they had played enough, and Benjamin's mom came in to let them know it was time to get ready for bed.

This part was strange for Elijah and Benjamin because usually Elijah would go home and sleep in his own bed, but tonight it was different.

They both went to the bathroom and brushed their teeth and combed their hair.

Then, they took turns going potty and getting their pajamas on so that they were ready to go to sleep.

Once they were ready, Elijah and Benjamin helped Benjamin's mom set up a sleeping cot in Benjamin's room.

The cot was a small camp cot that had lots of blankets on it to make it comfortable and warm.

Benjamin also let Elijah use one of his pillows, and Elijah's dad had brought over Elijah's favorite stuffed bear for Elijah to sleep with that night.

This made Elijah really happy!

Before they fell asleep, Benjamin's mom let Elijah call his parents to say goodnight.

He called them at the hospital and talked to his dad on the phone.

"Hi, dad! I am going to bed now. Is my little brother ready yet?" he asked.

"Almost kiddo." Elijah's dad answered.

"Is he here?" Elijah asked.

"He is!" his dad said, "do you want to talk to him?" he added.

"Yes, I do!" Elijah said.

Elijah's dad put him on the speakerphone and Elijah talked to his mom and his baby brother for the first time.

"Hello, baby brother! How are you?" Elijah asked.

"We are good." Elijah's mom answered.

"What is my baby brother's name?" Elijah asked.

"Nathaniel." his mom answered.

"Wow, Nathaniel. I like that name!" Elijah said, excited.

"Me too!" Benjamin said from across the room.

"Okay, we need to go to bed now, you get a good rest too, Elijah." his dad said, saying goodnight.

"Sounds good dad, love you, goodnight!"

"We love you too, Elijah. Goodnight." his parents said.

Benjamin's mom hung up the phone.

Elijah and Benjamin laid down, and Benjamin's mom turned out the lights.

It seemed weird sleeping in a different room, and it was even weirder to sleep in the same room as Benjamin, Elijah thought.

Benjamin seemed to think the same thing because as soon as Elijah thought that he said, "it's weird to hear you breathing when I'm trying to sleep!" and giggled.

Elijah giggled, too.

Then, they started talking about Elijah's new little brother, Nathaniel.

Finally, a while later, they both fell asleep.

They slept soundly through the entire night.

All night, Elijah dreamt about what it would be like to go meet his new little brother.

He dreamt about what his brother looked like, and sounded like, and how small he would really be.

In the morning, Elijah and Benjamin woke up.

They made their beds, brushed their teeth, and went into the kitchen to have some breakfast.

After they were done eating, Benjamin's mom told Elijah and Benjamin that they could go meet Nathaniel!

They were so excited that they immediately went and got ready and put their shoes on so that they could leave.

Elijah also put all of his clothes and belongings away so that he could bring them with him because their sleepover was now done.

When everyone was ready to leave, they went to the car, and Benjamin's mom drove them all to the hospital.

Once they were there, they went in through big sliding doors and made their way all the way up to the room where Elijah's mom, dad, and baby brother were waiting.

As soon as they walked in, Elijah was so excited to meet his baby brother.

"Hello Nathaniel!" he said excitedly, waving at his little brother.

He got close and looked and realized his brother was even smaller than he thought!

“I think he likes you,” Elijah’s mom said as his baby brother reached up to touch Elijah’s face.

Elijah stood very still and giggled as Nathaniel touched his cheeks and grabbed his hair.

Then, Elijah stepped away so that Benjamin could see Nathaniel.

Benjamin was shocked at how small he was and realized that Elijah was right: it would be a while before Nathaniel was big enough to play with them.

The two boys sat quietly in the corner of the room while Benjamin’s mom met Nathaniel.

She held him and played with his little hands, then when she was done, gave him back to Elijah’s mom.

Before Benjamin and his mom left, Elijah’s dad brought Nathaniel over and let each of the boys hold him for the first time.

One at a time, they carefully cradled baby Nathaniel in their arms, making sure not to move him too quickly or hurt him.

It was a big task, but they were both very careful and kind to Nathaniel and Elijah’s mom said they were doing a great job.

Then, it was time for baby Nathaniel to eat, and it was time for Benjamin and his mom to leave.

They said their goodbyes, then left. Elijah, Nathaniel, and their parents sat quietly in the hospital room while Nathaniel nursed and then slept.

Then, while he was sleeping, Elijah’s dad took him down to the café to get something to eat.

“So, how was your first sleepover?” his dad asked.

“It was awesome!” Elijah said.

“We played so much, and we talked all night about Nathaniel. I cannot wait to bring him home and show him my toys and play with him and Benjamin.” Elijah said.

His dad just giggled.

They ordered hot chocolates and lunches and ate them in the café so that Nathaniel could get a good sleep.

Then, before they went back to the room, they got a tea and a sandwich for Elijah’s mom, too.

It was a great sleepover and a great day for Elijah.

He could not wait to have more sleepovers, and to one day bring his baby brother Nathaniel with him on sleepovers.

The end!

Chapter 9: The Dragon King

Feyr was creeping closer to the dragon egg. Every part of her body was burning. It felt like lightning was passing through her veins. The little girl smelt iron in the air, as if there was a thunderstorm brewing in between them. She could have sworn that lightning was crackling in her hair. And when Feyr stretched out her fingertips, the dragon egg shot a small bolt of electricity at her. But it didn't hurt...

"Why doesn't it hurt, Giant?" Feyr asked the talking mountain giant without looking away. The dragon egg was mesmerizing. It was pulsing and beating, like a living storm. The heart of the dragon inside was strong and full of power. It made the girl's heart race. The glow of the crystal shell glimmered in the girl's blue eyes. The lightning reflected in her gaze like two polished mirrors. Was it the dragon inside that captured the girl's attention? Or was there something deeper? A bond of some kind.

"I'm not sure, little girl. I've never seen anything like this in my life. And I've lived for over five thousand years! Maybe the Dragon Prince likes you? Or maybe there is something connecting you two? Tell me... How were you born, child? I see the lightning in your eyes."

"It's funny you mention that, sir. I was thinking about that too. On the night I was born, there was a fierce storm. Terrible and powerful. The rains howled, and the roofs were torn off buildings. The roads were flooded and carried cars down the hill. And lightning! It was everywhere! Striking the ground wherever it could. Setting trees and houses on fire. That was the night I was born. And at the very moment I was born, midnight exactly, a giant bolt of lightning struck the ground right outside my house. Turned it right into glass. My parents told me that I was carried down from heaven by that storm. That it gave me my strength of spirit and body. They call me living lightning." The girl watched the lightning flicker through the crystal of the dragon egg, smiling.

"Hm..." The giant said thoughtfully. The moss on his face and the trees on his head swayed in the wind. Curiosity danced behind the giant's glowing eyes. "I wonder..."

"What do you wonder, Giant?" Feyr asked, looking away from the dragon egg for just a moment. At that moment, the little girl could swear she heard a whisper come from inside the egg. As if the baby dragon was calling to her. She almost missed what the Mountain Giant said next.

"Well, there is a Prophecy, you see. It was created long ago by one of the Wisest Wizards in the land. Of course, he wasn't wise enough to know exactly who would fulfill the prophecy, but that's how these things work. The way the story goes, the Dragon Prince has very powerful magic. Dream Magic, it's called. Dream Magic has the power to make dreams come true and even grant your deepest, craziest wishes. But it also has the power to make nightmares come to life. You can imagine how that worked out. The Dragon Prince, before he ever hatched, was making the dreams and nightmares of beings all around the world come true. It was chaos. Madness! Trees were coming to life, deer were turning to solid gold, and clouds were sprouting wings. I won't even mention the nightmares and monsters. Things had to be fixed. The world needed to be made right. And that couldn't be done with the Dragon Prince's Dream Magic turning the world upside down. The only solution the Wise Wizard could think of was to curse the Dragon Prince."

"What?! The wizard cursed this baby dragon? Why would he do that? If he was so wise, why didn't he come up with something better? And why didn't the Dragon King stop him?"

"Are you a Queen, little girl?" The giant said, furrowing his brows. They looked like two might cliffs colliding.

“What? No way. I’m just a kid.”

“Then what would you know of the responsibilities a king or queen must take. It was a difficult decision, but the Dragon King wanted to protect his kingdom and the world. Not just for the citizens. He wanted his son to arrive in a kingdom he could rule. As for the wizard, magic is beyond me. The old man probably looked through countless spells and enchantments. But if an old man older than I am decided a sleeping curse was the best way to solve the issue, who am I to question it? And from what I know, the Dragon Queen and Dragon Queen were constantly asking the human for help.”

“So they cursed the baby dragon? The Dragon Prince is cursed?”

“Yes, the Dragon Prince is cursed. But the kingdom, maybe the entire world, was saved from the wild magic. And the prophecy states that a dream come true from someone with a pure heart will save the Dragon Prince. Not only that, it will save the entire world. And that why I ask how you were born. Because the Dragon Prince was also born in a storm like that. A strong, ruthless storm that tore down mountains and set fire to fields with lightning. The Dragon Prince was also born at midnight. You two may be connected. As two bolts of lightning are still connected to the storm.”

“You know... It’s funny; you say that. When I look at the Dragon Prince’s egg, I see something odd in it. A reflection of myself, like in a mirror. It’s me, but it’s not me. It’s more like a feeling. And when I see the lightning strike in the egg, I feel the lightning strikes inside of me.”

“What else? What else do you feel?”

I feel a lot, but I’m also hearing something. A whisper. Almost like a song. Not in my ears, but in my head. Like the Dragon Prince is singing in my mind.”

“By the Stones! This is amazing. I’ve seen many beings meet with this egg, hoping they would be the answer to the prophecy.

None have experienced what you have. Tell me more! What is the Dragon Prince singing about, Feyr?"

"He's telling me about my dream. And how it is a good dream to chase. He's' telling me about his dreams. He says we share a dream, Giant."

"Hohohoho! I'll be darned! Who'd have thought that a lil' human crawling in my earholes would have something to do with the Dragon Prince? Not me, that's for sure! No, sir. Doesn't fate work in the most wonderful ways? It's been thousands of years. Thousands have tried. And the child who comes along wishing for nothing more than a little adventure is the one who could save us all. What's your dream, little girl?" The giant was laughing heartily now. The gusts of wind coming from his stony lungs made the clouds below them swirl and fluff up.

"Well, it's nothing special. Honest, it isn't. I feel like most kids have this dream. All I want is-"

"Wait! Nope! Hold that thought. Don't tell me. Tell him." And without warning, the Mountain Giant dropped the Dragon Prince's egg into Feyr's lap.

The moment the egg touched Feyr's hands, lightning began to run up and down her arms. The lightning changed color as it moved. Blue to purple to red to orange to yellow to green, all the way through every color imaginable. Feyr could feel the lightning crackling at the tips of her hair, which was starting to float up towards the sky. And then the girl started to float too. Little bolts of lightning jumped from the bottom of her feet and zapped the hands of the giant, who just laughed merrily. As lightning filled her body and made her mind race, the girl started to spin around and laugh. She'd never felt anything like this in her life. She could feel the life force of the baby dragon in the egg. She could feel the warmth and beat of its heart. Its heart was beating at the same time of her own.

“This is amazing! I never imagined I’d get to hold a dragon egg. The Dragon Prince, no less! No in a million years, no sir. And... am I flying?”

“We are flying, actually.” The voice came from inside Feyr’s head, just like before. But this time it was much clearer. It was the sweetest sound you could ever imagine. A siren’s song. An angel’s call. A mother’s lullaby.

“Who are you?” Feyr whispered out loud.

“It’s me. The Dragon Prince. The one in the egg.” The voice answered told her.

“Oh yeah, duh. I guess that was a dumb question.”

“No, it’s fine! Don’t worry about it. You’re actually the first person I’ve ever been able to speak with, even though my dreams.”

“Really? The first one?”

“Yep! I’ve been trapped in this Dreamscape for as long as I can remember. I’ve heard some people call out to me from the physical realm. People asking me to make their dreams come true. Sometimes I do and sometimes I don’t. But I’ve never been able to actually feel, see, and speak to someone from your side of the shell.”

“A dream that lasts forever, huh? That must be pretty nice.” Feyr wondered if the dragon wanted to wake up at all. After all, who’d want to leave their dreams behind?

“Yeah, sometimes it’s great. But it’s not as great as you think. In the real world, you can make your dreams a reality if you try hard enough. They can come to life, even without me. You can touch them and feel them. They’re not something you made up anymore. But here in the Dreamscape, it’s never like that. Dreams never become real here. They’re always just dreams. And there’s so much I’ve dreamed about that I’ve never gotten to experience." The dragon's beautiful voice sounded sort of sad now.

"Oh man, I'm sorry. What sort of dreams do you have, Dragon Prince?" Feyr could feel the Dragon Prince's sadness through the shell.

"My dreams? Nobody's ever asked about my dreams before. They're always asking me to make their dreams come true. You really are different." The girl could hear a bit of shock in the dragon's voice as it echoed through her mind. She hugged the Dragon Prince's egg a little closer. "I have lots of dreams. I dream of seeing my mom and dad for real. I've never seen their eyes. I dream of knowing what real flight is like. I don't want to just imagine any more. What does fresh meat taste like? And what about the sun warming your scales? That's gotta feel great!"

"I don't really have scales, but the sun does feel awesome. Don't worry, Dragon Prince. We'll get you out of there and you'll get the chance to make your dreams come true for once." Feyr pet the egg softly, before floating slowly down to the ground again. The lighting was still passing through the egg and into her body, but it was calmer now. And so was the Dragon Prince. The girl could feel it.

"I believe you. I really do." The Dragon Prince's voice was a soft whisper now. And then, after a few minutes of Feyr sitting with the egg in her lap and the giant watching this conversation with awe on his face, the voice asked her the same question. "What sort of dreams do you have, Feyr?"

"Well, it's like I was telling Mister Giant here. My dreams really aren't that special. I feel like they are dreams everyone has. You know, something every kid wants at one point."

"You'd be surprised what most people want. Go ahead, lay it on me."

"Okay, I will." Feyr sits there for a few more moments. She gathers her breath and appreciates all the magical things she has seen in just this day. "I'm pretty lucky, huh?"

"Luck has nothing to do with it, little girl." The Mountain Giant says, smiling at her with his mouth full of crystals. "You were meant to be here. You've been guided by fate."

"You really think so, Mister Giant?"

"I sure do. Nobody just happens to stumble upon a giant that's been sleeping for thousands of years. Nobody happens to just talk with a Dragon Prince trapped in his egg by a sleeping curse. Nothing happens by chance. Not stuff like this. You're lucky, sure. But you're also a believer. And I think that's why you're here."

"He's right." The Dragon Prince's voice filled the girl's head again. "There's something special about you. And that's why I want to hear your dream. So please tell me about it."

"Okay, okay. So, you know how humans and magical beings used to live together in peace? Well, I want that back. But better. I want us all to be one kingdom, one strong family together. Elves, humans, dwarves, gnomes, fairies, wizards, giants, dragons, and everything else you can imagine. I want us all to find peace together. Happiness and peace. Because I just know that everyone has something to teach someone else. And if we all learn just one thing from someone new, we could all be wise like that wizard."

Lightning flashed across the dragon egg. The giant sat there with eyes wide, looking down at the child sitting in his palms. The only sound that broke the silence was the howl of the wind against the giant's mossy head. The trees whispered to each other in the wind.

"Yes." The voice from the egg said to Feyr.

"Yes? Yes what, Dragon Prince?"

"Yes, let's make it happen. Let's make that dream come true. I've heard a lot of dumb dreams. I've made a lot of selfish dreams come true. Not this time. This time, let's have a good dream come to life."

Feyr was in shock. Could the Dragon Prince really do that? Such a little dragon? One still stuck in his crystal egg. How could he make a giant dream like that come true? But he could! Suddenly, something strange began to happen. Beautiful bolts of lightning began to swirl around the girl and the dragon prince. Bolts of light and life started to spread out along the hands of the Mountain Giant. The lightning spread further and got bright. Soon bolts were bursting and flying off in every direction. Feyr's body was warm like she was sitting next to a campfire, and she started to shake. Then, before she could ask the giant or the Dragon Prince what was happening, a bolt of lightning bright as the sun blasts straight into the sky, sending rainbow rays of light spread out across heavens.

Everything went black. Darkness and shock made the girl faint. And when she woke up, she found a whole new world in front of her eyes. She was still laying down in the Mountain Giant's palms, but the dragon egg was gone. Also, the Mountain Giant wasn't the only giant staring at her. There was a whole ring of them! Their giant, crystal eyes were full of wonder and amazement.

"You did it, girl..." The Mountain Giant whispered. Or he tried to, at least. Giants aren't exactly known for being soft-spoken! "You brought them back... My family. All the beings of the realms. Magical beings are everywhere!"

"That's amazing! But where is the Dragon Prince? If it worked, it's all thanks to him. He has saved the entire world. And made my dream come to life!"

Overhead, a flock of elves with bright golden wings flew about. They were singing songs in a language the girl did not know. Everything was different. Small beings that glowed. Some looked like snakes, and some looked like dragons. Others could be fish if you squinted hard enough. One bubbly critter looked like a floating jellyfish!

And then Feyr heard something. It was like the clap of thunder, but it repeated over and over. The little girl whipped her head around, but there were no clouds in sight. Where could that storm be coming from? But the child didn't have to wait long for the answer to burst through the cloud below. A massive dragon with scales of a bright blue crystal shout out of the sea of clouds, rising high into the blue skies. Its wings crackled with lightning and its eyes shimmered a beautiful mix of colors. For a few moments, the dragon hovered overhead. The thunderclaps were coming from its wings! And then the dragon opened its mouth and the most beautiful voice came out.

"Hello again, child! Do you like my wings! I have them thanks to you!" The dragon sang out with all its heart.

"Dragon Prince!" Feyr clapped her hands, hopping up and down.

"I'm the Dragon King now, Feyr! And you are the one who gave them to me. All of this is thanks to you! You made my dreams come true. You made all of our dreams come true!" The Dragon King flapped his wings a few more times, then settled down on the Mountain Giant's hands. The Mountain Giant was smiling so bright that wrinkles were stretching across his stony skin.

Feyr ran over to the Dragon King, who lowered his head so she could hug him. "Oh, Dragon King. I'm so happy. It's all so beautiful. Like a dream! Wait. This isn't a dream, right?" The girl was scared for a moment. Scared that this was all a dream.

But the Dragon King hissed softly at the girl, reassuring her. "No, child. This is real. This is all very real. What you see here is the power of a pure-hearted child's dream. Never doubt yourself or your dreams, Feyr. With them, you can make the impossible possible."

The little girl began to cry. But they were not sad tears. They were happy tears. Tears of joy and love. She was so glad that the Dragon Prince was free of his egg. She was glad that the world was once again magical. “How is everyone, Dragon King? Are they happy? Is the world at peace.”

“It’s better than you could ever imagine, child. The world isn’t just at peace. There are no more wars. Nobody is poor or homeless. There is no more pain or suffering. Nobody gets sick here and everyone lives for hundreds of years. Even humans! It’s a paradise, Feyr. Your dream, everything you hoped for, is here.”

And my family? What about them?”

“What about them, girl? They are back in the forest, the same as always. Though you might be surprised at how they’ve changed.” The Mountain Giant told her.

“What do you mean?” The girl blinked in confusion, looking at the Mountain Giant with her bright blue eyes.

The Dragon King laughed a bit, the sound echoing through the girl’s mind. It was a beautiful sound. “Climb on my back, and we’ll go see them.”

“Really? You’ll let me fly with you?”

“Of course! I can only fly because of you, my child. Let’s go.” The Dragon King held out a clawed hand. Feyr climbed onto his palms and felt herself being raised up into the air. “Hold onto my claws. The Breaker of the Curse can’t fall.”

Without warning, the thunderous sound of the dragon’s wings filled her ears. Feyr felt her belly roll over a bit, but that was no big deal. She barely had time to wave goodbye to the Mountain Giants and his other giant friends before they disappeared in a sea of clouds.

“I can’t believe it! I’m flying. And not in an airplane or anything. I’m really flying.” Feyr’s heart was racing a million miles per minute. The forest stretched out below them, glowing in the morning sunlight. Magical birds were flying beside them. Their feathers were a brilliant color, like a peacock! Their tails were long and flowing like a pheasant. And their bodies were big and powerful, like an eagle!

“Fun fact, there aren’t any more airplanes. People fly around on griffins and other winged creatures. Some people have a bond with dragons.”

“Amazing... Absolutely amazing. Oh, look, there’s our camp!” Feyr pointed her finger down at the ground, where the morning campfire was flickering and whispering softly.

As they landed down on the ground, the trees bent over to make room for the Dragon King. He was careful not to crush the van or anything, but one of the tents almost blew off! At the sound of thunder crashing and the ground shaking, Mom and Dad came running out of the tents.

“What in the world is going on here?” Dad called out. He looked different. His hair was longer and woven into an elaborate braid. His clothes were more elaborate, like something out of the past.

“Feyr? Is that you? What are you doing with the Dragon King?” Mom looked different too. Her eyes were even a different color. A bright purple that almost glowed in the light. Her hair was woven into fancy braids also.

“Mom! Dad! I missed you!” Feyr said, jumping off the Dragon King’s hand and hugging them both as tight as she could. “You’ll never guess what I did this morning.”

“Got into trouble, no doubt. Why else would you be with the Dragon King?” Dad said, laughing softly.

“Wait. You know the Dragon King, Dad?” Feyr was confused. How could her father know about the Dragon King when the dragon just hatched?

“Know him? He’s our King! Everyone knows him!” Feyr’s dad spoke as if the answer was obvious.

"How do you know him, little lightning?" Feyr's mother asked her.

But the little girl couldn't answer. She was still confused. How did Mom and Dad know the Dragon King? Why were their clothes different? What was going on?

"I think I can clear things up a bit. Sir. Madame. Your daughter is the Breaker of the Curse."

"What?!" They both gasped. Now the two adults looked shocked and confused. They looked at the Dragon King, then Feyr, then back to the Dragon King.

"Yes. She was the one who changed the world. It was her dream that I granted. It was her dream that made the world this way."

"I can't believe it..." Dad whispered softly, looking at his little girl.

Mom hugged Feyr tighter than ever, tears of joy in her eyes. "I always knew you were special, but..."

"Dragon King? I'm still confused..." Feyr said to the dragon, though the words were a little hard to hear through her mother's hug.

"It's pretty simple, Feyr. When you made your wish, the world changed. But it changed to the way things were always meant to be. The magical beings never left. I became King, and we all became one kingdom. We all became one family like you wanted. But to your Mom and Dad, it's always been this way. Nobody remembers the Old World, except for you. You saved the world, my child."

Feyr still didn't understand, but that was okay. She had her Mom and Dad. But something was different. When the little girl looked up at her Mom, she noticed something.

"Mom... Your ears. They are pointy!"

"Well, of course, they are pointy, sweetheart! I'm an elf, silly. Your ears are pointy too. Don't you know that?"

When Feyr reached up to her ears, she found out that her mom was right! But that was just the beginning of the changes. The world was different now. Really different. Beautiful and magical, but everything had changed. That took Feyr a long time to get used to. For Mom and Dad, the world had always been magical. Nothing had changed for them. But the little girl still remembered the world without magic. That was okay with her. Those memories were special and helped her love this new world even more! It's what helped remind her that this wasn't all in her head. That it was really happening.

After that day, the Dragon King took was always by Feyr's side. He invited her family to move into the castle with him, where they could all live together as one big family. The Dragon King taught Feyr magic and showed her all the new wonders in this world. And from then on, every day was a dream. For the Dragon King. And for the little girl who was born in a lightning storm. And they all lived happily ever after.

Chapter 10: The Halloween Night and the Little Vampire

High up on a hill stands an old house. The house is very run down because little Vladi and his family have been living here for a long time. It's exactly 200 years this Halloween. Yes, you heard right, little Vladi has lived here for 200 years, because Vladi is a vampire.

From the hill he can look over all the houses of the long winding road. Vladi sits at the window every day watching the kids. All year round - day out one day.

He observes them on their way to school, while playing and cycling, building snowmobiles and sledding - they laugh and rejoice. Some of the children have a lot of friends. Vladi does not have a single friend. At least no human. Only a spider and a cat keep him company.

Vladi would love to play with the other kids, but he cannot. Not only that the other children are afraid of him, because Vladi is very pale and also has sharp teeth.

No, he cannot. Because Vladi does not tolerate sunlight. It itches on the skin, that he wants to scratch constantly. And at night, when the sun is not shining, the other children lie in bed and sleep.

Vladi never sleeps. He does not have to, because he is a vampire. And vampires do not sleep. Oh dear, so Vladi has more time to get bored.

But once a year - for Halloween - Vladi sneaks out of the house. Because on Halloween, all children are on the streets at night and frighten each other happily. Disguised in spooky costumes, the children run around laughing. Since Vladi does not stand out. In this one night he walks around with the other children.

Tonight, it is time again. It's Halloween. Vladi is very excited. In his cupboard he has hidden a small stuffed bag for the sweets. At nightfall he gets her out and storms to the door. One more look in the mirror - oh yes, that does not help. Vladi cannot see himself in the mirror - that's the way it is with vampires. Of course, it's hard to say, if you look good, too.

Vladi turns to his cat: "And Klara? How do I look? "The cat meows happily and strolls around his legs. "Perfect, I knew it," says Vladi. "I'm a pretty little vampire!" And then he shines all over his face before disappearing through the door into the night.

On the streets there is joyful bustle. So many kids in such great costumes. Then Vladi is suddenly stumped from behind: "Man, that's a blatant costume!" He hears a girl's voice. Vladi turns around. Behind him is a girl dressed as a witch.

"I did not manage my costume so much," she says, pulling on Vladis shirt. "That looks like it's already a million years old." Then she wants to grab Vladi's teeth: "Wow, they look really real." Vladi recoils and tries to step backwards. But his body is faster than his legs and so he plops on the butt.

"Sorry, I did not want that!" Says the girl, holding out her hand to Vladi. Vladi takes his hand and helps himself up. "But you have cold hands. Are you cold? "Asks the girl. Vladi quickly pulls his hand back and plops again on the butt. He had completely forgotten that. Vampires are much colder than other kids.

Vladi is quite confused. Something about the girl makes him rash and even clumsy. Normally he would never fall. He is way too fast for that. Because vampires are also much faster and stronger than other children.

"Why are you leaving?" Asks the girl. But Vladi does not answer. "Hm, you do not want to answer me?" She asks. But

Vladi does not get a word out. He stands still and confused and looks at the girl with wide eyes.

As Vladi continues to make no sound, the girl pulls a pout and she looks at Vladi thoughtfully: "Hmm, well, then I'll start. I am Lana! But tonight, I'm a witch, as you can see. "Lana turns around once to show her costume. Then she laughs shrilly and horribly: "Hi hi hi hi hi! Oh, that was a really good witch laughter. Now you! "Says Lana, thinks for a moment and then goes on:" I just noticed, I do not even know how a vampire laugh.

Since Vladi has to laugh: "Hu hu huuu." The laugh came out a little funny from Vladis mouth, that he is immediately embarrassed, that he laughed. "No!" Says Lana. "I do not think the vampires laugh like that. I think they laugh more like us. "

When Lana says so, Vladi looks at her again with wide eyes. He does not know what to answer. He can hardly say that he is a vampire and therefore vampires laugh just as he has just done. So, he just smiles at Lana. At the same time his big teeth stick out in the corners of his mouth.

"That's a nice smile!" Says Lana. "You're right. Vampires are sure to smile sweetly. "Then she nudges Vladi, who becomes quite embarrassed:" Come on, you great vampire, let's collect sweets. "And so, she pushes Vladi in front of her.

"Hey, I can walk myself." Says Vladi. "I believe you, but it is so much funnier!" Replies Lana and pushes on. Both run laughing through the streets. Vladi has never enjoyed collecting candies as much as she did with Lana. They are running from door to door and Vladi's bag is getting fuller. The adults love Vladi's costume so much that he always gets a little candy extra.

Arriving at the last house on the street, Lana says, "I have to go home!" That makes Vladi sad. "But we'll see each other tomorrow at school. You just have to tell me who you are. "

Vladi hesitates. Then he says, "Oh, I'm not from here, you know? We're just visiting for Halloween. "Now Lana is sad too.

"That's a pity," she says. Vladi thinks. "But I'll be back next Halloween," he says, cheering Lana up. "Next year? That's really long, "says Lana. "But I'm glad we'll meet again." And she smiles at Vladi. Vladi smiles back - with his big teeth protruding from the corners of his mouth.

On the way home blows Vladi Trübsaal. A whole year is really long, he thinks. "So stupid," he mumbles to himself and kicks a stone away. The stone lands in front of a couple of big boys who are annoying a little boy in a clown costume. "I want to go home," says the little boy. But one of the big boys does not let him pass. "Before you go home, you leave us your sweets here," the big boy says with a nasty grin.

Well, that suits me right now, Vladi thinks. "Hey! Here you can have my sweets, "he says, offering his sweets to the big boy. Then he takes the little boy's hand and wants to bring him home.

The big boy, however, stands in his way. "Hey, wait a minute. Do you think, just because you give us your sweets, can the little one keeps his own? I still want his. "Vladi looks at the big boy," Leave him his. You have mine. That must be enough. "Then he passes the big boy.

The big boy grabs Vladi's shoulder. Lightning fast, Vladi turns and grabs the big boy's arm. And so firmly that he cannot move. Then he looks him in the eye - Vladi's eyes start to glow red. "I'll let you go now," says Vladi. As the big boys see the shining eyes, they get scared and run away.

But the little boy is totally excited about Vladi: "You're fast. How did you do this? I did not see how you move. And so strong. And the bright eyes. "

With big eyes there is a little boy in front of Vladi. In his eyes, Vladi can see the enthusiasm. "Yes," says Vladi. "I am fast and strong. But we will not tell anyone, ok? "

When Vladi looks up, Lana stands in front of him. Immediately he is pleased to see Lana. But then he notices that Lana has probably seen everything, and he freezes. If he was not already so pale, he would be white now.

The little boy runs to her and falls into her arms: "Lana! Good that you are there. A couple of boys did not want to let me home. "Lana nods," Yes, Erik, I saw that. Are you alright? "She asks. The little boy shines and points to Vladi: "Yes, I'm fine. He chased away the bad guys. "Lana looks at Vladi:" Yes, he did. "Then she looks at Erik again:" Mom and Dad are looking for you everywhere. They're really sick of worry. "

Lana's little brother leaves his head sad. "Oh dear, now I'm sure I'll get in trouble." But then he stands straight up and says, "But the bad guys will never annoy me again." Lana almost laughs when she sees her little brother standing so proudly in front of him, then she looks at Vladi: "This is my little brother. My parents are already looking for him. "

Vladi starts to stammer: "La Lana. I can explain that to you. "But Lana puts her index finger on her mouth. Then she looks down at Erik: "Hey Erik, are you going to go over there for a moment?" Lana points to a bench. Erik is not enthusiastic. But he still listens to his big sister. He goes to the bench, sits on it and rocks his legs.

Then Lana turns back to Vladi. For a short time, there is icy silence. Lana just looks at Vladi but says nothing. Vladi is getting more and more restless. Then Lana gets air: "I ask you know what and you answer honestly, ok?" Vladi nods. "Are you ... are you a real vampire?"

Vladi hesitates and nods again. "But I do not do anything to anyone. These guys did not want to leave your brother home and ... "Lana interrupts Vladi:" It's alright, I believe you! "

Vladi looks at Lana: "Are you scared of me now?" Lana shakes her head: "Nonsense with sauce! I'm not scared. I think it's great! I really like vampires! I just always thought there are no real ones. And now I'm meeting such a nice vampire like you! If I had not gone as a witch, I would have disguised myself as a vampire. "Lana hesitates," Oh, rubbish, what am I talking about, you're not disguised - I have to get used to that. " she smiles and continues, "I've never had such a great Halloween like today. And what you did for my brother is really great! "

Vladi looks at the floor. "Yes, but I lied to you. I'm from here. "Now he points to the house on the hill. "I live up there. And only for Halloween I go out. That's why I told you I was just coming for Halloween. Because otherwise the children sleep at night and during the day I cannot get out because I cannot tolerate the sun. "Now Lana smiles:" But that's great. "

Vladi is confused: "It's great that I cannot tolerate the sun?" "No." Shakes Lana's head. "Not that." Lana hides her voice to act sternly, waving her index finger, "And not that you lied to me. That this never happens again to my little vampire. "Then she bumps Vladi in the side and both have to laugh. "But it's great that I can visit you every day now."

Vladi beaming all over his face: "You would do that?" Lana bends Vladi again in the side: "Of course. As much fun as we had today, we will have every day from now on. And you have to tell me everything about vampires. Are you doing that? "Vladi can hardly believe it. "Of course, I do that!" And he shines again all over his face. And his big teeth are out again in the corners of his mouth. Lana beams, too. "But now I have to bring my little brother home. My parents are already crazy with worry. "She says and gives Vladi a kiss on the cheek. That's when Vladi turns red for the first time in his life.

Immediately Erik points to Vladi and shouts: "Look Lana. It starts again. What he did before with his eyes. Now he does it with his whole head - look how red that is already. "And Lana laughs:" No Erik, come now. "She throws one last look at Vladi, who looks down and beckons bashfully.

Vladi walks happily home. Finally, he has a girlfriend who plays with him all year round. That was the best Halloween for 200 years!

Chapter 11: The Fearless Willbi

There used to be a little mouse in Africa. She lived in a small village on the edge of the jungle. In Africa it was very hot and, in the village, where the mouse lived there was no waterhole, no lake or even a small pond nearby. "Phew," the mouse snorted. "I have to get out of here." Said, done and so the mouse decided to visit her brother in the jungle.

There were many waterholes in the jungle. In her mind, the mouse was already swimming in the cool water and a smile crossed her face. "Brrrrr, the water is pretty cool." She thought. Quickly the bathing trunks packed into a small suitcase and off we went.

When she arrived in the jungle with her brother, the little mouse wondered about the house. All windows were tight, and light was burning inside. The mouse knocked. Inside it rumbled and then it was quiet. The mouse knocked again: "Hey!" She called. "I heard you. Now get on Jonas! "The door opened a little gap. First there was a sniffing nose, then the blinking of small eyes.

Jonas threw open the door and jumped into his brother's arms, "Oh, Willbi. You are s. That's nice to see you. "Then Jonas looked around left and right. "Okay, come in quickly," he said and closed the door. Willbi looked around. Everything was pretty dark. "Why do you have the windows ... oh no," said Willbi. "I am here for a beach holiday! Nobody can handle the heat! So, grab your swimsuit and off you go!"

Jonas looked at Willbi anxiously, "You want to go swimming? To the water hole? But Willbi, that's where all the animals go. It's dangerous in the jungle! "" Excuse me? Pappalapapp, come on! "Jonas tugged on Willbi's arm:" No Willbi - really - it's too dangerous. So many animals are stronger than us and want to eat us. "But Willbi was not deterred. "If you do not pack your swimsuit, I'll do it!" He said, pulling Jonas after him.

The first thing they encountered was a lion. "Ahhh!" Yelled Jonas and scurried behind Willbi. Willbi looked at the lion. "What? Are you afraid of that? "Then he pulled his ears apart, stuck out his tongue, and made:" Bölölölölöl. "But the lion just looked at him bored. "What?" Said Willbi. "You are not afraid of me?" The lion smiled tiredly: "I am the king of the jungle; why should I be afraid of a little mouse like you? "

"What, little mouse?" Said Willbi, pulling up his sleeves. "You're pretty naughty for such a hairy litter cat." Jonas tugged on Willbis shirt: "Listen to Willbi. He's much taller than us. "But Willbi waved his hand." Oh, pappalapap. People run away when I do that. Who really believes who he is? "

The lion looked at Willbi in amazement: "The people are afraid of you?" Willbi plumped proudly: "And whether! They jump on chairs and tables - if they see me! "The lion laughed loudly. Then he took a deep breath and yelled in the direction of the mice. Willbis ears fluttered in the wind of roar. It was so loud that all the birds nearby were startled and flying away.

But Willbi was unimpressed: "Pah, was that all? You should brush your teeth again! "Now the lion was startled. With a thoughtful look, he studied Willbi again. "You are not afraid of me? he asked. "Nope!" Willbi said firmly. "Why should I? You should be afraid of me! "

The lion did not really know what was happening. There was a small mouse with rolled-up sleeves in front of him, looking at him angrily. "You say: people are afraid of you? Prove it! "The lion finally said. "Pah." Willbi said. "No problem!"

They sneaked into the nearby village. The lion was afraid of humans and stopped more often the closer they came to the village. "What's wrong? Did the courage leave you? "Willbi called cheekily." "The little mouse really does not seem to be afraid," thought the lion.

When he arrived in the village, Willbi said: "Okay, Pussycat. You look through the window. I go in and show you how to deal with people. Jonas, you stay with the rental cat. "" What? "Jonas asked. "But he's eating me." "Oh, my," said Willbi. "The Mietze is not afraid of hunger." And went into the house.

The lion did not believe his eyes when he saw people jumping over tables and benches when they saw the little mouse. Willbi ran back and forth and made his face: "Bölölölölö". Then he came out again: "Na Mietzi? Now you, "he said. But the lion was too scared. And so, they sneaked back into the jungle.

At the waterhole, Willbi jumped directly into the cool water: "Juhuuu!" - Splash - Other animals gathered around the waterhole when they saw the mice, but they did not dare, because the big lion stood there. Hyenas, Jackals, Wildcats ... everyone was waiting for their chance.

When the lion saw that, he just said, "Keep calm. Attack the mice - I will not stop you. "The hyenas were looking forward to a delicious snack. "But be warned," said the lion further. "I would not do it. These are the strongest mice I have ever seen. All humans have fled from them. I've watched it with my own eyes! "

The other animals were confused and looked questioningly at. A hyena lisped, "Alas, if the lion does not even eat it, I'll leave it." Another hyena stuttered back, "Well, there you are. If the lion d does not do that mmm ma, I will not do it either.

Willbi swam on his back through the waterhole and trumpeted: "What's going on? Just dare. You will experience your blue miracle! "But the animals slowly crept away. They were too scared of the mice - even people were afraid of them.

And even after Willbi had driven back to the village on the edge of the jungle, no one dared approach Jonas. He no longer hid himself, let in the bright sunlight through all the windows, and lived happily ever after.

Chapter 12: The Strange Girl

One day a new girl came to kindergarten. Everybody thought her strange because she spoke only in rhymes. "Why are you talking so weird?" Little Marla asked the girl. The girl replied, "I'm not talking funny, that would be awesome. Almost astronomical and somehow stupid. "Then she went on. Marla stood with her mouth open: "Astro ... what?" She asked - but the girl was already out of earshot.

The more the girl spoke, the more children began to speak in rhymes. "Hello, kindergarten teacher, I have something in mind. I would like to have another tea. Would that be okay?"

The kindergarten teachers wondered about the children, who now only spoke in rhymes, but they also found it funny. And so, they made themselves: "Hello dear children, we play a game now. The things of the inventor. Winning is the goal. "

It was not long before everyone in kindergarten spoke only in rhymes. When the parents picked up their children, they were very surprised that everything rhymed with what their children said: "We were almost only outside, I could barely catch my breath. It was so much fun. I did not think about the time. Now you are here and pick me up, can I still play short and sweet? "

The parents thought that was weird. Marla's mom asked Marla why she was talking so funny. Marla replied, "I'm not talking funny, that would be awesome. Almost astronomical and somehow stupid. "Marla's mom stood with her mouth open:" Astro ... what? "She asked - but Marla was already out of earshot.

The parents looked at each other in bewilderment. But then they began to rhyme themselves without realizing: "I see my child playing there. One among many. But it talks in rhymes. Will that stay that way? "Another mother turned around:" I cannot say that, at least I do not believe it. But you too were talking in rhymes right now - almost like a poem. "Then everybody laughed.

Now a father intervened: "What should I tell my wife when she hears the child talking? I do not want to complain, but I'm a bit confused. "" You say that's normal - it's all rhyming now. If it were not so, then it would be fatal, because then it would be strange child. "

And so, the parents began to rhyme. Then the parents' friends and it was not long before the whole country rhymed and those who did not rhyme were strange.

One day a strange girl came to kindergarten. It spoke without rhyming. Marla came and said: "You talk so funny. That's tremendous. Almost astronomical and somehow stupid. "

The strange girl asked in astonishment: "Astro ... what?" Marla looked at her: "I do not know what that means, but it sounds great," Marla said and shrugged her shoulders. Then the strange girl smiled and said, "I'm Luisa. Do you want to be my girlfriend, even if not everything rhymes what I say? "Marla thought for a moment. Then she took Luisa by the hand and said, "Sure! Let's play. I'll show you our great play area. "

And so, the children gradually stopped rhyming. Then the kindergarten teachers stopped rhyming. Then the parents, the friends of the parents and soon the whole country.

And what do we learn from history? So, it becomes strangely normal and normal becomes strange. But no matter how you are, it's as good as it is.

Chapter 13: The Deer and the Bear

Once, a long time ago, when animals roamed the earth and humans were not around, there was an animal named Meg. Meg was a deer, she walked on four legs and her body was covered in fur, she had a bushy white tail. She was very quick and could hop around the forest on her four legs. She spent most of her time by the forest lake with other plant-eaters like her. One of her friends was Murry, the moose. She was also friends with Ella, the elk. And Donnie, another deer like her except he was a boy deer and had antlers. These animals loved eating plants, drinking water, and playing by the banks. That is until some new animals appeared.

It was common knowledge that if the new animals, the meat-eaters, came in that the plant-eating animals would have to leave. Meg was a young deer and didn't understand that this was the way of life for all the animals who ate plants. Plant eaters had to leave if the meat-eaters came in. Her mother had always told her that everyone was equally important. If the plant-eaters must move out of the way for the animals who ate meat, then id didn't sound to Meg like they were all equal. She decided to ask some of the other animals why this was. After all, it sounded like they were not equal to her. Meg headed over deeper into the forest to speak to other animals and see what they had to say. They must know because she thought that the animals that lived deeper in the woods were older and many of them were different than her.

"I don't get it, why do we always have to run away whenever those who eat meat appear?" Mag asked old Gus and Ajax the beavers who were busy building a dam in the busy river.

"Well," Gus began. "It's just how it is." Then Gus put his head underwater to grab some mud from the bottom.

"It's always been that way," Ajax explained, "As soon as someone sees that the meat-eaters are coming, we have to hide." He busied himself patting on the dam to make sure it was secure.

"Or else, we might get eaten, Gus continued as he joined Ajax in building the dam, "Nobody wants to be dinner, you see, Little Meg."

"Well, I certainly do not want to be dinner," Meg said. "But it doesn't seem right. It isn't fair!"

"No, it doesn't," Old Ajax agreed, his mouth full of twigs. "And no, it is not fair either."

"It's just the way it is," Gus said, and the old beavers continued building.

Meg moved on to a field where some other older deer were lying about and enjoying the sun.

"Hi guys," Meg said as she greeted them.

"Hi, dear Meg," said her uncle Barney. "What can we do for you today?" Uncle Barney was laying in clover and eating bits of clover as he lay in the sun soaking up the warmth.

“I was wondering why we always have to move when the meat-eaters show up. My mom said that everyone is equal, are we not equal to them.”

“Well, you see,” Byron, a buck with the biggest antlers in the field said, “It’s simple, really. None of us want to get eaten.”

"I don't get it, what makes them so important?" Meg asked. "What gives them the right to eat us?"

"Well, they are bigger and stronger than we are," Byron explained. "It's just the way it is."

"They are smaller than a moose!" Megs argued, "Moose are the largest of all of us!"

"Well," Barney said, "While that is true, the meat-eaters can move very fast and are more aggressive."

Meg thought about this for a moment.

"What if we made friends with them to show them that we are just as good as they are?" Meg asked.

"That won't happen," Barney continued. "They are bigger and stronger and fiercer than we are, and it is just better that we stay out of their way."

This was going nowhere, so Meg decided it was time to move on.

As Meg moved along, she hoped she would find some plant-eaters that had more courage.

Soon she found Steve the ram grazing with some of his friends.

"I have a question," Meg began. "Why are we less important than the meat-eaters?"

"I don't think we are," said Ollie the ram. "But they always push everyone else around."

"But there are more of us than there are of them," Meg said." What if we stood up to them?"

"That might not work," Steve said. "Everyone is afraid of getting eaten."

"What if we made friends with them, then they might not eat us," suggested Meg again, hoping for a better response. And she got one.

"It's worth a try," Steve said. "But don't get your hopes up because it's never been that way before."

"We'll go with you," Ollie said. "We'll help to try to make friends with them, and we will protect you if it doesn't work."

"Thanks!" said Meg hoping that it would work. And off the three friends went.

Soon they found a young bear. Even though the bear was young, he was gigantic. He was just standing around roaring. It was loud enough to give anyone a headache. The three friends were just about to run away when Meg noticed a tear dripping down the bear's face. He was crying. Why he is just a big baby, thought Meg. She walked toward the big crying bear cub.

"Be careful!" Ollie and Steve warned. "Even though he is a baby, he is still a bear."

"Are you alright?" asked Meg carefully approaching the crying giant.

"No!" sobbed the bear. "I'm lost, and I can't find my mommy! I keep calling her, but she isn't here, and I'm so frightened I don't know what to do!" And then the bear cub continued to sob and wale so loud that Meg was sure that he could be heard all over the world!

"We'll help you," said Meg. "We can find your mother, and we will make sure that you are safe."

"We will?" Ollie asked, surprised that anything that large had a mommy.

"We can?" Steve asked. He was not so sure that they should help a gigantic baby find his even more gigantic meat-eating mother.

"Yes, we can, and yes, we will," Meg said. "If we want everyone to be equal, we have to show that we are. If we want kindness from meat-eaters like his mother, we have to show them kindness."

"I don't know," said Steve. "I am in favor of a kind act, but this is a bear we are talking about." He was worried about how a mother bear would feel about three plant-eaters escorting her baby. "What if she thinks we are trying to harm the big baby?"

"We have to try," said Meg. Then she turned to the weeping bear, "My name is Meg."

"I'm Ron," sniveled Ron.

"Please to meet you, Ron," Meg said, smiling. "This is Steve and Ollie, and we are going to get you back to your mother."

The four new friends took no time to find Ron's mother, who was so happy to see Ron safe that she proceeded to give the biggest bear hug in the world to Meg, Steve, and Ollie as well as Ron.

"Momma!" Ron roared happily.

"Thank you so much for bringing my little baby back to me!" Momma said to Meg, Steve, and Ollie, who were all sure that there was nothing little about the baby.

"You are welcome," Meg said.

"I don't mean to be rude, because I am so grateful that you found him," Momma said. "But why did you help him? I know that your kind and mine never get along?"

"We wanted to change that," Meg said. "I believe that we are all equal and that nobody is more important than anyone else, and we all deserve the same rights and privileges. I wanted to see if we could make friends with someone like you and that your kind might not chase us away or eat us."

"Well, now you have two new friends," Momma said, "and we will make sure that you have many friends with us meat-eaters. Besides we're bears, we usually eat fish"

The next day, Ron and Momma appeared at the big river. The beavers started to go underwater. The rams prepared to strike with their horns. The bucks lowered their antlered heads, ready to charge. Meg ran over to her new friends with Steve and Ollie.

"No! Stay! These are our friends!" Meg called out to the others. "There is no need to be afraid!"

"They are going to eat us!" yelled a rabbit.

"No! They are here to visit us and talk!" Meg said. "They are our new friends!"

"They want to tell us that we all belong too!" Steve called out.

"Remember, we are all equal!" Ollie said. "We have to show our acceptance of them, and they will accept up as equal to them!"

"You are my friends," Ron said.

"We never eat friends!" Momma said. "I promise, from now on, our kind will treat your kind as equals and friends. We only want to celebrate our friendship with a drink from the lake."

Soon the plant-eaters began to approach Ron and Momma to shake hands.

And so, the entire group moved to the river, and each took a long drink. Then they played and splashed in the water for hours afterward. By the end of the day, every animal was covered in mud and ready for a night of good night's sleep. And they were also all friends.

True to her word, Momma made sure that her new friends would be accepted and treated with kindness and equality by all the other meat-eaters instead of bullying them and eating them. And from then on, whenever meat-eaters approached the lake or the river, the plant-eaters did not run away in fear. Instead, they all lived together peacefully. Ron and Meg played all day every day. And at the end of each day, they curled up together and fell asleep counting the stars. They dreamed of adventures in the sky, water, and forests.

Sweet dreams little one.

Chapter 14: Mountains of Fun

Once upon a time, there lived twins that loved each other very much. Their names were Alia, and she was very feisty and very adventurous, and Arthur, who was very proud of himself, but also quite cautious. The twins were practically inseparable! They would do everything together! They were also very special twins, for they shared something that was greater than just sharing a birthday; they shared a very special power with each other! It was a very unique power that helped them greatly, for these twins traveled constantly. They were never put in a school the way most children are; rather, these two children spent their time traveling with their parents and doing their schoolwork on the go!

But that is not their power. What is their very special power, though, is the ability to speak to animals! These twins were very good at talking to the animals around them. The animals were always a little surprised to hear a human speaking to them, but they were happy to talk. Some animals would be very kind to the twins; they helped the twins out when they were in trouble. But, other animals did not like the twins much, and they did not like that the twins could talk to them.

No matter where they went, however, the twins knew one thing; they would never be alone so long as they were together and so long as they could continue to speak to animals. After all, animals were everywhere! They were found on the highest peaks of the mountains, and on the desert floor. They knew that, no matter where they went, they could find an animal to talk to; all they would have to do was work hard to find one that would ***want*** to talk. If they could do that, they could do anything.

One day, Alia and Arthur were brought somewhere new. They were brought to a strange, new mountain range that they had never been to before. It was called the Rocky Mountains, and it went through the United States. Now, the twins were born in the United States, but, they did not spend much time there, as their parents worked very hard as diplomats, going to meet important people in some of the most remote places in the world! But, this time, they were taking a little break. They were there for work, but it was not as busy of work as usual. This time, they were there to meet up with another worker for their company, and that meant that they would get more time than usual with their parents!

This was very exciting for Alia and Arthur, for they loved that very special time with their parents. They loved to be able to walk with them wherever they were going and talk to them without being told, “Hang on; I’m working.” And, that very day, they were going to go somewhere very special! They were going to take a hike up the mountain! Alia and Arthur were incredibly happy about this!

So, on the morning of the hike, they all woke up very early, for if you want to be able to complete the whole hike before dark, you have to leave shortly after the sun goes up, and they all got ready to go. Mom packed all sorts of good foods and water. Dad packed lots of sunscreen and bug repellent, and he carried the great, big backpack filled with all of the supplies. Alia and Arthur put on their clothes and their best hiking boots and were ready to go! They could not be more excited to get going than they were right that moment! So, off they ran toward the door, waiting for their parents to follow.

But then, it happened.

The dreaded phone rings. The phone always rang, and their parents would always answer it, and then they’d always have to work. Alia and Arthur looked at each other sadly, knowing what was about to happen. They were very used to being told that things were changing and that they would have to try again another time.

But, that time, the phone was ignored and of they went!

“Where are we hiking to?” asked Arthur, standing next to his father. They were all in a cabin near the bottom of the mountain.

“You see that peak? The one that looks a little funny on the top. We are going to that one,” replied his father, looking at a map and a compass.

“Woah, all the way to the top?” asked Alia, peering up at the great, big, blue sky with wide eyes. She didn’t’ think that she’d be able to climb up that high on her own.

“Only if you want to!” answered their mother.

So, off they all went together on their hike. It was the perfect day for one, too; it was late spring, so it was not yet too hot, but also not too cold to go all the way up the mountain. The sun was shining, and they could not see a single cloud in the sky. They could hear birds chirping their songs everywhere behind them, sounding as beautiful as ever, and the children were very happy that their parents were finally going along with them on one of their nature adventures! Usually, the adventures were just for Alia and Arthur.

But, on this particular adventure, they had to remember something; they were going to be with their parents, and that meant that they could not make use of their very special power. There was to be no talking to any animals at all.

As they all walked together, Alia stopped to look at something, as she loved to do. There was a patch of the most beautiful white wildflowers growing on the side of the trail! It had purple petals that extended out from the center, and white petals surrounding the calyx within them. The flower was very beautiful, and it smelled very nice as well. The smell filled up the air, and it seemed that Alia was not the only one that wanted to stop to smell it. A little bumblebee came buzzing over as well, landing on one of the flowers to suck up some nectar. And, a little further into the patch, Alia could see a hummingbird, dancing through the air. She could hear the soft hum of its tiny wings that flapped faster than any other bird.

Behind her, her mother laughed. “Those are columbine flowers,” she said softly. “They are the state flower for Colorado.”

“Colorado? Where’s that?” Alia asked.

“Here!” answered Arthur. “I think you fell asleep on the plane when we were talking about it. But, we’re in the Rocky Mountains in Colorado!

Alia blinked in surprise, but then shrugged her shoulders. “I was tired, okay?” she answered. Then, she heard something—the hummingbird was saying something behind her! It said that it was very tired and very thirsty. But Alia could not speak back, because her parents were there. A quick glance over at Arthur said that he had heard the little hummingbird, too, and he walked over to stand in front of the flower patch, blocking it out of view just right so that their parents could not see what they were about to do. He reached out his hand for the hummingbird, and whispered, as quietly as he could to the bird to land on his hand.

The bird was very surprised to hear a little boy talking, but happily obliged, and Arthur moved the poor tired hummingbird to a branch to stop to rest without it having to fall to the ground. The bird sung it thanks you to the young children and then settled down for a break. So, off they went to keep on exploring all around the mountains.

They traveled even further away than ever—they were looking for something great and new. So, they kept on hiking along the trial. As they hiked, there were some very pretty birds singing in the trees. Alia could hear some chickadees singing in one, and they could see a blue jay in another. They were very happy to see all of the birds that were in the trees around them, and they all sounded very pretty to listen to. But then, they heard something else. They heard a little voice in the distance, crying out, "Help! Help!"

"Do you hear that?" asked the twins' father.

The children looked at him in surprise. Could he hear the animal, too? So, they all followed their father through the big mountain trail. He was leading them somewhere that was very far away, and they left the trail that they had been on, too. They could still hear the crying sounds, and their father still kept on moving forward. Alia and Arthur would look at each other every now and then; they were curious if their father had heard the words too, or if he was only following the sounds of the woods. But there was no way to know for sure unless they asked.

They went up a slope and then turned and went down another way. They went around some big trees and through some trees that were losing all their leaves. They went over a creek, one by one, splashing in the water, and then, they all stopped! They looked around for what they could find around them, and then they saw it—there was a tiny little raccoon with its head stuck in those little plastic rings that are used to hold together cans at the store when they are bought in packs of six!

The raccoon was stuck on the ground, looking very sad, as it had gotten its head stuck on one end, and the other loops, behind him, were stuck to a branch! It could not get out at all on its own, and it would not be able to do anything at all if they did not help it, and quickly! They were going to have to work very hard to get it untangled from the line, but it seemed like the twins' dad had an idea!

He got very close to the raccoon, who continued to cry and ask to be left alone. But then, the twins were very surprised to see that the raccoon stopped! It was looking up at their dad in awe! It looked at him and stopped moving, looking down at the ground, even when their dad picked up his pocketknife and sliced up the plastic! He then quickly pushed the plastic into his own pocket so they would be able to dispose of it themselves and stood up.

They heard the little raccoon squeak out a thank you. And, then, something even more magical happened—their father smiled at it and seemed to nod his own head! Could he hear the raccoon too? They stared up at their father in shock as the raccoon ran away, deeper and deeper into the woods on its own.

Their father, noticing the children staring at him, raised an eyebrow. “What is it?” he asked them curiously, watching as the children seemed very unsure of how they should answer their father.

Alia shook her head. She didn’t want to ask! The last time that they had tried to tell someone that they could talk to animals, they thought she was crazy.

But Arthur was braver. “Wow, dad!” he said, very carefully picking out his words. “It was like you were able to talk to that little raccoon to make it stop moving! I’ve never seen that happen before!” He grinned up at his dad, watching very closely to see if his dad did anything or said anything that would make him doubt that his dad could, in fact, talk to animals just like he could. But, his father did nothing of the sort.

Instead, the twins’ father smiled back and patted them on the heads. “You’ll understand someday,” he said without another word about the subject. “So! It’s time for us to finish up our hike, isn’t it?”

“Do we have time, dear?” asked their mother, glancing at the sun. It was already more than halfway down; they had spent a lot of their time just looking for the raccoon, and then, helping the raccoon. They weren’t upset about it at all, either; they were very happy that they helped save an animal, but it was kind of disappointing to not get to make it to the top of the peak.

"No, I don't think so," he said sadly. "But maybe we can call in tomorrow and schedule another hike! One where we don't get so sidetracked by animals that are in need of help!"

The children looked up longingly at their parents. Getting one day with them was already a pretty big treat—but to get two days in a row? That was almost magical and that was something that almost never happened at all! But, if he could make it happen, they would be more than glad to do so!

So, the family hiked back to their cabin together and spent the evening watching their favorite movies, and the next day, they all spent time hiking right back up the mountain. When they made it all the way to the top, they felt like they were on the top of the world! They could see for miles and miles all around them and it was one of the greatest sights that they had ever seen!

Chapter 15: Story of the Young Triton

Once there was a young triton that liked to walk around, visiting all his friends until late in the evening. This kid was now becoming a serious problem, and his parents were getting worried. He was warned about the risky walks to different places around the sea, but he would not listen.

"My son, there are different kinds of animals under the sea, so anytime you move around alone, you risk your life. Are you with me?" his dad told him.

"Yes, dad, I get you very well," the young triton replied.

That night, Kevin went out to bed so early after the long talk from his parents about the dangers around him whenever he walks alone. The undersea world had so many risks, and now that Kevin's dad was the king, everyone would do anything possible just to hurt him. At the same time, his parents were willing to do anything to protect their only son, who was the next in line to the throne of his dad.

"Let's go visit Daniel, then come back," said Kevin's friend.

He had just been told about not going out, but it's like all that fell to a deaf ear. As always, he was just playing outside their home, and then he would disappear and leave with his friend to visit another friend. His parents never noticed the visits, and he thought he was winning. One day, he was playing with his friends. Then the idea of wandering came up; as always, he agreed and left with his friends to go out and play.

"Kevin! It's lunchtime; where are you?" his mother called.

She thought that her son was playing outside the house only to realize that after calling for more than four times, there was no response. Kevin wasn't around, which was something that she knew would not happen. Kevin would always let her know where he is going after the lecture he had been given, so she was sure Kevin was just around. Kevin's mother came out of the house to check what was happening with his son or if he had been sleeping. When she came out of the house, no one was around, and that's when she decided to check at the neighbor's place.

"Have you seen Kevin?" she asked the neighbor.

"They left out in a large group to play," neighbor responded.

Her mother was so angry and felt so bad about Kevin. She thought her son was disrespectful about what they told him and maybe needed to be punished. Kevin, on the other hand, was having so much fun with his friends; everyone was showing their tricks of swimming and how to hunt. His mum went home, furious, waiting for her husband to return so she could report the incident. After some time, the husband came back, and upon hearing the news, he left to find where his son was. The mother was unsettled and just wanted to see her son back home.

The dad was out in the sea, and the mum was in the house when Kevin came back. Her mum couldn't hide the fury in her, so she jumped onto her son and slapped him.

"How many times do we have to tell you that it is perilous outside?" Kevin's mum shouted as she kept on slapping him.

Kevin tried to escape, but her mum had a hold on him so tightly that he couldn't escape. The beatings were so thorough that he could not hold on to his tears. He screamed for help, trying to apologize, but no one could help him. The beatings showed how much her mum was frustrated and, at the same time, worried.

"They were just playing here and left for home," a member of the community told Kevin's dad, who was asking everyone about his whereabouts.

"I don't know what is wrong with this boy; he is not aware of the risks he is putting on him out here," Kevin's dad told himself.

He went straight home, knowing that he would find his son safe from any injuries or harm. Upon reaching home, he had already calmed down and was not furious about what happened. The dad found him crying and embraced him. After some time, it was time for dinner. And as always, the dad had something to tell him after the mistake he had done during the day.

"My son, you have to be respectful of the things we tell you; out there is very dangerous, and you are our only son, so we have to take good care of you and make sure you are always safe. That is why we are strict on you about going out. Do you understand?" said his dad to Kevin.

"Yes, dad, I am sorry I left without getting permission from mum. I won't do it again, and I won't be disrespectful to you," Kevin said to his parents.

That night after dinner, Kevin's parents were left wondering why their son kept on going out, even when it is dangerous in the open sea. After a lot of talks between them, they decided that they will get their son a tutor who will be there to guide their son on what to do. So, the father brought his younger brother home to help look after their son. Kevin felt disappointed during the first days, as this move gave him limitations on where to go. He could spend time sleeping in the house or just swimming around the house because of his uncle, who was always with him and keen on his moves.

His days became so sad, and he could not complain as this was going to lead to either being punished or something severe, which he was not ready to have. He started getting along with his uncle, and this was now going to be an advantage to him, as he would easily convince him to let him go out and play with his friends. The uncle, too, liked him, and their friendship was getting on so well, and with time, they started going out to eat the seafood at the bottom of the sea. This was now a routine they couldn't miss, and Kevin's parents had no issue about it as long as his uncle was with him.

The excursion started becoming so random that the uncle adopted Kevin's ways. They could visit more dangerous places where other animals could eat them, and his dad started getting worried about the trips they were making. Kevin's mum was getting worried, too, and it was getting out of hand that the parents couldn't take it anymore.

"Kevin, we are getting worried about your trips with your uncle; please don't go that far. It's risky, and you may be eaten by other creatures," said Kevin's dad as they listened silently with his uncle.

They had lunch and left for some walk just outside the house. Kevin's dad was getting old, and someone was needed to take over the crown, and that was Kevin. His dad could teach him leadership skills and how to be a good and respected leader. They would go out to the deep sides of the ocean for lessons about good leadership skills. This was the best moment for Kevin as he could be under the protection of the dad and his uncle. He was learning so much daily, and this was a great achievement for him and his dad. The mother, too, was so happy about how his son was doing great when it comes to learning from his dad.

As always, they left for training, and Kevin asked his dad if he could invite his friends to come along. His dad accepted, and Kevin felt so happy about it. His friends got the information, and that afternoon, everyone was ready to go see how skillful Kevin was developing daily. After some preparations, they left for the deep-sea training. The trip was full of learning as Kevin's dad educated the crew about the sea and everything in the sea. The journey was full of questions, thus making it so much fun and educational. They got to the training ground, and his young friends sat aside to watch how Kevin was being trained.

Kevin showed the swimming skills that he had learned, and all his friends cheered for him as he swam swiftly in the sea. His dad was also amused by the progress of his son. The training was going on well until waves started blowing strongly. This was dangerous, as many of the young ones could not swim under such conditions and could be easily washed away. Kevin's dad tried to protect the young kids from the waves, but it was getting rougher that he could not control it. Some of the kids were being carried away, and it was worrying. As they tried to escape from the storm, one of the young ones got washed away and was struggling so much. The whole crew watched pitifully, unable to help. Kevin swam at high speed and risked his life to save his friend. He swam through the waves and could not be seen as he went after his friend. The waves calmed down, and everyone was safe, except for Kevin and his friend. His dad looked worried; he knew his son had died, and he blamed himself for it.

"Kevin! Kevin! Kevin!" his dad called out several times, but there was no response.

He ordered the other kids to go home with the help of his brother while he remained to look for his son. As they were leaving, Kevin came out with his friend, who was also okay. Kevin thanked his dad for the skills he taught him, and the whole neighborhood felt good and happy for his generous act. He was getting ready to be the next leader after his dad, indeed.

Chapter 16: Paw Island and Coco

Archie left with Maggie and found himself in a magic land. Archie was not willing to take another step unless Maggie explained to him where she was taking him. Archie was right because we should never trust anyone blindly. Sometimes unquestioned truth can lead us to danger. And being careful can help keep us from future danger.

Maggie explained that dogs govern Paw Island. And every dog had some special mission to fulfill and a purpose to serve. The dogs who felt an inner calling were worthy of staying and getting trained on Paw Island. And only the old wizard could decide which dogs were truly righteous. Archie did not believe in the whole thing, but he managed to follow Maggie anyway.

After reaching the wizard's house, Archie learned some startling revelations. The wizard was none other than Paul's lost dog, Coco. Maggie and Coco were very ancient, but they had managed to stay youthful by using special magic to serve their purposes. Archie also came to know about his long-lost siblings. Coco asked Archie to take a test to prove his worthiness. Archie agreed unwillingly, just because he wanted to meet his family.

The test made Archie realized the many problems of having too much anger and hatred. He felt the bliss of helping others. He also came to realize that humans, dogs, and all other creatures were dependent on each other. The best way to live a life was through proper cooperation. The test unburdened him from his hatred. It gave him some relief.

Hating someone cannot harm that person that we hate. But it is harmful to us. Hatred and anger stop us from focusing on good things and the character attributes of others. We spend time hating each other and keeping our right sides veiled. It is okay to feel victimized, but revenge can only lead us to destruction. One hateful act causes us to make another wrong decision, and soon we become drawn into an unbreakable chain of unethical activities. Forgiveness frees us from this vicious cycle. We should always nurture the values we have, such as forgiveness. It frees us from our inner hatred and anger.

Archie had initially trusted Maggie before he set out on his journey. He knew that he did not have any particular destination in mind except possibly to find his siblings one day. He was lost and clueless about his life. He had known Maggie for only two days. And Maggie surprisingly had convinced him to start a journey towards the unknown and she had brought him to a strange land called 'Paw Island.' After crossing the entrance, they saw a lovely city with no trace of humans. Archie was beyond astonished and completely delighted. For some time, Archie thought he must be dreaming because what he was observing was illogical and irrational. Maggie was still maintaining her calmness and composure, which meant this was not the first time Maggie had been here in this weird place.

Archie finally broke his silence and asked, "Don't you think I deserve some explanation about this place?"

Maggie's reply was vague. "You really have some serious trust issues. Have I done anything wrong or harmful to you yet?"

Archie hated twisted and cynical answers. And above all, he had no reason to trust Maggie blindly. He said, "I want to trust you. But trust is something that needs to be earned. You are not pushing me in front of a car or leaving me alone, because that is the right gesture of any sane person. That does not mean I will blindly trust you, whatever you say. And there is a difference between trust and blind trust. Having blind trust is never a wise decision to make."

Maggie knew that Archie was right, and he deserved the truth. Maggie said, "This is Paw Island. You already know the name. This is the paw world. We have our schools, universities, community centers, a special training center, and everything a civilized society needs. Everything is run by Dogs only. This is a special dog land where dogs like you and me can feel safe. We all have a mission. We are gate-trained here, and then we enter the human world in order to fulfill our missions."

Archie listened to every word carefully but hardly understood anything. He had never heard of it. If dogs already had a special land, then why would they choose to be the lapdog of others? This was a lot to believe and understand. Eating thrown-out food and crossing a road full of cars were much easier to accept than this. Maggie was not older than Archie - she was just a puppy like him. She had been living a good life in that house, cuddling with Izzy. If she had already known about Paw Island, then why would she have been living with Izzy? Now she was talking about some secret mission - how was that even possible? Either she was lying, or this entire thing was a bad dream!

Maggie was waiting for Archie to ask questions. She knew that understanding this whole situation was a bit challenging for Archie. Even worse, Archie had a choice - he could run away from here. But Archie did nothing like that. He just stood still, totally silent, because he did not know what questions to ask her. Finally, Maggie could wait no longer. She asked, "Do you want to know more? Don't you have anything to ask me? I think you have finally got your home."

Archie shook his head in disagreement and replied, "Look, Maggie, I appreciate your help. I know that you want to help me and have sympathy for me because of my past and all, but that doesn't give you the right to play sick games with me. Yes, I have something to ask. Who gave you the right to mess with my brain? I am feeling lost for now, but why you have misguided me?!"

Maggie had thought that Archie would be happy. She had not been expecting this reaction, but she also knew that this revelation was intimidating, as well. So, she tried to convince him again. She said, "I have already told you that I do not have any sympathy for you because you are my friend, and that is why I am willing to help you. I also know that this is hard to believe - what I am telling you it is beyond your imagination. My secret mission is to bring people like you to this island. I am very old, but I always keep looking tiny due to magic. It helps me to keep doing my job and fulfill my mission, and Izzy's home was not the first home where I lived with a family. I keep changing families to search for worthy puppies like you who feel that they have some purpose in life to serve, or that there is a hole in their life. Our wisest wizard decides whom to keep and train here." She waited for a reply, but there was none.

Maggie continued, "I know that I have not given you the chance to trust me blindly, but I did not ruin your beliefs either. I am just asking you to follow me for some time, and then to go with me to see the wizard. You can have all the answers you have been seeking for so long," Maggie continued.

Archie was unsure, but there was a sincerity in her voice. She deserved another chance, so Archie replied, "Ok. I will come with you, but I have one condition. If I feel that this whole thing is nothing, but a hoax and your old wise Wizard is nothing but a con artist, then I will leave immediately, and you will not be able to stop me, or try to convince me, either. You will help me to get out of this hocus-pocus land. Deal!"

Maggie knew one thing about Archie - arguing with him would never end well. Archie was a stubborn one. He would not go one step further without making that deal. So, Maggie nodded in agreement. All the dogs of Paw Island were busy doing their everyday chores, and no one was paying attention to the new puppy roaming around with Maggie. Maggie and Archie came in front of an ancient Castle. Dogwood trees surrounded the castle. The castle was made of stones, and old creepers were everywhere on its outer wall. The island was covered with snow, and everyone was getting ready for Christmas. Even the Castle was being decorated for Christmas. Archie saw that the wreaths on the door were made of bone-shaped wooden artifacts instead of dry flowers. They noticed the door was half shut. Maggie walked towards the door and knocked softly. An ancient and wrinkled dog opened the door. There was a serene smile on his face, and he looked at Archie eagerly, as if he had been expecting him for a long time.

Maggie bowed down in front of the old dog, but Archie did not feel the urge to do anything. He had no reason to be respectful, but he was intrigued by the wizard's expression. The wizard asked, "Dear child, who is our guest today? And what took you so long in bringing him here?"

Maggie was also perplexed by the wizard's manner, but she managed to gather herself together. She replied, "Wizard, most of the dogs are happy and comfortable with their present domestic lives. They are getting enough food, a warm place to sleep, and walks around clean parks. No one is feeling the urge to be better, or to do something for others. They are not willing to give back to this society, or to humans, or even to us. They are contented. After a long time, I met him; his name is Archie. He feels that he has some mission; he is aimless but feels that he has some purpose. He was ready to leave all the comforts behind him without any attachment. He was ready to start his journey to get his answer."

The wizard smiled and said, "I see. So, Archie, may I give you a test to see whether you are worthy or not? But, before that, tell me - how are you feeling?"

Archie had expected an elaborate introductory speech on how to be worthy and why to help others. But the wizard preferred to stay on point. Archie replied, "Ok. Before you give me some weird test, is it ok if I ask you something? Maggie had told me that you have some magical power or something, and you are very ancient. If that is true, then why are you all wrinkled? Why are you not magically changing yourself into a young dog? And I cannot call you Wizard, so I guess you must have a name!?"

The wizard smiled and said, "You are wise. You know what to ask and when to ask it. I do not bother to use magic to stay young anymore because I have not taken any missions in the outer world for some time. One thing is clear from this conversation, though - you do not believe anything blindly, and that is a great virtue. We should always ask questions until we feel that there is nothing left to ask. Curiosity leads us to wisdom, child. I am not transforming myself into a younger-looking dog because I don't feel the need. Maggie needs to stay young because she needs to stay with families. And no one is willing to take responsibility for an old and feeble dog. It doesn't matter whether I am very young or very old looking; wisdom is everything for me. If you are wise, then being beautiful or being ugly doesn't matter. People will always respect you and come to you for your suggestions. I have a name, and my name is Coco!"

Archie was shocked to know the name. He asked, "Coco! Are you Paul's Coco? You were lost, and he still misses you. If you are wise and all, then why did you leave that house? I think they are good people. And you said you no longer go in the outer world, but if you are that Coco, then this whole thing does not make any sense."

Wizard coco's smile became broader. Archie had the qualities to be able to connect all the dots. He replied, "You are right; I am Paul's Coco. You see, on Paw Island, we are all driven by some mission, and we are bound to fulfill that. No matter how we feel about it, we have to come back to this land after fulfilling every mission. Three years ago, I had envisioned a prophecy that a wise puppy was about to born. And one family helped him to reach us. I had to make sure that the family was kind enough to take care of that prophesied puppy. So, I went there and lived with them for some time. When I became satisfied, I had to leave. I think you know who that prophesied dog is. I have lived here for 12 lifetimes. And I can live fourteen lifetimes in total. Archie, you are supposed to be the next wizard of Paw Island. But that's a long way to go. Tell me, why did you feel the urge to leave all the comforts behind?

Archie was still processing everything, and he was silent. He thought, 'These people are mad. How can I turn into a wizard? Are they lying to me?' But he did not utter anything and instead replied absentmindedly, "I was not at all comfortable there. I hate humans. They are rude and unkind. Paul and his family were kind to me, but that does not mean I trust them. Living inside a comfortable house can never satisfy me. I started my journey to find out my siblings, especially my little sister Katty. But then I realized I have no idea where to find her. I stayed on the road for one night. Then Paul took me in."

Coco smiled mysteriously. "If I say that living on-road and meeting Tobby was part of our bigger plan, will you believe me?"

"I think I can believe anything you say at this point. Because you already know Tobby's name and I am guessing he was also part of some secret mission. I still do not know what I am doing here. And why should I be the next wizard of Paw Island?" Archie asked.

Coco requested that Maggie leave them alone. Maggie knew that her job was done here for now, so she said goodbye and left. Coco said, "Katty lives here with us, and all your siblings are here, too, because your parents were senior ministers of this land. Your bloodline has been serving the missions of Paw Island for many generations now. And I know that one day you will also feel the same urge to do so. And I know you have a trust issue. You do not need to trust me unless I prove myself worthy of your trust. But you need to know one thing. I am your great-great-great grandfather. Now it is time for your test."

Not so long ago, Archie had nothing. He was all alone, with no family and no one to depend on. And now he was standing in front of his heretofore unknown great-great-great grandfather. He could not say anything, and he was choked up. He knew that, in spite of his being family, Coco would never let him meet his siblings before this stupid test. So, he agreed.

Coco took him to a room full of antiques and talismans. There was a crystal globe in the center of the room. Coco asked Archie to focus on that globe. Archie concentrated on the globe, but nothing was happening. He was still standing with Coco, inside that room. After some time, Coco requested that he stop concentrating and go outside for some air. Archie was confused about this whole testing process. He still did not know what the test was. Nothing happened at all.

When he came out, he saw there was a gate in front of Wizard's house. He had not noticed the entrance before. But the gate was not important because he was lost in thought. He was still thinking about all the information he had to digest. How could this wizard be his great-great-great grandfather? How could his siblings be in this weird place? He absentmindedly crossed through the gate. Suddenly he heard a loud noise. He found himself standing beside a road. The road was being repaired, and a lot of people were working.

Archie gathered himself and noticed what was going on around him. He was no longer in Paw Island. He was in the city and standing in front of an under-construction building. A crane had lost its control and banged a wall. Now it was trying to pull itself up, as its one part was stuck in the mud.

He noticed a blind schoolboy was walking alone towards the crane. No one noticed him because everyone was busy pulling the crane up. Archie realized if the boy kept walking in that direction, he would be severely injured.

Archie ran towards the boy and began to bark loudly. He reached the boy in no time and grabbed the boy's umbrella with his teeth. Then, he started pulling the boy with all his might. The boy followed Archie's lead and finally reached a safe area, away from the construction site. Archie had saved the boy's life.

This was the first time Archie felt the magic of real bliss, a bliss of saving someone's life. He had never felt that before. Archie realized why Paul had helped him, and why people supported and helped one another. No matter how much Archie had believed he hated humans, he could not let that boy get hurt. Every creature on earth needs help from the other ones. And to survive, we should all live together and support each other. Archie felt like a veil was lifted from his eyes; he had been blind in his rage. He also felt like a burden had been lifted from his heart. He was relieved. Hatred could not give him anything besides pain. He realized that instantly. Archie sighed and closed his eyes to relish the moment.

When he opened his eyes, he found himself in Coco's room. His test was complete. Archie had learned a simple truth of life. He was worthy. He was ready to be trained for his mission for the greater good.

Chapter 17: An Orphan

Once upon a time, there was a student living in an orphanage. His name was Alex. His parents had died in an accident when he was too young. There was no one to look after him, his uncle leaves him to the orphanage. He raised in an orphanage. He always thought where his parents had gone and left him alone, but as time passes, he became used to, to live there. he likes to explore new things. He always feels alone and has not many friends.

One day he decided to go out from orphanage to explore the world. He never goes outside. But there was no permission to go outside. He decided to go out when everyone would be sleeping. He went out of the room at night to check whether everyone is sleeping. When no one was there, then he unlocked the door slightly and went outside. He used to jump over the orphanage's boundary wall and roam around. So, he jumped over the wall. He saw shops which were closed and no traffic on the road because he went outside at mid of night. He has to return back to the orphanage before dawn. He roamed here and there and got afraid because the night was dark. He had to return. He jumped over the boundary wall of the orphanage and slowly moved to his room without making any noise and get back to sleep.

The next day he again decided to go outside with courage, then he again climbed to the boundary wall of the orphanage and jumped outside. He walked two miles. There he saw a boy sitting alone on the road. He went close to him and asked him "why are you sitting here alone, and what is your name?" The boy replied, "My name is Sam, and this is the place I live". He told him that his mother had died 4 days before. And there was no one who looked after him and gave food to him.

Alex said, “why won't you come with me, I'm also an orphan and my parents have died in an accident”. The boy agreed to go with him. He said, “I have not taken permission from Father to go outside”. Alex said “you should come to the orphanage tomorrow. And we will meet tomorrow at the orphanage”. The boy replied, “ok”. Alex said, “I’m getting late I should go now”. The sun rises. Alex runs speedily back to the orphanage and goes to his room. The day arises the boy came to the church and told the Father about his mother and all situations he faced. The Father decided to take that child to the orphanage. Then in the evening, he met Alex. They both became good friends. They played together, ate together, studied together. Alex said to Sam that he again wanted to go outside and explore things.

At night they both jumped over the boundary wall of the orphanage and go outside. There Sam takes Alex to the park where they play games and then they decided to go three miles far where they found a fruit shop which was opened late at night. They became hungry. And go to that shop and asked the shop keeper to give them one apple, but they have no money the shopkeeper refuses to give them an apple. The sun was about to rise. They decided to go back to the orphanage.

The next day Sam refuses to go with Alex because he realizes that it is not a good thing to go outside without taking permission from Father. But Alex said I'm getting tired from this place I want to see the world. Alex decided to go out alone. And that night father was awake, and he had seen Alex going out. He got up to stop him, but he was gone. After a few hours later when he gets back to the orphanage, he opened the door and he saw Father was looking at him.

He became scared. But Father told him that "son, at least you should take a warm shawl, because you know when you go at night, it is cold outside.” Fathers gentle manner made Alex realize his own folly. He feels ashamed and guilty. He apologized to the Father and promised him that he would never go outside without taking permission from him.

Chapter 18: Hailey Goes on a Nature Walk

Hailey loved nature and everything about the outdoors.

When she was just a baby, her mom used to strap her to a baby carrier and carry Hailey along some of the coolest hikes in the Pacific North West.

They would climb mountains, scale trails, and check out incredible waterfalls that decorated the sides of the cliffs they hiked near.

As she got older, Hailey was able to start walking the trails herself, and soon, it became her favorite hobby.

Hailey loved getting to see the outdoors and all of the curious wonders of the world when she was out in nature, so much so that she was always asking to go on nature hikes with her mom.

One day, Hailey realized they had not been on a nature hike in a while.

Life had been busy for her mom, and she had not been able to make much time for the two of them to do anything together.

Hailey felt sad and wanted to go on a walk, so she asked her mom if they could go soon.

Hailey's mom said yes, and the two went for a nature walk that very next weekend.

At first, Hailey was surprised because they did not get in the car to go anywhere.

When they went on hikes, Hailey's mom would always pack the car, and they would drive away to the trail and then do their hike.

This time, Hailey's mom never packed anything, and they never got into the car.

Instead, they put on their shoes and their sweaters and started walking down the road.

"Where are we going?" Hailey asked, following her mom down the road.

"On a nature walk." Hailey's mom answered.

"Where?" Hailey asked.

"You'll see!" Hailey's mom said.

Confused, Hailey kept walking with her mom down the road.

At first, she had no idea what was going on.

Then, Hailey grew frustrated and angry with her mom.

This is not what she wanted; Hailey wanted to go on a nature walk, not a walk down the road.

What was her mom thinking? Hailey wondered.

"This suck, I want to go home!" Hailey said, growing annoyed with their walk.

By now, they had turned several corners, but they were still just on the road; there was not a trail to be found.

"Just wait, Hailey, be patient, please. You will see what we are doing." Hailey's mom answered, continuing to walk.

Hailey reluctantly followed, although by now, she was not having any fun.

She wanted to go home and play with her toys and pretend this day had never happened.

All she wanted was to go on a nature walk with her mom, and instead, they were walking around the neighborhood, and she had no idea where they were going.

After a few more turns, Hailey's mom turned into a small trail that opened up into a field.

"We're here!" she said, looking around.

Still confused, Hailey looked around at where they were.

They had made their way to one of the local parks.

"Where?" Hailey asked.

"On a nature walk, silly!" Hailey's mom smiled.

"This is not a nature walk, mom, this is a park," Hailey said, matter of fact.

"Oh, really? Well, then, what is this!" Hailey's mom said, pointing to a strange plant that lined the trails.

Hailey rolled her eyes at her mom and then looked closer.

As she looked, she realized the plant was unlike anything she saw before.

It's purple-black leaves curled in every which direction and had tiny hairs on them that made it look like they were little hairy plant hands reaching up for sunlight.

Hailey giggled and stood back up.

"Okay, cool plant. But what now?" Hailey asked.

"Do you hear that?" Hailey's mom asked.

"Hear what?" "That sound, that bird!" Hailey's mom said.

"Yes, I do!" Hailey answered, starting to get excited about the park they were in.

"Let's go find it!" Hailey's mom said.

The two of them began walking toward where the sound was coming from.

As they followed the path, they came across the bird that was up in a tree chirping at them.

It was a red-crested woodpecker, calling to his friends before pecking the side of a tree to get a meal.

"Cool!" Hailey said, watching him as he called and then pecked the side of the tree.

Hailey and her mom started walking down the path through the park a little further, and as they did, they started seeing several different types of plants and birds all around them.

Then, they started seeing cool bugs.

First, Hailey saw a fancy spider that was spinning its web.

Then, she saw a little caterpillar chewing on a leaf.

As they kept walking, they also saw a beaver in the nearby creek, three more spiders, a ladybug, two grasshoppers, and several bumblebees.

Hailey started counting out all of the different things she saw as they walked around the park.

Her mom also stopped to take a few pictures of the birds and the beautiful plants that were all around the park they were in.

When they got to the end of the trail, they made their way back to the street.

Hailey was sure the nature walk was over and started to feel sad again, but her mom assured her there was plenty more to see.

"There is so much nature in our own back yard!" Hailey's mom grinned, pointing out several different plants, bugs, and birds along the way.

Hailey continued looking for cool species that were all around their walk.

She was surprised to realize that there were so many cool things to see in their own neighborhood.

In the past, she only noticed the houses, driveways, and cars.

But now, she could see that her own neighborhood had so many incredible pieces of nature woven into it.

She knew that she would never see her own neighborhood the same way again.

As they approached their home, Hailey's mom asked her if she enjoyed the nature walk, they had.

"I did!" Hailey's smiled.

"I wished we were going on a nature hike because I wanted to go see a waterfall or a mountain, but this was a really fun walk, too. Thank you for taking me, mom." Hailey said.

"I know you wanted to go on a hike, Hailey, but sometimes life gets busy, and we cannot go do things like that. I know you are disappointed, but I am grateful that you are so kind about it. If you are patient for just a little bit longer, everything at work will settle down, and we will be able to go on a real hike again real soon. Until then, I hope you are ok with us just going on nature walks around our own neighborhood. There are so many cool things to see here, too!" her mom said.

"I am sad we didn't go, but I know. It was a fun walk. I did not know we had so many things in our own neighborhood!" Hailey said.

"Me neither." her mom smiled, hugging her.

When they were done talking, Hailey's mom got them both a cup of juice and some snacks to help fill their bellies after a long walk.

The two enjoyed their juice and snacks and talked about all of the cool things they saw, and about what they hoped to see when they went for another walk the following weekend.

And, when things got more calm at work, Hailey's mom took her on a hike as she promised, and they both got to enjoy a wonderful trip together watching waterfalls falling down cliffs and seeing mountains rising high into the sky.

Chapter 19: Dino Chef and the Great Soufflé

Dino puttered around the kitchen, gathering some of the tools and ingredients he would need for his next project. He picked up some flour, some eggs, a bowl, a whisk, and a measuring cup. He set them down on the counter and laid them out neatly so he could get to work.

"Today, I'm going to make a soufflé! It's a light and fluffy dessert that tastes so sweet and yummy, and it's so light and fluffy that only the best chefs can get them right every single time!"

Dino spun one of the eggs in a little circle on the countertop as he thumbed through his cookbook for the perfect soufflé recipe. When he found the page, he set the book down and studied the instructions carefully.

"It says here that I will need to make sure the oven is preheated to exactly the right temperature, and that I will need some baking dishes." Dino hurried around the kitchen, preparing everything for his delicious soufflé.

"I've made stew, I've made pizza, I've made ***lots*** of pasta, and I've even made my own pies! I'll bet that a great chef like me can make the perfect soufflé on the very first try!" Dino hummed to himself as he followed the directions in his cookbook.

Finally, Dino was ready to put his creation into the oven to bake. Just some patient waiting and there would be a delicious dessert waiting for him at the end of it.

Dino set the timer as he sat down in a chair he had in the kitchen. He picked up a book, kicked up his feet, and read while he waited for the timer to go off. Soufflés take a long time to bake, so Dino was sure he could finish his book by the time it was done!

Sometime later, when the timer was ticking down its last minutes, Dino had forgotten all about his book and was staring into the oven through the little window on the front. The soufflé looked like it was getting nice and fluffy on top! It almost looked like a giant muffin in its big dish.

The timer dinged and Dino flung open the door to the oven, slapped mitts on his hands, and took the delicious dessert out of the oven. He held up the dish, admiring the golden sweet fluff in front of him. Happily, he set down the soufflé, shut the door to the oven, turned off the heat, and turned around.

To Dino's horror, the soufflé had caved in on itself when his back was turned! Dino panicked as he watched all the air seep out of his fluffy dessert. Soon, the top of the dessert settled in near the bottom of the dish, leaving nothing behind but a sweet crater in the center of the bowl.

Dino paused for a moment, looking at the dish and the dessert he has been working on all afternoon. Soon, tears filled his eyes and he put his head down on the counter to cry.

"I just wanted to make the most delicious soufflé that ever was! I followed all the directions perfectly and it looked so beautiful when I took it out of the oven." Dino cried and cried. He read the directions for the soufflé recipe once again, to make sure that he hadn't missed anything when he was making it. He couldn't find anywhere that he had gone wrong.

Dino sat up and wiped his tears. He looked down at his flattened soufflé and then looked back at the cookbook. With a spoon from his drawer, Dino took a small piece of the soufflé and tasted it. His mouth closed around the spoon and his eyes glittered, his cheeks blushed, and his spirits soared. It was an absolutely ***delicious*** dessert and Dino was so proud of it.

"How could something this delicious still be wrong?" Dino asked himself. He continued to eat the soufflé as he read through the directions. “I know! This means that I’ve almost got it right. The flavor is perfect, all the ingredients are right, I just have to fix the way it puffs up. I can make a better one!” Dino zipped around the kitchen, picking up everything he would need in order to make another soufflé.

Carefully, he put all his ingredients together in just the right way. He got everything ready to go, he popped the soufflé into the oven, and he set his timer. Once again, Dino sat down in the kitchen with his book. This time, he was sure he would finish the book. Things were just starting to get really good in the story and he couldn’t wait to see how it ended!

Sometime later, the kitchen timer was just about to go off and Dino had once again completely forgotten all about his book. He hopped around the kitchen, from foot to foot, waiting for the timer to go off so he could look at his creation. He just knew that this time, he would get everything right and it would look just as great as it tasted.

Finally, the timer sounded, and Dino pulled the oven door open. He carefully pulled the soufflé from the oven and set it down on the counter as gently as he could. He switched off the oven and closed the door, all without taking his eyes off of the soufflé. Slowly, he took off his oven mitts and put them back in their place, never looking away from his dessert. When he was done, he put his hands on his hips and stood in front of the soufflé. He let out a relieved sigh and said, “I think I got it this time!” He closed his eyes and threw his hands in the air.

Just as he looked away, as though the soufflé heard what he said, it caved in on itself, forcing all the air out of it. Dino flopped onto the floor and sat, looking up at the dish on the counter.

“Well isn’t that just... SOMETHING. What am I missing with my soufflé? Something must be wrong.

Dino hopped back up onto his feet and grabbed the oven mitts once more. He grabbed the baking dish and put it into his bag with some foil on top. He raced out to his Vespa and drove straight to the bakery where Pietro was getting ready to lock up for the evening.

“Pietro! I need your help with my latest creation. Do you have some time?” Pietro, whose key was in the lock to his bakery, unlocked the door once more and gestured for Dino to go inside.

“I always have time to help a friend! What can I help you with, Dino?”

“Thank you so much for being here, Pietro.” Dino slipped the mitts back onto his dinosaur claws and pulled the soufflé out of the bag. He set it on the counter and pulled the foil off of it. “This is the second one I’ve made, and it won’t stop falling apart like this! Can you tell me what I’m doing wrong?”

“A-ha! I already know the answer, just by looking at it. It’s too dry.”

“Dry?” Dino asked. “But it’s so delicious. There’s nothing dry about it when I eat it.

“Well the ***inside*** is moist, but the outside is too dry and the crust up at the top is too dry to hold a shape, so its ***frump*** falls in on itself.” Dino looked at the soufflé and poked at the top of it with his claw, noticing that it was a bit dry.

“How do I fix it? I followed the recipe in my book exactly. Should I add more milk?”

“Absolutely not.” Pietro stepped forward and grabbed one of the spoons from the counter. He tasted the soufflé. “It’s perfect inside. What you must do is bake a dish full of water along with your soufflé. When you bake the soufflé, it will have all that water in the air around it, keeping it fluffy and perfect.”

“That is pure genius, Pietro! I will try that. Thank you so much!” Dino put his mitts back on, grabbed his soufflé, and ran right back out the door. He would get this soufflé right, even if it took the whole night long! He got back up on his Vespa and drove back to his kitchen.

When he arrived, he threw all the ingredients together with no problem. When you have to make a recipe so many times, you start to remember all the steps without reading the book!

Dino placed a large baking pan filled with water into the oven and placed his soufflé dish right into the center of it. Once more, he set his timer. He looked at his book on the table and sighed. There was no way he could give the book the attention it needed. Even if he did finish the book now, he wouldn't be able to take it all in.

Dino laid on the floor of the kitchen and listened to his little timer ticking away the seconds until his soufflé was ready to be pulled out of the oven. He thought about the soufflé and how delicious it would be when he finally got it right. His tired eyes started to see little smiling soufflés dancing around before he dozed off, right on the kitchen floor.

Sometime later, Dino woke up to the ringing of his kitchen timer. It was time! The soufflé was cooked, and this was the moment of truth. He hopped up, turned off the oven, slipped the mitts onto his hands, opened the oven, and pulled out the beautiful, golden soufflé. Little swirls of steam curled up off of the dessert as he carefully placed it on the counter and admired its beautiful, strong shape.

He closed the oven, he turned it off once more, and he stood in front of the soufflé, watching it carefully. He walked around the kitchen, keeping his eye on it. He walked to another part of the kitchen and he kept looking at the soufflé. Carefully, he closed his eyes. When he opened them, he looked back up at the soufflé that sat there peacefully, billowing more sweet steam.

Dino smiled and, just as he was about to run over to look at it closely, he stopped himself. He walked over to the refrigerator and opened the door. He stood behind it, so his view of the soufflé was blocked. Slowly, he peeked out from behind the door, to see the soufflé sitting there, just as perfect as when he had pulled it out of the oven.

He walked to the door of the kitchen and pushed it open slowly. He walked out, looking cautiously at the soufflé. The door closed behind him and in an instant, he burst back through it to try to catch the soufflé deflating once again. But the soufflé didn't change! It sat on the counter, looking fluffy.

He knelt on his hands and knees and crawled over to the counter to sneak up on the soufflé. Just when the soufflé wouldn't be suspecting him, he jumped up and made a big dinosaur roar! But the soufflé stayed perfect!

Dino had finally done it! He had made a delicious soufflé that looked just as beautiful as the one in his cookbook! Dino walked to the middle of his kitchen and did a little victory dance. He wiggled his tail from side to side, he kicked his feet out to either side and pumped his fists.

"Dino is the greatest chef who ever was! This soufflé is the best thing ever and I have done something amazing in my kitchen today!" Dino kept dancing as he cleaned up the kitchen. He wiped down all the counters, he emptied his pan of water, he washed all his utensils, and he looked back at his perfect soufflé from time to time to keep his dancing going.

When he was all done, Dino fixed himself a little bit of dinner and sat down at the table to eat. He finished his food and he sat down with a nice piece of soufflé and his book. Now, he could finish the book, he would know what happened in the end, and he could pay attention now that he wasn't worried about making the most perfect soufflé!

What a wonderful way to spend an evening.

Chapter 20: Leopard and the four kids

Once upon a time, there was a Goat who after giving birth to her four kids died. They were left to take care of themselves.

All of them left their mother and they had to fend for themselves. At first, they were all walking together but later, they went on their separate ways.

As one of the kids kept walking on his own, he came across a leopard. The Leopard quickly went to him and made friends with him. The Leopard began to ask him questions and he told him that they are four but that they have separated and that he is in search of food. The Leopard quickly said to himself: "These kids won't be bad for food". He then told the kid that he should follow him and that he has food for him. He took him to his house and asked him to enter so that he can give him food. As soon as he entered, he pounced on him and ate him. When he finished eating him, he made up his mind to also go looking for the other ones and kill them.

The second kid also continued in his search for food. As he was walking, whatever he saw on the road, he ate. Before long, he met the Leopard who quickly made friends with him. "Hello, it seems you are new around" here says Leopard. He also responded and said, "Hi, yes, I am new here". What brought you to town asked the leopard. The kid went ahead to explain what happened to their mother and how they all separated to go and look for food. Leopard then asked him if he had a house and he said no and that he has just been sleeping around. He then offered him his house. With joy, the kid followed him. When they got to his house, he told the kid to make himself comfortable as he has nothing to be afraid of. He even gave him lunch. They talked and talked. When night came, he pounced on the kid and though, the kid begged him not to kill him, but he didn't answer, he killed and ate him immediately.

The third kid decided to build a house because he thought within himself that if he can build a house, he will not be attacked by wild animals and he will also have a place to rest. He went ahead to get all the materials needed and he then started building. When he was almost done, the leopard saw him carrying something so heavy and he exclaimed, " Why didn't you call for help? This is quite big for you". He then offered to help him. He helped him carry the material and when they got home, he assisted him in the building. The kid thanked him for helping out and asked to know where he was living. He then told the kid that he is trying to fix some things in his house and so, he is not sleeping at home that night. He said he was on his way to his friend's house when he saw the kid. The kid felt so sorry for him and asked him to move in with for as long as he wants. They both ate and slept.

Leopard began to stay with him. After a few days, when they were sleeping in the night, the leopard woke up and saw his friend sleeping. He killed him and ate him. When he was done eating, he left the house and went away.

The fourth kid decided to build a very strong house and then, stock it with enough food so that when he is inside, he will be safe from danger. He got all the material needed and took his time to build it.

Then came the Leopard again, as he got to the fourth kid's house, he called to him “Oh dear Goat, let me come in and stay with you till dawn. My house is very far from here and I need a place to stay until tomorrow.”

The Goat answered him from inside, "No, my dear Leopard, you have no place here. I don't want any visitor."

"I will pull down your house and come in. I will then feast on you", the Leopard said. "You can try your luck", the Goat replied.

Well, he tried everything, but he could not pull down the house. When he found that he could not, he was disappointed and angry at the same time and he made up his mind to do everything within his power to get the kid. He left and came back again at another time.

A few days after, he came to the kid's house and called out again, "Nice structure you've got here, kid. I need to build something as strong as this. Can you allow me in to take a look at the inside?" The kid replied to him from inside, "Well, Leopard, the way the outside is, is the way the inside is. You don't need to come in". The Leopard was angrier this time around and told himself that when next he comes; he is going to break the roof of the kid's house and kill him.

He came again after some days. As he got outside, he called out, "My friend, I am here again to give you a gift. Just come out and accept my token of love for you". The kid replied him from inside and said, "Oh thank you, that's quite thoughtful of you, I am coming." The Leopard was happy that at last, he is going to get him but unknown to him, the kid had kept a dagger by the window to use to kill him. Suddenly, the kid opened his window and threw the dagger, it hit the Leopard on the head, and he fell.

The kid then came down and killed it. He boiled him and ate him. He then lived in peace ever after.

Chapter 21: The Forest Boy and The Shepherd Girl

Once upon a time, there was a boy who grew up in the forest. The forest trees and flowers were his friends. They sang different songs to him. Sometimes, if he offends one of them, while others are singing for him, the one he offended will be saying bad things about him. He had never lived outside the forest. He ate and slept there. By himself, he will play with all the flowers and trees, they will also laugh and clap with him. He never thought there was another life outside the forest.

One day, as he was walking inside the forest, he saw some people and he decided to follow them. He kept following them from a distance. He was very surprised to see that there is a village not too far from where he lived. He has never seen humans before, so, he was surprised to see people. He saw their market and heard them buying and selling. He was moving from one place to another and he loved what he saw. After spending some time there, he made up his mind to come there sometimes. Day after day, he was coming to the market to see people. His friends in the forest were always missing him whenever he leaves them but whenever he is back, they kept singing for him.

One day, when he got to the market, he saw a woman selling flowers and saw that many people were buying. He was so surprised and then, he thought to himself that there are even more beautiful flowers from where he is coming. He then decided to come and be selling flowers in the market. When he got to the forest, he told the flowers what happened at the market and that he wants to be selling flowers. The flowers told him to go ahead and cut from them. He was very happy.

On the market day, he got up early and got plenty of flowers and carried it to the market. As soon as he got to the market, the villagers were fascinated by the scent of the flowers. As they were so beautiful, and for each of his flowers, he received a gold coin. Many villagers came to buy from him as they had never seen flowers so beautiful as that. He made plenty of money that day and as he got to the forest, he went straight to the flowers and told them what happened at the market and the plenty of money he made. They were so happy. They sang for him and also told him she can always come and pick from them.

He was always going to the market frequently and he was making a lot of money as many people were buying the flowers because they were very beautiful, much more than the ones they've always seen. One day, when he got to the market, he saw a shepherd boy who came to meet him to buy flowers. As the boy got to him, he smiled at him and greeted, the boy loved him immediately. That was how they became friends. Whenever he is done selling every day, the shepherd boy will see him off and after some time, turn back while he continues his journey into the forest. Each day, they look forward to seeing each other.

One day, after he finished selling flowers, he carried his container and money, as he was about leaving the market, the shepherd boy came with his sister to say hi to his newfound friend. He quickly made friends with the girl and that was how the three of them started meeting at the market square. When the shepherd boy and girl are done tending the sheep, they would come to the market square to see their friend. When he finishes selling, they will see him off and go back after some time.

The flowers in the forest continued to sing for him whenever he comes back from the market. They were his friends in the forest. He started liking the shepherd girl. One day, he decided to take the most beautiful of the flowers and give them to the girl. Before cutting it, he told the flower, "In this forest, you are the one I love most. May I give you to the girl I love?". The flower said, "Yes, go ahead". He thanked the flower and went ahead to pick a few of the flowers. When his friends came visiting, he gave the girl the special flower as a symbol of his love for her. The girl was very happy, and she thanked him.

Both of them began to plan on getting married and he agreed to leave the forest and come and stay in the village with the girl. When he got to the forest, he spoke to the trees and flowers. He thanked them for being his friends for years and how they have kept him company all the while. He told them about the girl he wants to marry and how much he loves him and that he wants to start living in the village after marrying her. All of them began to talk about how much they are going to miss him. One of the trees then said, "You have made so much money from selling flowers, use that money to build a house for yourself and the girl". All of them chorused, "That's a good idea". A flower also told him, "You can continue to sell your flowers. Come and be plucking us and we will keep increasing for you to get more every day". All of them agreed. He then thanked all of them for their support. They asked him to bring the girl so that they can do a farewell party for him when she comes.

He began to build the house in the village and when he finished, he brought the girl to the forest. All the trees and flowers sang many beautiful songs for both of them. The farewell party was great. When they finished, both of them left the forest and the boy and girl lived happily ever after.

Chapter 22: The Luck Dragon

Once upon a time, a boy named Matthew was lucky enough to travel all the way to China, half the world away from where he lived in the United States. His mom had to attend a business conference there—she worked for a large technology company—and decided to allow Matthew to tag along. There would be children of other businesspeople there, therefore, she thought it would be nice for Matthew to meet some new friends and experience some new cultural encounters. The timing of the conference happened to coincide with the celebration of Chinese New Year, or Lunar New Year - one of the biggest celebrations in China at any time of the year. Matthew was, needless to say, so excited he couldn't sleep the night before they left.

After a really, really long flight—truly, Matthew couldn't believe that he could sit on a plane for that many hours—they landed in Beijing, the big gray capital of China, home to millions and millions of people. Once they got their things settled in the hotel room, Matthew's mom and their guide took him around the main sights of the city where he got to see the enormous plaza called Tiananmen Square, with its huge posters of one of China's former leaders—other schoolchildren about Matthew's age crowded around him, curious to know where he was from. His blonde hair and gangly height made him stand out a bit in the crowd. The attention was a bit awkward but fun, and he got email addresses from a few would-be pen pals. They also visited the Forbidden City, which, despite its name, was no longer forbidden it was an inviting maze of ancient rooms and halls from which much of imperial China had been ruled.

It was a blur of a day, with so many grand sights and so very many people everywhere you went, rushing along to get to work or to school or to wherever they had to go. Matthew didn't think he'd seen so many people in his entire life as he'd seen in this one day. It was grand, but a little overwhelming. Besides all that, it was a bit hazy in the city, and it was hard to see very far in front of your face. The air felt thick.

After a rest in the room, Matthew got excited all over again, for tonight some Lunar New Year festivities were going to take place. There were lots of traditions associated with the Chinese holiday, such as honoring ancestors and eating dumplings filled with good fortune, but he was most excited about the fireworks and the parade. His mom assured him that it would go right along the street in front of the hotel and that they'd get out early to have a good spot from which to watch the action.

Matthew, indeed, was perched along the sidewalk right up front as the parade began to snake its way down the street. It was noisy and bright and wonderful! There were drummers banging rhythmically on drums, wearing bright costumes of red and gold; there were fireworks going off, here and there, sending bright sparks and showers of multi-colored glitter into the air; there were dancers and acrobats bounding down the street, again in elaborate costumes of bright colors; and, most impressively, there was a great red Chinese dragon (presumably helped along by human puppeteers) winding through the street. He was magnificent, all royal red with golden eyes and real smoke blowing out of its mouth! Unlike the images of European dragons that Matthew was more familiar with, this Chinese dragon was long and lean, like a snake, with four short legs to carry him about. He'd heard these kinds of dragons were also called luck dragons, and it filled his heart with longing. He wouldn't mind some better luck now and again. Sometimes life as a young person could be hard, and it would be nice to be better at sports or to have better grades. Or, turning his strict parents into parents who would let you do anything you wanted. He smiled at that thought not very likely.

Still, he was mesmerized by the dancing snake dragon in its brilliant red, so much so that he found himself slowly approaching it, not really aware of what he was doing, but he just felt he had to touch it, so convinced he was that it must be real. He could faintly hear his mom call his name in the background, but it was too late: Matthew was swept up in the happy chaos of the parade, and he was jostled on all sides by the dancers and performers who were running alongside the dragon. While he was a little bit startled, he was mostly deliriously excited to be caught up in the chaos. After a moment, he found himself quite near the dragon's head—and that's when something truly extraordinary happened. The dragon turned his head to Matthew, looked directly into his eyes, and winked.

At that same moment, Matthew felt a hand on his arm and a good, hard yank as the guide his mom had hired for their trip pulled him out of the parade. He walked him back to his rather stern mom, who, once she was assured that Matthew was okay, was actually pleased to see how happy her sometimes quiet son was.

"Mom, you wouldn't ***believe*** it," he almost yelled. "The dragon ***winked*** at me! It did! It winked at ***me***." His mom laughed, not wanting to burst his bubble of happiness.

"I'm sure he did, son," she ruffled his hair. "You, my dear, are very special."

After the parade was over, and the last of the fireworks burst gloriously into the air, leaving trails of smoke behind, Matthew and his mom trudged up to bed, tired from all the excitement. Matthew still felt like he wouldn't ever get to sleep, thinking about that amazing dragon, but really, as soon as his head hit the pillow, he was out like a light.

Sometime in the middle of the night, Matthew grunted a bit and rolled over, halfway waking up. As he settled back in to fall back asleep, he heard a soft tapping at the window next to him, followed by a snuffling sound. He lay very still for a moment, sure that he was imagining it, but after a minute, there it was again: tap-tap-tap, snuffle snort, tap-tap-tap, snuffle snort. He listened to this for a while—what felt like a very long time to him—deciding whether he should be afraid or whether he should look. In the end, curiosity got the best of him and he crept quietly out of bed to peek out the window.

It was the dragon! His golden eye was pressed up against the window, peering into study Matthew. Matthew jumped backward, almost falling over the chair behind him, in his surprise. After a second, he looked around to see that his mom was still sleeping, and crept quietly up to the window, pushing it open slightly to see and hear better.

"Hello, lad," the dragon said in a deep and growling voice. "I just had to come see you. It's not often that someone is brave enough to jump into the crowd and stand right next to me." He laughed softly, a low chortle that sounded both amused and impressed. "Why don't you come with me for a while? I'll show you something that tourists almost never get to see."

Matthew hesitated for the briefest of moments, looking back to the sleeping figure of his mom, then grabbed his hoodie and a pair of sneakers and leapt out to the landing.

The long red dragon was floating there, suspended in space—how, Matthew did not know, for it had no wings that he could see—and invited him to jump on his back.

"You, my young friend," he said in his growling voice, "are getting out of the city for a while." With that, he glided off on some mysterious power, soaring higher up into the sky. Matthew could see that, even in the middle of the night, Beijing was filled with lights, from huge buildings and billboards and streets and homes. Eventually, they were just distant twinkles below him as the dragon soared ever higher. It had happened so quickly that Matthew didn't have time to worry or to be afraid. Besides, for some reason, he felt he could trust the dragon; after all, he was a luck dragon.

After a while, the lights started to fade and then there was just blackness below and about them, as they flew outside the city. The dragon was humming a foreign tune and gliding along smoothly, with seemingly no effort at all. Finally, he started to circle what looked like a hilltop and began to descend toward the ground. They landed with a soft thud, and Matthew slipped off the dragon's back.

"Where are we?" he whispered, looking around him at what looked like the densest forest he had ever seen.

"We are in the Hushan Mountains," the dragon replied. "Down below us is part of the Great Wall of China. Wait for a few minutes, and you will start to see." With that, the dragon flew up above him a few feet, and spun three times backwards in a circle; the sun crept slowly upwards from the wrong part of the sky, giving off what felt like late evening light.

Matthew began to see all around him, these mountains so old and worn with time. They were dense with low-growing trees, but he couldn't sense a lot of wildlife in them. They felt alone and empty, but profoundly old and wise.

"Here, lad," the dragon landed next to him again. "Climb back up, and I'll show you around."

The view as the dragon hovered a hundred feet above the mountain was magnificent. Matthew could see what looked like the endless outline of the Great Wall, one of the few things that humans have built that can be seen from outer space, so big was it. But he also noticed something else: the air was so clean and pure that he felt like he was breathing better than he had in days.

The dragon nodded, seemingly reading his thoughts. "Yes, lad, the air here is pure as it isn't in the city." He shook his head. "Too many people, too much pollution. It will surely be the end of us if we aren't careful. That's why I wanted to show you this place, up in the mountains. Surely you understand that these mountains have existed long before humans, and they have seen and known just about everything there is to know. They should be respected and protected."

Matthew nodded in agreement. He could feel how important this place was, and how small he was in it. He was just one small speck amid such a magnificent setting. It was humbling and peaceful at the same time.

“We must get you back. I can’t stop time forever, you know,” the dragon laughed, and tendrils of smoke curled out of his nostrils. Matthew hopped on for one last magnificent ride, as they glided back into the blackness of night and then, shortly, over the vast lights of the city below them. The dragon glided up to the landing, letting Matthew slide off his back and thump gently down.

“I’ll never forget you, luck dragon,” Matthew said solemnly. “Or those mountains. Thank you for taking me on such a wonderful journey.”

“You are welcome, lad,” said the dragon. “And thank you for your bravery. And for caring.” With that, the dragon soared upward quickly, as the first faint streaks of dawn started to light the sky. Within a moment, all that was left was a fading puff of smoke.

Matthew crawled back inside, closed the window, and buried himself under the covers. He felt like just about the luckiest person in the world. That’s the power of a luck dragon. He drifted off to sleep, dreaming of flying about the greenest mountains in the whole wide world.

Chapter 23: Butterfly Fairy

Once there was a Butterfly Fairy with wonderful wings. She was driven pixie. Her name was Juana. She was a library overseer of the delightful castle of the Butterfly Fairyland. She adored her activity. She was fond of perusing, so she accepted that her activity is ideal for her. Attractive Prince Turgut was found of perusing as well. He was dazzled by her characteristics.

Butterfly Fairies feared Crystal Fairies, they all accepted that Crystal Fairies are their adversary. One day Queen of Butterfly Fairies welcomed Juana on supper. During supper, Queen talks about Crystal Fairies and she wanted for exchanges with Crystal Fairies. Everything was astonished "How could that be" top dog stated, " Those are troublemakers". In any case, Juana affirmed them the genuine history from the old book, "Years back, Crystal Fairies and Butterfly Fairies were companions, one day a misconception was made between them about gestures of recognition Crystals of Crystal-land and from that time both didn't meet one another" Juana let them know.

Sovereign pick Juana to send Crystal-land for companion transport. Presently, she was all set Crystal-land. Sovereign gave her a sparkling Glass Ball as a guide for voyaging. After voyaging, a night and a day she came to Crystal castle. It was delightfully designed with precious stones and sparkles. Yet, everybody feared Butterfly Fairy, and nobody needed to meet her as they suspected her a troublemaker. Thus, she becomes vexed.

Be that as it may, Merry, King's girl, was a benevolent Crystal Fairy Princess. She became the companion to Juana. She utilized a pixie pony to fly as her wings were harmed. Her amicable conduct made Juana certain. Cheerful welcomed her on supper where she could purchase the message of kinship, from Butterfly Fairy Queen to Crystal-land's King. She came to supper. What's more, gave the message of fellowship to Crystal King. But since of Juana's huge wings, a few bungles have occurred in the royal residence. That drove the King crazy. She got irritated.

Following day, Merry purchased Juana to the most excellent spot of the Crystal-land. It was brimming with shinning precious stones and sparkles. Happy gifted her an excellent Crystal jewelry. In gratitude, Juana gave her shinning Glass Ball. They played there and delighted in a great deal. Joyful enlightened her concerning the yearly Crystal party in the royal residence.

In the night, Juana was all set in the gathering. Joyful made Juana's dress sparkling. She was looking lovely. The gathering was magnificent. It was brimming with happiness. Nevertheless, a pixie saw Crystal neckband in Juana's neck. She cried "That butterfly pixie is a cheat she has taken Crystal jewelry from Crystal-land" King became angry and requested her to return to Butterfly land, there can be no fellowship."

In stress, she was returning. Out of nowhere, she saw a Witch who was setting off to the Crystal castle. She thought "Perhaps she is going to hurt Crystal Fairies." So, she returned to the royal residence where she saw the witch is obliterating shinning Crystals into dark stones with her dark enchantment. It would be troubled for Crystal Fairies. Juana attempted her best to capture the Witch. Be that as it may, she proved unable. Juana went to Merry. She was aidless.

Juana made her certain to battle with the Witch. At that point without her pixie horse, she flies just because and battled with the Witch. It was difficult turned into the Witch was exceptionally amazing. In any case, Merry and Juana both captured her. In any case, it was past the point of no return as every Crystal was changed into dark stone except for a solitary Crystal. Cheerful and Juana went to that Crystal. They attempted to make it shine as it was previously yet futile. Out of nowhere, they saw the shinning Glass Ball is making the precious stones shinning and beautiful. They put it closer to the Crystal and soon all the Crystal-land got shinning and vivid.

Everybody got glad. Presently, Crystal King was dazzled by Butterfly Fairy Juana. He was appreciative of her fortitude. What's more, he requested to rebuff the Witch. In any case, Merry didn't permit him to do that. She said "Dear Father, you are committing a similar error as you did years prior. She approached only for a solitary Crystal and we have such a large number of, yet you didn't give her. Try not to rebuff her. We can make her a decent pixie."

At that point she talented her a piece of Crystal jewelry. This agreement completely changed the Witch. She became a companion to the Princess. Everything was glad. Lord acknowledged the companionship from Butterfly Fairies. Juana joyfully came back to Butterfly-land. Presently Butterfly Fairies and Crystal Fairies were companions.

Chapter 24: Archie's Sister is Kidnapped

Archie questioned Maggie's loyalty and expressed his irritation with her after he came out of the Wizard's house. The wizard had not given him any proper answers about his siblings or his larger mission. He had left it to Archie to find out all his answers. Archie also could not accept the lies Maggie had told him to bring him here. But Maggie told him that her intentions had been good all along, and she had to follow a protocol. She was not allowed to tell anyone about her mission.

This made Archie realize that sometimes, our friends and family might have to take some questionable steps to make us understand something or to help us out. It does not matter if we like that process or not. The only thing that matters is the outcome. Sometimes we feel like revolting against our parents for certain things they don't let us do, but in time, we will realize they did the right thing.

Archie was not in a position to understand about Paw Island or its rules. Maggie knew that, so she did not say anything. Maggie promised Archie that she would help him find his siblings. She took him to a quaint house in the woods.

That house belonged to Tobby, but Tobby was not a dirty street dog anymore. Tobby told Archie that there was one dog who could help Archie to get to his sister Katty. This dog's name was Doro. Doro was a pug who was Archie's sister, Katty's, best friend. Doro informed Archie and his friends that a circus company had kidnapped Katty.

Archie, Tobby, Maggie, and Doro tried to convince the Paw Island Council to allow them to undertake a rescue mission. But the Council would not allow it. However, they visited the

Wizard and asked for his advice. Wizard Coco told them to follow their hearts, to be there for each other, and, above all, to put family above all rules and protocols.

True friendship can be tested at a time of crisis. Archie's friends could let him go alone, but they helped him. A friend should always support another friend in need.

Archie's test was complete. And now his real journey was about to begin. Coco did not give any hint about what it would be. He just suggested that he find Maggie. Maggie would guide him accordingly. Archie had a lot of questions to ask. But he felt that Coco was not in the mood to answer any questions. Coco was about to leave when Archie asked, "You said my siblings are here - what they are doing here? Who brought them here? And what if I do not feel the urge to go on the given mission or stay here? Are my parents alive?"

Coco stopped on his way out and turned to answer. He said, "Archie, patience is the key to success. You will get all the answers when the time is right. But you need to be prepared first. This test proved that you are worthy of being trained. But you need to be worthy to receive these answers. Now you know the source. It is your job to find out the rest. I am not going to serve you everything you need on a silver platter. We believe in determination, discipline, and persistence. Do not rush."

Coco stormed out of the room, and Archie stood there silently. His head was spinning. He was confused and a bit frustrated. He hated twisted and riddle-like answers. There was no point in standing in that room anymore, so he also stormed out of the house. He saw Maggie was waiting outside eagerly, as though she had already known Archie was going to need her.

This strange land and its strange dogs, Archie thought.

"What are you doing here?" asked Archie. Maggie was waiting for Archie; she was curious to know how the test had gone. But Archie's expression showed his inner irritation about the whole situation. So, she decided to remain silent. Archie repeated his question more insistently.

Maggie suppressed her curiosity. She replied casually, "I am actually waiting for you. I know that the wizard must have told you to come to me for further guidance to tour the island. You still do not know about this island and its roads. So, I thought I could wait here for you. So how was your experience? Have you discovered anything interesting? You can share with me, you know!"

Archie realized there was no point in being mad at Maggie because she'd had nothing to do with the entire test or Coco's reluctance to reply to his questions. After all, this whole trial was about anger, hatred, and these types of emotions - and how he should fight them. So, he took some deep breaths and replied, "I finally realized the futility of being angry with someone for so long, and the disadvantages of hatred. I also realized that humans are not all bad or our enemies. To survive, we should always help each other and cooperate with each other. There is a hidden bliss in the ability to help others. I had a lot of questions, though, and the wizard refused to answer any of them. He said I must get my answers through persistence and patience. And I have no idea what to do next. So, tell me, are you going to help me in my pursuit?"

Maggie knew that the wizard loved riddles. And unfortunately, she had no idea how to help her friend. But she also realized her friend needed motivation and emotional support. He was already feeling lost. So, she said carefully, "I do not know how to help you, but if you decide to do something, I will always be there for you because that's what a friend should do. But you have to decide - what is the first thing you need to do? According to the law here, now is the time you should be visiting the training center and meeting the instructors. But if you feel that there is something more important than that, then do it; otherwise, you will always feel restless inside yourself."

Archie smiled and replied, "I know that you want to support me, and you consider me a friend. I also care about you, but I need to know something from you. Did you know that my entire experience was crafted by a Wizard or by a prophecy of this island? You had asked me to trust you, but you never told me that I am nothing but one of your missions. So, tell me, how can I can trust you!? What if I don't feel like fulfilling some stupid prophecy of this land? I don't even know whether my siblings are here or not. You played me once - now tell me, Maggie, how I can consider you as a friend and guardian angel after all your lies."

Archie had every right to be mad about the whole situation. And now was not a good time to make him appreciate the implications and reasoning behind the situation. Maggie replied calmly, "You will get all your answers soon; then, you will understand why I couldn't tell you about my secret mission. The wizard can never lie, so if he said that your siblings are here, then it is true. And no one can give you all the solutions, as the wizard said. I know you have no reason to trust me again, but you have to realize one thing - whatever we have done, everything was related only to your safety. I cannot tell you where your siblings are right now because I do not know. But I can take you to someone who can help you to figure out all these answers, or at least tell you about your siblings. Come with me."

The calmness of Maggie's voice somehow pacified Archie's resentment. Sometimes our friends and family have to take steps to protect us or to teach us something, and it is not necessary that we will always like their methods. But before we start judging them, we should always try to understand the intention behind their actions. Then, Archie remembered a story Paul had told him.

It had been Paul's birthday. In the morning, when his mother was busy baking a cake for him, he took her favorite paintings and used them in making a house for Coco. His mother was very sad after discovering what he had done with the painting, but she did not rebuke him or say anything. However, she took some of his favorite toy cars and hid those for a few days. He was angry and frustrated when he failed to find his toys. But after two days, he realized how his mother had felt when he spoiled her paintings. Though he didn't like the method, his mother had to make him understand the lesson. But, Paul thought, it was better than scolding or ill-treatment. Carol's intentions were good.

Coco's methods of making Archie understand the problems with feelings like hatred and anger were also questionable. But his attempt had, indeed, been successful. Archie would never forget the teaching.

So, Archie did not argue with Maggie anymore. He simply nodded in agreement. Maggie took him to a small house in the woods and knocked on the door. It was Tobby who opened the door.

The Tobby Archie had known a dirty and street dog. But this Tobby was a healthy, clean, and well-maintained dog. Archie quickly recognized him from his doe-shaped eyes. His eyes expressed how eagerly he had been waiting for Archie.

Archie and Maggie entered Tobby's modest hut. It was a quaint little house. The Tobby Archie had known was messy and rude. He had seemed like a rogue street dog, but his present-day living conveyed a whole new story. Tobby knew Archie had a lot to ask him. Tobby served them both hot bone broth and said, "Archie, first of all, I am happy to see that you finally reached Paw Island. I had a mission to bring you here. But those two boys chased you and hurt you. It was unexpected. That was not included in our plan. But when I came to know that Maggie had discovered you, I felt relieved. I know I have deceived you. But that was not the right time to make you understand what was happening. You are very important to everyone here. We have been waiting for you for so long."

Tobby had already anticipated the questions and Archie's thoughts about everything. His honest confession brought a broad smile to Archie's face. He replied, "I have no complaints. I may not understand your ways, but I know that you tried to protect me. You people are weird - but in a good way! However,

I want to meet my siblings and especially my little sister Katty. You know how much I wanted to meet her. Maggie told me that you could help me in locating them."

Tobby smiled and said, "Your sister has been living with us for quite some time, and she is already on her first mission! Let me call Doro - he knows her exact location. But you are not trained yet. So, I do not know whether the authorities will allow you to go outside Paw Island or not. But I will try my best to help you, my friend."

Tobby called his aides and asked him to bring in Doro. After a while, Doro came in. Doro was a tiny puppy with a small tail. He had the face of someone who is always happy. Tobby introduced Doro to Archie. But Archie was not expecting the greeting Doro gave him.

Doro jumped up to hug Archie and hugged him so hard he was about to suffocate him. Archie had no idea what was happening. Then Doro started crying. Tobby and Maggie were also confused. Doro said, "Katty is my best friend, and she is always talking about you. I am just coming from the council office. I went there to get an update on Katty's mission. It is her first mission, so I was very worried. But then I got the unexpected news. I have no heart to tell it to you, Archie."

Archie, Tobby, and Maggie did not say anything, and Doro continued sobbing. Archie's heart was racing, and he was imagining all the worst scenarios he could imagine. Doro continued, "Katty was carrying out a mission of rescuing a litter of abandoned newborns. But some people from Coast Circus kidnapped her. The council is sending a team to rescue her, but I do not know exactly what is happening to her. I am so sorry, Archie! I know how long you have been waiting to see your sister."

Maggie and Tobby fell silent after this unexpected twist of events. They had been expecting a happy reunion, but they now did not know how to react. Archie snarled, "See, Maggie, why I do not believe in your stupid missions? My sister has been kidnapped because of the strange way of life of this fantasy land."

Tobby tried to mollify him and said, "It is because of this land that you are getting another chance to see your sister. These missions and training empower us and unify us. We are not just meant to be the pets of humans. We play a great role in society. We help military soldiers in their livelihood, we help blind people to walk, we keep lonely people company, and we help as guard dogs. Again, as you can see, we are an important part of society. You are new here, and I do not expect you to understand everything instantly. I know you are upset after getting this news. But your sister is our sister. We will do everything we can to free her from the circus company."

Archie was upset, but his brain was working. He realized they would need as much help as possible to rescue his sister. He could never just rely on the council and their typical rescue missions. It was his family, and he had to go. So, he remained silent and did not argue with Tobby. Archie, Maggie, Tobby, and Doro rushed towards the Council office. Tobby said to the officer, "Hi, we have received the news of Katty's kidnap. This is Archie, Katty's brother. He came here today, and the Wizard has already tested his worthiness. Four of us want to come with the search party to rescue Katty."

Archie had no plans for a group search; however, he felt the keenness in Tobby's voice. That convinced him to stay silent. He could trust them. This was the first time Archie had felt like he had real friends. They were even willing to risk their lives and well-being for the well-being of Archie's sister. Archie was not alone anymore. He had good friends who would always be with him. Good friends always help a friend in need. They support in bad times and keep us motivated. They encourage us to be better and do well.

The officer replied, "Tobby, I understand. Every brother wants to take care of his sister. And Katty's other siblings are not here; for now, they are involved in other missions. But I cannot allow

Archie to go on this rescue mission without any proper training. This is against protocol."

Archie finally said, "Ma'am, I understand the whole "protocol thing." But I am not officially part of the Paw Island way of life. So, no protocol can stop me from protecting my sister. I respect your rules, but you cannot tell me what to do. I am going."

Tobby, Doro, and Maggie knew they were bound to follow the rules of Paw Island. But they could not leave Archie alone. Tobby said, "Archie, we must go to the wizard. He is wise and old. He can give us good advice."

Archie and his friends revisited Coco's house. Coco had already got the news of Katty's kidnap, and he was expecting Archie. Doro asked, "Wizard, we know it is wrong to disobey the council. But we want to help Archie. What should we do?"

The wizard replied, "Disobeying rules is wrong. But not helping a friend in need is unethical. We should always prioritize our family. Katty is alone and probably scared. You should help Archie to get her back. Take this cloak with you. It will help you to be invisible. And these potions will give you strength as per your capabilities. You will need these. My blessing is with you. And Archie, son, you do not need the training to help Katty. Because it is not a mission - it is a real-life crisis. Always stay calm. God bless you."

Just after sunset, Archie, Tobby, Maggie, and Doro began a new journey - the journey to rescue Katty.

Chapter 25: Dagi the Happy Shark

Far out in the heart of the big blue sea, there lived a shark whose name was Dagi. Dagi was a beautiful blue shark, with a wide, big-toothed smile. He was also an excellent swimmer.

When Dagi was a baby shark, he loved swimming around the sea and exploring what lay in the water near their home. Every day, Dagi would wake up, and after having breakfast, he would wave goodbye to his mother with his little fins and dart outside their underwater cave to look for a new adventure.

Outside, he would be joined by his friends, Pago and Tina. They would first go around the neighborhood to see what's new, and then they would extend their forays into the nearby forest of seaweed and coral reefs. Every so often, a family would have new kids, and it was always fun to meet them and welcome them to the neighborhood. Pago was a little older, and Tina was a little younger than Dagi, but that was never a problem for them, and they always found many things that they liked in common. Sometimes, they would notice a new growth on a coral or a missing branch in the seaweed, and they would play guessing games on what might have happened to it.

"Maybe a sea cow ate it," Dagi would say.

"Or maybe someone made a nest with it," Tina would say.

"Or, or, or, maybe Miss Simone, the octopus, took it to sweep the floor with," Pago would say excitedly, then they would move to the next area to see what's new.

Sometimes, they would notice a pufferfish nest and go to marvel at it and try to count the circles and ridges.

“One, two, three, four, five,” counted Tina.

“Six, seven, eight, nine,” continued Dagi.

“Ten!!” They all said in unison. “But what comes after ten?” Did they wonder? “Oh well, we’ll be going to school soon, and we will learn everything there.”

And so, it came to be. They started school in the next season, and everything was lovely. They liked their new schoolmates and made friends with most of them. There was a lot to learn, and the teachers were accommodating and kind, and Miss Tocci was even funny!

However, there was this one classmate named Rah. He did not seem to like the others very much, and he kept mostly to himself even during recess. Whenever anyone came close, he would swim away, and he hardly ever spoke in class. One day, Dagi approached him and said, in a friendly manner, “Hello Rah, how are you today?” but Rah did not answer him. He just turned away and continued to sulk.

When Dagi got home, and they were talking about how the day was, Dagi asked his parents why some people are sulky, and he related to them his short encounter with Rah earlier in the day.

“Maybe he is having a problem adjusting to the new school,” said his mom.

“Or maybe he has a speech problem.” said his dad. “You know, some people stutter or stammer, but it goes away with time and with practice,” he added.

Dagi always marveled at how wise and insightful his parents were. “And what can I do to help him?” he asked.

“Just keep being his friend,” answered his dad.

“And maybe try teaching him a new song, like the one we taught you when you were learning to swim and would sometimes be afraid. Do you remember it?” asked his mom.

"Oh, yes! I had forgotten about that song. Let's sing it, mama; remind me the words please," Dagi pleaded.

"Oh, alright," said his mom. But first, go get ready for bed, then I'll be with you shortly to sing the song.

"Yay!" said Dagi, and off he went to get ready for bed.

When his mom came in, Dagi was ready to start right away. "Okay, do you remember how we start?" Mom asked.

"Yes," replied Dagi.

"Breathe in, and hold,

One, two, three, then breathe out

"Good job!" said mom.

"Breathe in, and hold,

Four, five, six, whistle out," sang mom

"Yes, yes, I remember now!" cried Dagi. Then in unison, they sang.

Breathe in, and hold,

Seven, eight, nine, flap your fins

Breathe in, and hold,

Up to ten, let's return."

"Now, I remember it all," said Dagi, "Can we sing it one more time?"

"Alright, dear; just this once, then it's bedtime," said his mom.

"Breathe in, and hold,

One, two, three, then breathe out

Breathe in, and hold,

Four, five, six, whistle out

Breathe in, and hold,

Seven, eight, nine, flap your fins

Breathe in, and hold,

Up to ten, let's return."

"You two sound terrific." said dad. "But it's bedtime now, so goodnight, son," he said as he kissed Dagi goodnight. Dad and mom both went out. Dagi was glad to have remembered the breathing song and couldn't wait to teach it to Rah. He thought about the song lyrics again as he drifted off to sleep.

The next day was the beginning of a long weekend. As usual, Tina and Pago came around, and the trio went seeking adventure. They swam much further than they were used to, and Pago noticed that Dagi was quiet most of the way.

"Hey, Dagi, what's up, buddy? You are very quiet today."

"Oh, nothing," said Dagi as he swept a pebble aside with his fin, and they continued in silence. Tina, Dagi, and Pago did not realize how far they were from home until they tried to ascend and found that they were already deep inside a cavern. "What do we do now?" asked Tina with fear in her voice.

"Oh, my! I was so deep in thought about Rah that I did not even realize where we are!" shouted Dagi, who had just now snapped from his reverie.

"What about Rah? And what d-d-d-do we do now?" Asked Pago

"Oh, you know, how he's always quiet at school, in class, and at recess."

Just then, they heard a loud splashing from the darker part of the cave, moving swiftly toward them. The three turned and swam as fast as their little fins could carry them, but they were not fast enough. They heard growling and turned back to see what it was. A great white shark with pointy, gleaming teeth was coming toward them.

"What itty bitty little dudes! Go get them, bro!" He growled.

From the little light streaming into the cave, the youngsters saw a familiar figure swimming toward them. When he got closer, they saw it was Rah! He swam hesitatingly toward them but growled just like his brother. Taking advantage of his slower pace, they turned and fled out of the cave. They heard a loud, angry growl behind them, but they did not turn back, and neither did he come after them. For the rest of the weekend, the three friends played close to home and were a little apprehensive about going back to school when it restarted.

Come the next school day, Dagi, Tina, and Pago swam to school together and kept close together all day, making sure to steer clear of Rah. They did the same on the following day. The school was no longer fun for them. They were always afraid that Rah would do something to scare them even more. Dagi was very unhappy with the situation, and he said to his friends, "Tina, Pago, let us try to do something about this. Maybe we can ask Rah why he behaved that way in the cave."

"Ummm, well, alright," they agreed half-heartedly.

At recess, they slowly swam toward where Rah was, and this time, he did not swim away or growl at them.

"Hello, Rah," They said timidly, but he did not answer.

"That day at the cave, you were very mean to us. Why?" asked Dagi.

Rah was silent for a while, then he told them that his big brother, Basa, was the bully in their neighborhood, and he wanted Rah to be just like him. He added that Basa had told him to have no other friend but him.

"Oh, how sad, said Dagi. "Here, I will teach you a song that my mom taught me; it helps me not to be afraid. Okay?"

"'Okay!" said Tina, who always liked songs. Dagi remembered then that he had not yet taught it to his friends.

"Pago, Rah, wanna learn it, too?

"Sure," said Pago.

"Okay," said Rah.

Okay. It is called the breathing song. Breathe in, hold, and breath out. Now sing after me."

"Breathe in, and hold,

One, two, three, then breathe out

Breathe in, and hold,

Four, five, six, whistle out

Breathe in, and hold,

Seven, eight, nine, flap your fins

Breathe in, and hold,

Up to ten, let's return."

Oh, it is such a good song! said Tina. "It makes me feel relaxed," added Pago.

"How about you, Rah?" asked Dagi.

It's alright, I guess," said Rah.

Okay, let's sing it again.

"Breathe in, and hold,

One, two, three, then breathe out

Breathe in, and hold,

Four, five, six, whistle out

Breathe in, and hold,

Seven, eight, nine, flap your fins

Breathe in, and hold,

Up to ten, let's return."

"I actually do feel much better," said Rah.

The three friends looked at each other happily.

"Told you, it works!" Said Dagi.

"Okay, fins in. Friends on three! One, two, three!"

"Friends!" they all shouted happily and went back to class, giggling.

After that, every day at recess, Rah joined them, and they always started and ended the recess with the breathing song. Sometimes, when Rah couldn't' sleep at night, too, he sang it to himself. One day, his brother, Basa, heard him and gruffly asked him, "What are you singing? Why are you singing?

"My friend at school taught me a breathing song. I sing it to relax and not to feel afraid," Rah replied. He was no longer afraid to stand up to his brother. Basa noticed this and was also perplexed that his little brother had friends at school. The tune for the breathing song, however, was so catchy, Basa asked Rah to teach it to him.

"Breathe in, and hold,

One, two, three, then breathe out

Breathe in, and hold,

Four, five, six, whistle out

Breathe in, and hold,

Seven, eight, nine, flap your fins

Breathe in, and hold,

Up to ten, let's return."

At the very same time, Dagi was singing the same song with his parents at bedtime. He was no longer afraid or anxious, but he was glad that the song had brought joy to his friends, and especially Rah.

"Breathe in, and hold,

One, two, three, then breathe out

Breathe in, and hold,

Four, five, six, whistle out

Breathe in, and hold,

Seven, eight, nine, flap your fins

Breathe in, and hold,

Up to ten, let's return."

Conclusion

Thank you for reading all the way to the end of this book.I hope that it was enjoyable for you and your kids, and you were able to learn from the different stories we covered in this book.

Remember that the grounding and meditation exercises that have been provided in this book can be useful for both you and your children. The physical and mental benefits of meditation are very real and can improve the quality of life for children and adults alike. As you and your child get into this book, feel free to mix and match the exercises to tailor the book for you both. You know your child best. We want you to get the best possible result as you can from this book, so use it however you think is best!

This book has set out to entertain you and your little one while teaching valuable meditative techniques for relaxation. Every story was crafted with a particular moral lesson in mind. Children have such a capacity for creativity. That powerful imagination can be used as a vehicle by which to teach them the values that you wish to impart. I am honored that you have chosen this book to assist you in making those fundamental connections with your children. I also hope that you have found these tales useful and that they have made bedtime a more relaxed experience.

We have covered several stories in the book to help you and your child relax with a series of meditational content. The stories will also enable your children to become critical thinkers as they evaluate and understand the moral of the stories. This book has offered a very powerful tool to promote understanding of different meditational techniques and how to become heroes. You are now acquainted with different oceanic creatures, including angelfish, blue crab, the sea cod, the barracuda, and the dotty back. In order for your children to master the concepts and morals in this book, it is vital that you read it to them every single night and repeat the stories several times.